Sirenz

Sirenz

Charlotte Bennardo & Natalie Zaman

Woodbury, Minnesota

First Edition
First Printing, 2011

Cover design by Lisa Novak
Cover images: pedestal © iStockphoto.com/James Martin;
feathers © iStockphoto.com/Saoly, Katarzyna Krawiec, Максим Ширин;
shoe © iStockphoto.com/CarlssonInc. Photography;
label © iStockphoto.com/Nilgun Bostanci

Flux, an imprint of Llewellyn Worldwide Ltd.

Library of Congress Cataloging-in-Publication Data
Bennardo, Charlotte.
  Sirenz / Charlotte Bennardo & Natalie Zaman.—1st ed.
    p. cm.
  Summary: Bickering New York City roommates and high school seniors Meg and Shar must find a way to balance their love of fashion with the drudgery of being special-assignment Sirens, luring to the Underworld those whose unholy contracts are up.
  ISBN 978-0-7387-2319-8
[1. Sirens (Mythology)—Fiction. 2. Mythology, Greek—Fiction. 3. Hades (Greek deity)—Fiction. 4. Fashion—Fiction. 5. New York (N.Y.)—Fiction.] I. Zaman, Natalie. II. Title.
  PZ7.B4352Sir 2011
  [Fic]—dc22

                                                    2010054516

Flux
Llewellyn Worldwide Ltd.
2143 Wooddale Drive
Woodbury, MN 55125-2989
www.fluxnow.com

Printed in the United States of America

Shar

A Mismatched Pair

God, you're wearing those clunky things again? How stupid, wearing five-inch wedge heels on cracked and frozen New York City sidewalks. What if you break an ankle?

"Great shoes," I said, faking a beauty queen smile at Meg.

"I think I paid five dollars for them. They're from the seventies," she said absentmindedly.

No kidding. You should have left them there.

"Feet cold?" I wiggled my toasty toes in my crystal-studded Ugg boots. *My* feet were warm, *and* they looked good.

She shrugged.

Poor toesies.

Last spring, when I scored a spot in the coveted Fourth

Year Live-In, a program our alternative school offers to twelfth grade students who "show promise, initiative, and vision in their chosen field of study," I was psyched. It's a sweet deal that includes the perk of on-campus housing, just like college—no parents, no curfew, and Manhattan living for nine months! Only top students are offered the opportunity. I knew I had to have a roommate, but I figured, how awful could that be?

Then I got paired with Meg Wiley.

We couldn't be more mismatched—black hair, black clothes, *old* clothes, not to mention voodoo, hoodoo, or whatever else she was into. The Academically Independent High School of New York had saddled me with a vampire out of a 1940s horror movie, and an argumentative one, too. She always had some smart-ass remark about my love of cashmere or my Starbucks addiction. As if she had no habits to complain about.

I looked at her now, clomping along the sidewalk in those outrageous wood-soled Kabuki shoes and completely black ensemble, and shuddered. On my tall and fair-skinned body, that much black would make me look like the walking dead. At least I knew my skinny jeans, ballet flats, and Victoria's Secret PJs were safe; Meg could never squeeze her curvy frame into my pink sweaters even if she wanted to, plus she only wore clothes that made her look like she was in a perpetual state of mourning. I shrugged it off.

The wind blasted us as we turned the corner of Fifth and Broadway. We bent into it, clutching our sleeves and wiping our tearing eyes. It made the holiday lights look blurry. Good thing my mascara was water resistant. Who knew who we'd meet? Lots of celebrities came to these sales. Not that Meg cared; she hated the rich and the "ostentatious."

We'd learned a lot about each other during weeks of petty bickering this fall, but I thought it was time for some sort of truce, since we had to live together for the rest of the year. There was no switching roommates at Live-In; any irreconcilable differences were resolved via removal from the program, and I was not about to let Vampirella stand between me and independence. So, as a peace offering, I called her at home over winter break and invited her out shopping. It was either that or put up with my family for the entire time, which was too depressing to consider. Meg actually agreed—with great reluctance—to come with me to an after-Christmas sample sale. One-of-a-kind creations at undreamed-of prices! Even if she wasn't interested in a designer bag, something might catch her eye.

And anyway, since she'd gotten into the Live-In program, we had to have something in common. I was determined to find out what that was. So I would be the bigger person and make the first move; we'd do a little shopping, get to know each other better, and who knew—by the end of the night we'd be swapping style tips over a couple of hot lattes. Maybe I could get her to lighten up a bit. Literally.

I tugged on Meg's coat sleeve to get her attention. "What time is it?" I asked.

She drew an ancient-looking pocket watch out of her purse. "About ten thirty."

"We have some time to kill before the sale starts," I said, my teeth chattering.

As Meg snapped the watch shut, her foot caught on the uneven sidewalk. But she quickly recovered.

See, bad shoes! Maybe you'll find a decent pair at the sale.

"So let's do something first, then eat, then go," Meg suggested casually, as if she didn't almost kiss the sidewalk. I suppressed a smirk behind my pink pashmina scarf. It would be too cruel to ask how her feet were holding up.

"Wait!" She held up a hand, stopping short in front of a little shop. An orange neon sign cast a strange glow against her face: *TAROT.* "I want a reading."

"Okay." I shrugged. If that's what she wanted to do, I could be magnanimous as long as I was going to be warm and they kept me out of it. Who really believed that stuff anyway?

A silver bell tinkled brightly as we rushed inside. The shop was cozy and redolent with the spicy aroma of cinnamon incense—*the joy of Cinnabons without the temptation.* My stomach grumbled. The walls were lined with bookcases and cluttered with hanging stone and brass sculptures of pentagrams, angelic goddesses, and leafy-faced men. Colorful glass globes and wind chimes dangled from the ceiling, while the center of the store was crammed with displays of pouches, stones in baskets, and other hocuspocus tchotchkes.

A woman walked out from the back room. "Hi," she said.

She'd avoided the stereotypical fortune-teller look.

No jangly earrings, India-print skirts, or head scarves. I breathed a sigh of relief. She looked like an average New Yorker—great jeans, vintage cream Irish cable knit sweater, and sexy, black-heeled, not-too-high boots. I didn't think she'd be giving Meg the "you'll-meet-a-stranger" B.S.

"Hi," Meg said matter-of-factly. "Can I get a reading?"

"Come on back. I'm Katharine." *A nice normal name.* I relaxed a little more. No bizarre madame, no Hollyweirdness.

We sat at a round table covered with a celestial-print cloth. Katharine took a deck of cards from a stone box carved with a skull. I looked around. Were there a lot of skulls around here, or was I just...? No, there were a lot of skulls.

Katharine caught me staring and grinned. "I love cemetery art."

Meg nodded. "It's intense."

"Uh, yuh," I said.

"Think of a question as you shuffle the cards," said Katharine, handing them to Meg. "Put them on the table when you feel it's right."

Meg's face lit up, an expression I never liked and one she always wore when talking about weird stuff. She shuffled the cards for several minutes, then gingerly placed them on the table in front of Katharine, who laid them out in a five-pointed star pattern. I dug through my Coach bag and searched for pen and paper to list the outfits I wanted to find, the shoes to go with them, and things I had to do that weekend. I didn't want to listen to this even if I could hear it.

"You're at a turning point. The Wheel of Fortune indicates that a change of events is going to alter your current situation," Katharine murmured. I peeked over as she pointed to the first card and flicked a glance my way. "If you've been having a tough time, say, in a relationship with a friend, things are going to improve."

She lifted the second card and held it up—a picture of a man who appeared distraught at three overturned cups. "In the past, it seems that you didn't get what you wanted or expected."

Meg's eyes widened, and drawn in against my common sense, I scooched over so that I could see better.

Katharine smiled and shook her head. "Look at the picture. There are still two perfectly good cups behind him and he's ignoring them. Your situation has a lot of good in it, but you're just not seeing it. This one," and she pointed to a card that pictured a single man fighting with a staff on a hill, "tells me that you have a challenge coming up. Nothing you can't handle. If you take the higher ground, you'll prevail."

Sooo mystical, I pooh-poohed. *That could be applied to anyone.* I tuned the conversation out and went back to my lists. Finally, Meg stood up to leave.

"Nice meeting you." I thrust my hand into Katharine's, quickly shook it, and tried to hurry Meg along before she asked yet another question, or worse, put me on the spot to get a reading too. As genial as Katharine was, all this psychic stuff was a tad too creepy for me.

"At least she didn't say you'd meet a handsome stranger and fall deeply in love," I quipped after Meg paid and we left the store. "I would have thrown up."

Meg's forehead creased. I could almost hear the wheels spinning inside her head.

"Don't worry about anything she said, Meg. I'll bet every fortune-teller—"

"Katharine isn't a fortune-teller, Shar. She's a *psychic*."

"And you know this for sure just because she told you?"

"I'm in for a big challenge. I—"

"Oh please! Your only challenge is going to be to find something that's not black!"

"You're so skeptical!" Meg huffed. "Don't you believe in anything other than what you see?"

"Right now I'm so hungry the only thing I want to believe is that I'll find food before I faint. How about pizza?"

Meg brightened. "I know a great place."

A block or two down the street, she steered us toward a grimy-looking storefront hung with garish holiday garlands that had seen better days. I could barely make out the red, green, and gold through the tarnish. I was about to protest when she dragged me in. It looked roachy; the floors were gritty and it reeked of garlic. But the instant we walked through the door, I was glad she hadn't given me a chance to say no. Standing at the counter, ordering a slice with extra peppers was … a god.

At least he looked like it from his profile. A rippling

cascade of smooth dark locks tumbled to his shoulders, just brushing the collar of his perfectly distressed leather jacket. What kind of jeans was he wearing? It didn't matter; they fit his lean but obviously muscular legs. Now if he would only turn around, so I could see all of his face.

"Bad-ass jacket," Meg murmured under her breath.

"Sweet jeans," I whispered. We exchanged glances. *Yummo!* But there was only one of him. I didn't know if Meg was into sharing, but I wasn't.

Sweet Jeans turned around and I heard Meg catch her breath. His front was even better than his backside. A fringe of hair somewhere between black and dark chocolate dipped above his large, cerulean eyes, which were smudged with a bit of dark liner. He caught me staring and grinned. There was a hint of stubble on his chin that made the eyeliner *so* work for him. Normally I wasn't into makeup on guys, even rock stars, but for him I would totally make an exception.

"Hello ladies," he said, looking from me to Meg.

"Hey," Meg breathed. She always knew what to say and how to say it, even if it was a one-line hello. Meanwhile, I couldn't untie the knot from my tongue. Sweet Jeans took his pizza and made his way over to a counter that ran along the window. Both of us watched him as he leaned his studly body over the narrow ledge. The soft glow of Christmas lights reflected in his hair.

I've been a good girl, Santa...

"What can I getchya?" I barely heard the voice behind the counter. "Girls?"

A shrill whistle made me jump. I turned my attention back to the pizza. A squat older man in a smudgy apron cocked his eye at me knowingly.

"Are you here for pizza, sweetheart," he asked, jerking his head in Sweet Jeans' direction, "or dessert—'cause he ain't on the menu."

"One plain slice and a Diet Coke," I answered primly, trying not to blush.

"And your friend there?" he asked, plopping a cheesy wedge onto a paper plate. I glanced at Meg, who looked like she'd forgotten about being hungry. I nudged her in the ribs. Hard.

"Ow!" She glared at me.

I inclined my head toward the counter.

"Oh. Oh! Uh, a mushroom slice and . . . a Diet Coke."

Meg never did diet anything. That was another one of her lectures—that I'd probably already preserved myself for eternity from ingesting all those artificial sugars and additives.

She was definitely distracted.

Pizza Man shook his head and slid a plate and a cup in her direction.

"Follow me," she ordered, quickly grabbing her food.

"Where?" I whispered.

She grinned. "To make a new friend." And she started moving toward the window counter.

"No! Wait!" I whispered as loudly as I could. I needed to run to the bathroom and check my makeup, but I had serious doubts about the restrooms in this place. They were probably unisex and I do *not* use man bathrooms. Too late. Meg had already positioned herself on one side of Sweet Jeans. I had no choice but to join them, as is.

"How did you manage to get passes to that?" I heard Meg say as I settled myself on the only other empty seat, which was on his other side. Bad-boy sandwich. *Delicioso! Who would get the first bite?*

"I know the manager there," he answered in a throaty, sexy voice.

God, I hope my mascara hasn't smudged.

He tucked a stray lock behind his ear and turned to me. My face got hot.

"Do you like Elysian Fields?"

I had no idea what he was talking about, so I smiled prettily, nodded, and took a bite of my pizza so I wouldn't have to elaborate.

"They're probably the best new prog band from this area. They *never* do club shows!" Meg purred.

Okay. He was talking about a band.

He turned back to Meg and proceeded to trade notes with her on the nuances of techno. I was beginning to think that I might ask her to burn a CD for me when Sweet Jeans asked, "Hey, you two wanna come? They're only playing tonight. I'm sure I can talk all three of us in." He turned to me and tilted his head in such a cute way.

I knew what Meg wanted to do. She'd rather go to a club than out shopping. I was considering changing our plans, but we'd never be able to talk at a club, and we had to clear a few things up. And, it was a *designer* sale.

"Sorry," I said, making a sad face. "We already have a commitment."

Meg sighed loudly, but before she could protest, Sweet Jeans nodded, saying, "That's cool. Some other time." He stood to leave. I thought I could see steam coming from Meg's ears.

"Please," I mouthed. She clenched her teeth and shook her head.

"Catch you later." He waved and winked at us, then pushed his way out the door, letting in a blast of arctic air.

"Fantastic," Meg mumbled, taking her first bite of congealed pizza. Served her right for talking too much.

After a dinner in stony silence, we trudged the remaining blocks to the sample sale, arriving just as the doors opened. A crush of people pushed their way inside.

"If you wanted to go body surfing, we should have gone to that club. I should have gotten his name! Remind me again why I'm here with you?"

"You'll see," I assured her, but not with complete enthusiasm. Maybe we should have taken him up on his offer, but we were here now. I started to wonder how far two hundred dollars would go. I'd saved for over a month for this sale.

Once the crowd dispersed, Meg started to wander off, although not before I instructed her to call me if she found something I might like and vice versa. How did anyone shop before cell phones? After a last skeptical glance from her, I took off for the dresses.

An hour later, we caught up. Meg had a pair of over-sized

Chanel sunglasses propped on her head and several shoe boxes tucked under her arms. I hadn't found a little black dress. Or jeans. Or a sweater. Not even a belt. How could *I* come away from a sample sale with nothing?

"These looked interesting," she said in a voice that sounded like they didn't interest her at all. As she dumped the boxes in front of me, a ruby gleam caught my eye and I reached into the pile.

"I *love* these red patent heels! I'll take them." I pulled the lid off the box and caressed the shiny leather. Little gold charms. A sexy instep strap. Gorgeous. *Irresistible*.

She looked at me, shocked.

"I don't think so," she said.

I tilted the box upright to check the size. "They're a ten, you're a nine. They won't fit right."

"I'm a nine and a half." She paused and stole a glance at the printing on the side. "And they're Vivienne Westwood." She put her hands on the box.

I tugged back. "Since when do you care about labels?"

"They're too quirky for you!" Meg pulled again.

"They're too conservative for *you*," I argued, tightening my grip.

"I thought you said my challenge was to find something not black!"

"Since when do you ever listen to me?" I growled, not letting go.

"Katharine was right when she said that things hadn't turned out as I expected. I saw her look at you when she said that. She was referring to us."

"Don't be so dramatic."

"It's been so obvious that you don't want to be stuck with me." Meg compressed her lips and looked away.

"Look, I know we don't have that much in common, but—"

"Exactly," Meg scoffed. "Miss Teen Vogue."

"Like you've never looked at those magazines!" I shot back.

"Oh, yes—such great reading material. Everything I *don't* want to know about making up, making out, and making prom queen," she retorted with a sneer.

"That's so mean! And I did you a favor by bringing you here!" My lip started to tremble. I would *not* cry! Instead, I got mad. How dare she speak to me like that! I gave her my angriest scowl. "Why would you want these shoes? They're not fifty years old!"

The few people around us stopped to stare. Meg's face turned a pretty pink, like a storybook piglet.

"And they're designer, too! *Oooh*," I rushed on, "if you get them, won't you somehow be taking food out of the mouths of impoverished Far Eastern children and—"

"Big surprise," she said, cocking her head and puckering her lips in a sarcastic attitude. "Just like I always thought. Shallow and selfish in the same package." She shoved the shoes at me, then tore the sunglasses from her head and threw them on the ground. I whirled around to watch her storm out past the stragglers coming in late.

I scooped up the shoes. Someone had to get them at this price; it might as well be me. I nearly tripped over the mountain of boxes Meg left behind. In the center of the pile were the sunglasses she'd been using as a headband. I felt a sting of guilt—or was it that karma thing she was always talking about? Perhaps the last bit, about the starving children, was too much. But then, she did call me Miss Teen Vogue—as if! I'm more a Cosmo type.

I turned the glasses over in my hand. They were five dollars—her usual price limit. Getting them for her might help patch up this latest argument. I bought the shoes and the glasses.

The wind slapped me with a driving force as I bolted out the door. I strode quickly down the block, head down, gloved hands stuffed into my jacket. Looking up for a second to get my bearings, I spied the subway station with relief—and dread. I hated the subway. Down in its creepy depths, my footsteps echoed ominously. I swiped my metro card and slipped through the turnstile, praying my white down jacket wasn't getting grimy.

At first, the platform looked empty, but then someone stepped out from behind a tiled pillar. My heart jumped into my throat. *Sweet Jeans!* I thought about Meg's five-dollar sunglasses at the bottom of the shopping bag. Did good karma come this cheap?

She probably already caught a train, but maybe I won't have to ride home alone after all. This couldn't have worked out better if I'd planned it. Fate was on my side.

Meg

Oh. My. Gods!

*M*y face still burned, even after several brisk walks around the block. *Shar always acts like SHE got cheated being burdened with ME*, I thought furiously. *For four months I've dealt with her giggling girlfriends, OCD wardrobe, and coordinated bedding. And now this! I get publicly humiliated and miss a chance to see Elysian Fields with, oh, probably the most beautiful guy in the city. Talk about being divinely screwed. Why did I ever agree to go shopping with her? I'm insane, that's why. There's no other plausible explanation.*

I trudged down the subway steps behind a gaggle of clubbers. Half of me hoped she'd be down there, the other half hoped we'd miss each other. If I did see her, I had a few choice things to say.

One by one we passed through the turnstile. As the club kids moved out of my way and toward the back of the station, I saw her. There she was, standing near the platform—talking to *my* Bad-Ass Jacket!

She was deluding herself if she thought he was interested in her. And that sad attempt to act like she knew what we were talking about? Pathetic! At least, that's how it seemed back at the pizzeria. Shoes I could forget, but she'd made a mistake of global proportions by going after the guy. Apocalypse? NOW.

"Thanks for the great evening!" I said, stomping over to her. Bad-Ass Jacket backed up a step, while Shar gaped at me, mortified.

"Meg…" She trailed off and flicked her eyes at him. I hoped I was embarrassing her.

"I see you had time to buy *my* red shoes," I said, pointing at the shopping bag.

"I can't believe *you're* freaking out over a pair of shoes!" she shouted, moving away from me, toward the tracks.

"Get over yourself, Mary Poppins."

That earned me some applause from the club kids, a snicker from Bad-Ass Jacket, and a nasty glare from Shar. A muffled rumbling came from the tunnel. The train would be here any second.

"You want them so bad, come get them!" Shar taunted, waving the bag and clonking Bad-Ass in the chest with it.

He backed up a step into the yellow zone. "Hey, it's

just a pair of shoes," he started to say, but without warning I lunged for the bag, latched onto the handles, and pulled.

"Hands off!" Shar tugged.

I lost my balance and tottered backwards toward the tracks. Time seemed to slow as I felt my heart thudding in my chest and my legs starting to give way. The roar of the train grew louder. I turned my head—lights twinkled down the tunnel, growing larger and larger. It was coming up fast.

Death by train! Death by train! I squeezed my eyes shut, bracing myself for the inevitable smack of a subway car.

"Meg!" I heard Shar scream.

I felt my arm being yanked almost from its socket, then my whole body hitting something soft yet solid. Turning my head, I opened my eyes to see a wall of crackly leather and my nose filled with the scent of patchouli and sandalwood. I shrieked and fell sideways into Shar.

The thunder of the train filled the station, and we watched in horror as gorgeous Bad-Ass Jacket slash Sweet Jeans stumbled forward and teetered on the brink, his arms fluttering over the empty blackness.

He tumbled off the platform.

Instantly the train was there, racing through the station. *Didn't they see him? Wasn't it going to stop?* The cars screamed by like silver bullets and Katharine's prediction flooded my mind: *A chain of events is going to alter your current situation.*

The last car shot past, and the rumbling reverberated into a distant hum. Nobody spoke.

I realized then that Shar was holding my arm with both hands. The shopping bag with the shoes in it lay on its side a few feet away, the corner of the box peeking out of the top of the bag. She'd stopped me from going over the edge.

"Oh my God, oh my God," Shar's voice shook, breaking the silence. "He ... fell. He ..."

Unable to stop myself, I peered down at the tracks and gasped, waves of nausea coursing through me. He lay sprawled out over the tracks, a dark pool growing under him—both pieces. He'd been sliced in half more cleanly than a tomato. Now he was Mr. Sweet Jeans *and* Mr. Bad-Ass Jacket.

Up came dinner. I hurled over the platform, missing the body by mere inches. At least I'd spared him that last indignity. Then a crackling noise came up from the rails, along with a smell like pork rinds, and whatever was left in my stomach decided to vacate. Poor guy—this time I didn't miss him.

The club kids ran over to the edge of the yellow line and peered over. One of them screamed, and another stared at us and pointed. *They didn't think we did this on purpose, did they?*

"Don't look," I gagged, grabbing Shar's arm and dragging her back a few steps. "Why was he standing so close to the edge?"

"He's ... dead? Oh my God!" Shar choked, and put a hand over her mouth. "We—"

"Oh man!" one of the clubber girls shrieked. "Like, he

was just standing there…" She trailed off and started sobbing. Then she looked at us with angry, accusatory eyes. "You totally shoved him in there. Poor dude!"

"No!" shouted Shar. "That's not what happened!"

An acne-pocked boy in neon goggles cursed. "You were messing around and you killed this guy! He was trying to break you two apart!" The boy looked over the edge and gasped. "Look at the blood!"

The club kids huddled together and started pulling out cell phones.

"It was an accident," I insisted, but none of them listened to me. I turned to Shar, taking hold of her shoulders. "We didn't mean to hurt anyone. You saved me, I was falling—"

Shar looked at me helplessly. "What are we going to do? They're going to call the police!"

"I don't know. I don't know." My head dropped. Then I lifted it and stared up at the ceiling, blinking back tears. "I would give anything to make this go away. Anything."

"Me too," she sobbed. "*Anything!*"

"I believe I can assist you with that." A silky voice wafted through the murky silence. That's when I noticed that the station was uncannily quiet, and my heart stuck in my throat when I saw that the club kids were still gaping in horror on the brink of the platform. They were frozen in various poses. No one was moving.

"What's wrong with them?" Shar whispered, clutching my arms. Even with my winter coat on, her nails hurt.

"They're perfectly fine," the voice spoke again.

We turned around to see a tall man standing nonchalantly by the tiled wall. He wasn't just tall; he was towering tall, well over six-six, and dressed like the guys in the foreign fashion magazines that Shar always kept in our room. Long, elegant fingers hooked the collar of an expensive-looking black coat he held over his shoulder, and his gleaming white shirt was unbuttoned far enough to see a chest of rippling muscles and taut, olive-toned skin. He gazed at us with dark eyes. But where did he come from? He wasn't here before.

"Wh-what?" I stuttered in disbelief.

"That poor man was simply waiting for a train," he sighed. "Then you two came along. Now he's dead."

"Excuse me?" I didn't like what he was insinuating. "We are NOT responsible for this!"

He glanced down at the tracks and made a doleful face. "If he could, I think he'd argue that point."

"It was an accident!" whispered Shar.

"My dear Sharisse and Margaret, this poor soul is dead. You both had a hand in killing him. Do you think that will matter to his family and friends? To the courts?"

"How do you know our names?" My voice, steady until now, trembled slightly. I glanced over at Shar, who stared back, looking as pale as I felt.

"What should we do?" she whimpered.

The man turned to us with a saccharine smile. "That depends. I could call the police and tell them everything, and you can take your chances that they'll believe it was a tragic accident."

Impulsively, I grabbed Shar's hand and squeezed it. "It *was* an accident."

She nodded vigorously, and I turned back to GQ Man. "You saw what happened."

"Indeed I did. But I'm afraid I'll have to tell the authorities that I saw this man standing by himself. Then Sharisse and you attacked him, pushing him in front of the train just as it was going through the station. You waited until the last possible moment, giving him no time to react. And it sounds like these young people will back me up."

"That's not how it happened!" I stamped my foot. As badly as I felt about all this, I wasn't about to go to prison for it.

"Yes, it looks like the two of you killed him," he tsk-tsked and flicked his wrist. The club kids vanished. We were alone in the station, shaking like we'd spent the day downing double shots of espresso.

"Now," he said, casting an all-too-admiring glance at Shar, "let's attend to business."

"Who *are* you?" I demanded.

When he smiled, a full set of white, even teeth peeked out. Everything about him was uncannily perfect. His suit was spotless and he looked too polished, like a statue.

"Allow me to introduce myself, ladies. I am—"

"Deranged," I murmured.

He smiled easily. "Not in the least, Margaret. I am Hades, Lord of the Underworld."

"You mean like...the devil?" Shar trembled.

"No," he corrected her in a voice that sounded like

21

she'd just insulted him. "I am *not* the devil. He's a pale, corrupt version of me, created by humans. I can assure you that I am very real."

"The devil's real!" Shar insisted.

He clucked his tongue. "I suppose I can't fault you for believing what's been passed off as truth for thousands of years. But it's an inspiring piece of fiction, and it certainly worked for the people who invented it. There's no better way to scare people than to conjure up a devil! Fear is how to control people. It's how I got into my current business endeavor."

Shar and I clutched each other. This reality was very unreal.

"You see," the man continued, now circling around us like a wolf cornering its prey, "I liked the way that whole devil setup worked—a little temptation, some soul trading, and then, eternal servitude. And I thought, I should get into that! It's easy to find desperate people who'll sell their souls to me for fame, wealth, talent, revenge, whatever. Once they've attained a certain level of success, I call in their contract. When I first started out, I would collect them myself, but it was always so melodramatic. They'd plead their case to the other gods and we'd end up in negotiations. Too time consuming! That's when I came up with the idea of delegating, and hence, where you come in." He grimaced at my feet. "Those shoes have got to hurt."

"Everyone's a fashion critic," I snorted. "But seriously, soul selling? Are you joking? Who would sell their soul to you?"

He stopped moving and stroked his chin. "Cleopatra is a wonderful example. A more lusty and ambitious woman never lived. She wanted to preserve Egypt, no matter what the cost. That meant bringing Caesar, then Marc Antony, to heel. Romans!" he spat. "We Greeks brought civilization to the world, and then they come and change our names only to abandon us a few centuries later! They brought chaos and ruin!" He sniffed. "I was only too happy to deliver both those men to her. Of course, once she had what she wanted, her deal was complete, and I called in her contract. A nasty business—I had to transform myself into a serpent to finally get the job done. After that, I vowed never to make an *asp* of myself again!"

"Who else sold their souls?" Shar asked, seriously interested. She didn't really believe him, did she?

"You'd be surprised at the number of people who'd like to make a deal with me. Take a look around—they're not hard to pick out," Hades replied smoothly. "Rock stars and petty actors with no real talent. Multi-billionaires with no common sense and too much greed. How do you think people like that manage to achieve anything?"

"Hades plays Mephistopheles, is that it?" I interrupted boldly. "Look, I don't know who you are...or *what* you are, but we—"

Suddenly, a circle of flame danced all around us, and we huddled closer together.

"Please, Margaret, don't make me resort to parlor tricks. But let's get back on topic. You killed an innocent man." He grinned sardonically. "And if I heard you correctly, you both said that you would do anything to make this situation go away. I'm here to oblige you. I've never seen such natural talent!"

"Talent for what?" I asked.

"Think about what happened. You met that young man tonight, and you made quite an impression. He was going to take both of you to a music venue, yes? You saw what you wanted and wasted no time in engaging him. And then Sharisse"—he turned a lascivious grin on Shar—"not to be outdone, moved in, and all she had to do was smile. How could he stay away from either of you? He was completely enchanted. You lured him to his doom, and he happily followed!"

"Nooo," Shar stepped in. "We only talked to him for a couple of minutes over a slice of pizza."

Hades wagged a finger. "Oh, no no no! You two did much more than that. You were a duet of connivance. The fact that you don't realize just how beguiling you are makes you even more perfect. I have an offer you can't refuse."

"I'm not selling my soul," Shar declared dramatically, fingering the small gold cross dangling around her neck. "I'd rather die!"

He raised an eyebrow. "I don't want your soul. I want your service. You two will be my new Sirens."

Shar

The Fine Print

*Y*our *what*?" I asked.

"Greek Mythology, Shar," whispered Meg. "The Sirens were these bird women who sat on the rocks and sang. Sailors couldn't resist them, so they crashed their ships and drowned."

Meg and her occult studies. Who knew they would come in handy? She could converse with psychos.

"Hello? That's a fairy tale—the stuff they make a TV series out of!" *It's not real. It's not!* I refused to believe it, but the sinking feeling in the pit of my stomach told me that I was kidding myself. I turned to Hades.

"Fine. Okay, let's pretend that you're telling the truth—

hypothetically. Why would you need new Sirens? What happened to the originals?"

Hades shook his head sadly.

"Once Odysseus sailed past without succumbing to their call, they threw themselves into the sea and drowned. The same thing happened when Jason and the Argonauts resisted them. They didn't take rejection very well. So I kept replacing them. I need a steady workforce." Hades grinned and I felt sick all over again.

"You mean, they *died*??" I was only seventeen and not liking what I was hearing.

"Every profession has its risks." He straightened his immaculate Jerry Garcia—signed—tie. "No one's immortal but us gods."

"Get to the point," Meg said. "What would we have to do?"

"Oh it's easy," he purred. "You two will bring me a specified individual who executed an agreement with me, which, shall we say, is about to expire. You lure him to an underworld portal which will send him to Tartarus, my kingdom. In exchange, I will undo this terrible tragedy and you're off the hook. A one-shot deal. Simple, no?"

"Too simple," said Meg. "If it sounds too good to be true, it probably is. What happens if we can't do it?"

Hades looked sideways at us and grinned with a sly smile.

"If you fail, you must reside with me. In the Underworld. For all eternity. And I'll have another job for you—taking care of my pets."

"Pets?" I asked. "You have pets?"

"The hell hounds," he winked. "And they do so love a game of fetch. Especially Cerberus."

"What do they fetch?" I chewed my bottom lip.

"A stick, a rubber ball. Whatever else amuses them."

I am *so* not a dog person. Neither was Meg. At home, we both had cats.

"That's it? All we have to do is play with your dogs?" I ventured to ask. Greek gods always had some trick up their toga, although Hades wasn't wearing one now.

"Playing fetch is the fun part. You'll have to clean up after them, too. They leave quite a mess about the place."

"Don't you hate that?" I said. "Once you step in that stuff you can never get the smell out!"

"It is a problem," he agreed.

Meg stared at me, aghast. "We're pretty much doomed to either go to prison, wear orange jumpsuits, and be someone's girlfriend for twenty-five-to-life, or spend eternity on pooper-scooper duty for gigantic hell hounds—and you're worried about your *shoes*?"

"Oh, don't worry about the shoes." Hades lightly ran a finger down my arm. I flinched away. "I have a regulation uniform for those who take care of my babies—right down to the underwear. Tell me, do you care for industrial gray wool?"

I looked from Hades to Meg and back again, the horror dawning.

"Ah, you're getting the finer points," she snapped.

"That's torture," I breathed.

"Not quite," said Hades, looking around in distaste. "Please, let's discuss this in a more civilized place." He stepped away from the tiled wall and overflowing waste can. The smell of garbage and faint urine suddenly repulsed me, and I checked the bottom of my shoes. Meg rolled her eyes.

"Starbucks?" I asked hopefully.

Meg gave me a *duh* look. "I don't think we should discuss this in Starbucks, do you? We have to call someone about…" She jerked her head in the direction of the tracks.

I didn't want to look. "Let's go, please!"

Meg shrugged in resignation as she pulled out her cell. "Okay, Hades, lead us to a Starbucks. Shar likes chai tea and I want a—"

"I don't do Starbucks," he said haughtily. "And it wasn't a question. I was merely being polite. Now—" He flicked a wrist and Sweet Jeans was gone. Another flick and we were standing in a tropical garden. Hades was now wearing a very bright white polo shirt that looked custom-made, and cargo shorts. Throwing off my coat, gloves, sweater, scarf, and hat, I wriggled out of my boots to bury my toes in the warm white sand. *Ooh, nice!*

Meg put her cell back in her purse. "Some place you've got," she said, investigating every swaying palm tree and bright flower around her.

It seemed real enough. After a frigid New York night, this *was* heaven.

"Is this… Paradise?" I breathed. It sure looked like it

to me. The air was balmy and breezy and the azure ocean crashed just beyond the lush trees and undergrowth.

"Actually, this belongs to an acquaintance of mine," he began.

"Apollo?" asked Meg.

"God?" I said.

He gave us both a chiding look. "Hardly. It belongs to Arkady Romanov."

"The fashion guy? As in 'House of Romanov'?" I mused, staring out across the waves.

"Does it matter?" Meg put one hand on her hip. "Let's see, fabulous wealth, personal tropical island, both most likely ill-gotten—sounds like villain material to me." She pointed an accusing finger at Hades. " Why don't you take *him* down to Hell with you?"

"It's *Tartarus*, not Hell," said Hades with an annoyed voice. "Don't people study history anymore?" He snapped his fingers and lawn furniture materialized. Tropical drinks appeared in our hands. I sipped. *Pina Colada! The real thing!* I was about to take another taste when Meg kicked me, ogling my glass.

"Don't! Haven't you ever heard of 'Let's drink to that'? You'll be sealing a pact!"

I hastily slammed the drink down, spilling it.

Hades sighed morosely. "I don't do business that way. You must consent or I face certain ... unpleasantries." He frowned. "And I dislike unpleasantness, especially for myself."

I gave Meg a *see, I told you so* glance and picked up

my drink, which Hades had thoughtfully refreshed. Reluctantly, she picked up hers, a green concoction, sniffed, then tasted. I saw a small flush of pleasure. She looked away guiltily.

"Now, where were we? Ah, yes, Mr. Romanov. He's had a long time to enjoy this lovely place. That was his deal, you see. A regular mortal span wasn't enough for him, so I gave him a few extra years. But now his time's up. Next year he won't be spending any holidays on his island—I see him in a less *idyllic* location. You will send him to me." He twitched an elegant index finger with an obscenely large ruby. "Come, time grows short. The devil is in the details, as you humans say. We need to go over the particulars." A huge mahogany desk and three luxurious CEO-type leather chairs appeared on the sand. A tightly curled scroll lay on the desk.

He gestured. "Ladies, do have a seat. Let's wrap this up."

Gingerly, each of us took a chair and regarded Hades warily as he pushed the scroll toward us.

"Our agreement requires you two to lure Mr. Romanov to one of the many portals to my realm. To help you achieve this task, your natural talents will be enhanced." He looked from me to Meg and back again before continuing.

"As Margaret has so accurately described, the Sirens called to the sailors, who couldn't resist them. A word or a look drew their victims to them." He licked his full lips and gazed at me. "One look from you, Sharisse, is already captivating. From this moment forward, no mortal will be able to look away when you engage him. And you," he continued, turning to Meg, "so glib, Margaret. They'll hear you, and they'll obey."

"That's it?" I asked.

"I doubt it," Meg replied.

"Clever Margaret!" Hades drummed his fingers on the desk. "There is a time limit. Now let's see, when do your classes at school resume?" Instantly, a large open leather-bound datebook appeared, then floated down and gently rested on the desk. "You're a few days into your winter break. This is perfect. You must finish your task before you go back to school."

"But that's less than two weeks!" Meg cried.

I had to agree—it didn't seem like a lot of time to befriend and dispose of a renowned fashion mogul. It might take me that long to build an outfit around the red shoes. And what does a girl wear when sending someone to their doom?

"Why are you complaining? Most schools give a lot less time off than that. Ah, the perks of a private education! But you disappoint me," he continued. "That should be plenty of time for two clever young ladies like yourselves. When, or might I say *if*, you go back to school, read up on your ancient history. Now, I strongly suggest that you exercise your powers in moderation, and only on Mr. Romanov. They're quite potent. Oh, and there is a standard nondisclosure clause. You can't discuss any aspect of our dealings, or your powers, with anyone."

I shook my head, having a gut feeling that there was

still something that he wasn't telling us. It sounded too easy.

"What happens if we don't agree to do this?" Meg asked, staring at the scroll.

Hades chortled darkly. "Then this is your future."

Instantly, the blue sky turned the color of painted gray concrete and the balmy breeze became bitingly cold. I looked at Meg, who stood across from me. Two thick sets of bars and a stone hallway separated us. She wore a hideous orange jumpsuit and cheap prison slippers. I couldn't stop myself from laughing out loud.

"What's your problem?" she demanded.

"You ... you ..." I gasped, covering my mouth with my hand. "You look like a pumpkin!"

"Well, what do you think neon orange does for you?"

I looked down, and then we both started screaming.

A shrill whistle shut us up. There was Hades, pacing the wide hallway that divided my cell from Meg's.

"Do women still go for that 'man in uniform' thing?" he asked, parading around in front of us. Gone were the polo and cargo shorts. He brushed an imaginary fleck off his starched gray uniform, a bright *Death Row Detail* patch happily decorating the sleeve of his shirt.

"Death row?!" I shrieked. "But it was an accident!"

"Well, that's your opinion," Hades informed her coolly. "But really, enough of this nonsense, ladies. I'm offering you a way out of this horrible mess you've gotten yourselves into. Besides, it's not a hard job, and there are perks."

"Like what?" I challenged.

"Oh, limitless cash, an apartment on the Upper West Side, all at your disposal. Seems quite a bargain for you gals, really. All this for one special task. Make your choice—a good deal, or a last meal."

I snuck a peek at Meg. "Limitless cash!" she whispered.

"The Upper West Side!" I mouthed excitedly. So much for our poker faces for wheeling and dealing. *We were sooo easy.*

"Where do we sign?" we shouted.

"Excellent, ladies! So glad to have you on board!" Hades gestured for us to sit down. We were back on the island and in our own clothes. "Now let's address the matter of your formal consent." He unfurled the scroll and pointed to two blank lines at the bottom.

"Do you have a pen?" I asked, searching around.

"Pen?" Hades chuckled softly, and opened a drawer on his side of the desk. He placed a shiny silver stiletto blade in front of us. "Only blood will do."

We stared at each other. I hated the sight of blood, but this was no time to be squeamish. Stoically I took hold of the dagger and picked it up, and before I could stop myself, I put the tip to my finger, squeezed one eye shut and pressed it in. A few drops fell onto the parchment, sizzling as they landed. Meg gasped and pointed. The blood rolled along the first line, moving faster and faster as if it were being driven by an invisible pen. The leaden feeling in my stomach started creeping up into my throat as I saw my name form on the line in my all-too-familiar curly handwriting.

My hands shaking, I passed the blade to Meg. With the barest hesitation, she pricked her left thumb, then watched with a spellbound expression as her blood formed the precise letters of her name on the second blank.

"Perfect!" Hades whispered. "Let's not waste any time, shall we?"

Instantly we were back in the subway station, the club kids huddled in a corner, and Sweet Jeans—alive again!—standing between us. I clutched a shopping bag; it felt incredibly heavy. Looking down, I saw that Meg had hold of it as well. My head jerked up and we stared at each other, wide-eyed. I heard the rumble of the train a short way down the tunnel.

"It's just a pair of shoes." Sweet Jeans' voice echoed in my ear.

Meg laughed nervously, not taking her eyes off me. "You're right...and...red's not my color anyway." She let the bag go just as the train pulled into the station.

"My train," Sweet Jeans said, and turned to go. Rooted to the spot, we waved at him listlessly, and watched as he got on behind the club kids. The car doors closed. He was safe inside. The train lurched away with a squealing grind, and we were alone.

Meg let out a deep breath. "Okay, *that* was bizarre."

"No," I shook my head. "This is." I took hold of her wrist and raised her hand. She didn't realize that she was holding something: a shiny iPhone with a transparent envelope taped to it. Inside were two credit cards in slim leather cases, and two keys.

"There's something written here." Squinting, Meg passed it to me. What I thought was tape was a label. The spidery writing read:

S. Johnson, M. Wiley
Penthouse H2 at 100 West 81st Street.

Meg

Retail Therapy

*W*e waited until morning to take a look at Hades' apartment. I was hoping that this was all just a bad dream, but that was shattered when I woke up to find the iPhone, keys, and credit cards on my desk where I'd dropped them before going to bed. I called Shar at home and we agreed to meet outside my building.

I dashed off a note to my parents explaining that I'd be spending a few nights at Shar's, then I managed to get out the door before anyone else awoke. She was waiting outside, looking immaculately groomed and completely coordinated, whereas I'd barely taken the time to brush my teeth and hair.

"Let's do this," I said. The worried look in her eyes

must have been a perfect partner for the grim set of my mouth.

At Hades' building, the doorman ushered us into the festively decorated lobby without question, and we didn't pass anyone going up to the penthouse. The shiny key slid easily in and turned the lock of the heavy silver door.

We walked into a living room that was a montage of pale neutral colors, sparkling chrome, and huge vases of artfully arranged exotic flowers. It had one wall that was entirely glass; our view of Manhattan was spectacular for those not prone to vertigo.

Even so, I was about to swear that I wouldn't spend so much as a single night there when I noticed a door with a brass plaque that had my name etched onto it in gothic letters: my bedroom suite. Expecting another beige nightmare, I gasped when I saw the room I'd often sketched in my journal but hadn't shared with anyone else. There were the blood-red walls, the yards of black lace hanging from the ceiling like cobwebs, and my secret piece of lust-furniture, an ornately carved tester bed with scarlet drapings, all placed just as I'd imagined it. There was also a Victorian writing desk with secret compartments, each lacquered drawer stuffed with cash. I heard a squeal from Shar, who no doubt had gone to check out her room.

Taking a deep, reluctant breath, I slammed the door on my dream haven. There was a size-thirteen, triple-wide carbon footprint for all this materialism.

"I can never tell my mom about this place!" Shar said, throwing herself into a huge latte-colored leather chair near the wall of glass. Despite the panic in her voice, I could tell that she was thrilled with her bedroom suite. If she was that happy, I had no doubt it was decorated in every vicious shade of pink this side of Barbie.

I looked around the spacious living room and cringed; the place was impossibly high-end and sterile. With an all-powerful god as the landlord, it probably cleaned itself.

"We can't say anything to anyone. Ever," I told her.

"And how are we going to chase after Arkady? He's a celebrity! There are laws against stalking! It's going to be impossible!" Shar's voice had risen an octave.

"We'll figure it out." I raised a hand at her. "Please, don't have a panic attack."

I wandered over to the kitchen. Black marble tiled floors supported massive mahogany cabinets that stretched all the way to the ceiling. Along with the stainless steel fridge, I discovered, they were crammed with every sin-ful treat down to our favorite ice creams—Rocky Road for Shar and Cherry Garcia for me. How did he know? Ah, yes. God. Omniscient. Check.

"What have we done, Meg?" Shar said as I came back into the living room. She buried her face in her hands, then raised her head and looked around hopelessly. "How are we going to get that guy to a portal? He's rich and famous, and we're nobodies."

"We can't back out now, done is done." I sighed, mak-ing her scooch over. "This is probably one of those things that's a lot easier than it seems at first."

I mustn't have sounded convincing; Shar nodded thoughtfully, but she looked miserable.

"This is my fault, Meg, and I'm sorry!" A tear tracked down her porcelain cheek.

"I guess I'm just as much to blame, and hey"—I grinned crookedly—"the dark Underworld wouldn't be any fun alone. I was probably on my way there anyhow, and now I can drag you with me!"

Shar managed a feeble laugh, then leaned back and flipped on the TV, a wide-screen plasma monstrosity that almost covered the wall. We had one in every room, even the bathroom. I wasn't shocked to find that there was a seemingly endless collection of DVDs to go with them, but what was surprising was that Shar liked the same films I was into—pretty much anything with corsets, buff vampires, and bad-ass action heroes.

I got up and rummaged through my bag for the necessities I'd packed before I left home.

"What are you doing?" Shar asked as I pulled out a meat mallet from a kitchen drawer.

"Mmmmf," I mumbled, my mouth holding a tack. I took it out and banged it into the wall, then hung up a little mirror with a bright yellow frame.

"This is useless," she said, coming over and trying to see her reflection. "It doesn't go with the furniture, and it's ugly!"

"It's not meant to be pretty or used for checking eyeliner. It's a feng shui mirror. Hades' juju is in every corner of this place. You might not feel it, but I do."

She rolled her eyes and yanked the mallet out of my hand. "No more paranormal babble—"

"It's not babble! It's a—"

"*Science*, I know," she finished my sentence for me as I fixed her with an annoyed stare. "Do you have to hang things on the wall to feng-schweng this place?"

"Feng *shui*." I paused for a minute to think. "I *could* bring in a life element—"

"So buy a house plant. Oooh!" Shar grinned suddenly. "Why don't we do some serious damage to those credit cards?"

Against my instincts, five minutes later we were back outside and making our way to the department stores.

"Wait." I grabbed her arm, stopping her short. "First things first." I turned her around and steered her into a small coffee shop we'd passed by.

"A chai," she whispered in my ear, as the wreath on the door jingled when it slammed shut behind us.

I gave her a blistering look. "I *know*. Get a table." I sauntered up to the counter and excused myself to a man in a sharp suit who was still checking the menu, thinking, *geez, if you're not ready to order, let me go first.* He backed up a step. Smiling at the guy at the register, a sandy-haired grad-student type in a goofy Santa hat, I ordered, hoping he'd get it right. "Give me one large chai tea and one double mocha latte with skim milk, no whipped cream, please."

He stared at me and grinned.

"Um…" I said after a few moments, wondering when he was going to ring me up. "Can I get—"

"A large chai, and a double mocha *love* with skim." He cut me off in a dreamy monotone, then flung his head so that the pompom on his hat flicked back.

"Are you okay?" I asked, waving a hand in front of his face, thinking, *is he high?* I thought places like this had drug-testing policies.

"Sure." He continued to grin at me.

I felt a tap on my shoulder and turned to see a portly woman with velociraptor-length acrylic nails. Tiny reindeer were painted on them. She crossed her brawny arms over her huge and heaving chest and raised an over-penciled eyebrow at me.

"Can you place your order? I'm in a hurry!"

"I did!" I snapped, then turned back to Elf Boy, who had finally started entering my drinks into the register.

"How much is that?" I asked, taking out my wallet.

"I'm giving you our special discount, so you don't—"

"I'll take care of that!" Sharp Suit pushed past Dino Woman and whipped out a billfold.

"Hey!" she shouted, but a few more men stepped in front of her.

"There's no need." Elf Boy eyeballed Sharp Suit with a menacing expression. "I was about to say that she doesn't owe me anything."

"That's okay," I said firmly, tapping the counter and drawing their attention away from each other. "I can pay for my own drinks. Here." I handed him a $20. "Please put the rest in the tip jar."

I stepped aside and headed quickly for the coffee bar.

The barista, a slim pony-tailed blond girl with a lip piercing, looked at me, then peered down the length of the counter. The line was starting to snake around the shop. Alarmed, she darted over to the register. I heard some angry whispers, and then she came back, shaking her head.

"I'm so sorry. What was your order?"

I was too confused to be annoyed. Elf Boy had gone back to work and was waiting on Dino Woman, but he kept glancing my way. That I could tolerate, but not Sharp Suit, who waved and blew a kiss at me—he was old enough to be my dad! A guy next to me, also waiting for his order, caught my eye, and I mumbled, "Please save me from the weirdo convention that's come to town." What was wrong with these people?

I turned back to the barista.

"One large chai and a double mocha latte with skim, please."

"Coming up." She smiled, obviously relieved that I wasn't going to be difficult. Then she looked back at Elf Boy and rolled her eyes. "Men," she grumbled.

Cups finally in hand, I sashayed over to Shar, but my springy step died when I saw her. She sat, posed at the table, her long legs crossed and her slender fingers twisting her wavy blond locks. Her eyes flicked upwards toward the ceiling or down to the floor, but never at the tables around her—which were filled with guys of all ages. They were staring at her, drooly grins on their faces.

"Shar?" I whispered, standing there. "What's going

on?" I jerked my head as subtly as I could at the growing entourage.

"I was just sitting here, and they started crowding around!" she said in a low voice. "What about him?" She pointed to something behind me. It was Sharp Suit, pushing his way through the now-crowded shop as he eyed our table.

"He offered to pay for our drinks," I said, "but I have no idea who he is!"

"And him?" She jerked her head at someone standing behind me.

"I'm here to save you!" he gushed.

"We'd better go," Shar said, quickly getting up to leave. A few of the guys around us got up. It was too much.

"Please, leave us alone!" I said loudly. Several of the men sat back down as we hustled out the door, Shar giving one last glance back. When we were a few blocks away, we ducked into the recess of a closed docking bay.

"What happened back there?" she asked, breathless from our fast pace.

All I could do was hold up the palm of my free hand in confusion. Elf Boy was definitely in an altered state, but the others? Whatever it was, there had to be a logical explanation.

"Come on," Shar said. "I need some retail therapy to calm my nerves." She stepped out onto the sidewalk and I followed her. All seemed normal; people streamed around us, the usual pedestrian foot traffic. "We'll go to Bendel's first." She grinned at me. "They have this eco-friendly bath line that even you can't diss."

"Watch me," I chuckled, but the laughter died on my lips as a few guys turned their heads to look at us. We hurried along, and didn't stop until we reached the department store. We passed through the heavy doors and around the sparkling cases filled with rainbow-hued displays of leather gloves and overpriced hair accessories. Shar paused to look at a crystal-encrusted evening bag and waved down a sales person.

"Where are you ever going to use something like that?" I asked, but she ignored me and started chatting up the saleswoman, who took forever to unlock the case. Bored with waiting for her, my eyes started to wander around the vast atrium. I followed the line of tasteful garland, twisted with anti-holiday shades of slate gray and purple ribbon, around the ceiling to where it culminated in an elegant display over the main doors. Then I froze. When I could force myself to move, I groped for Shar's arm and clutched it fiercely.

"Wait a sec! Can't you see I'm—"

She stopped dead. Four or five guys from the coffee shop, including Elf Boy carrying two sloshing cups, had arrived, along with at least one man who I thought passed us when we were in the docking bay, and one or two I know we saw on the street. They were milling around the cases, slowly moving toward us.

"They weren't following us!" squeaked Shar, terrified. "I looked back!"

"There you are!" a male voice boomed. It was Sharp Suit. Shar blinked at him, like a rat taken by surprise when the dumpster's opened. "Do you like that bag?" He snatched it out of the saleswoman's hands. "Please, allow me." Out came the billfold.

"No!" another shouted. "I'll get it! And how about these earrings? Do you like these?"

"What do you want to do, buy us everything?!" I shouted. They froze and gaped at me for three long seconds, then ran around wildly, grabbing every black thing they could lay their hands on and throwing them at my feet. More wallets came out.

"You want me to get that for you, don't you?" A cute guy about our age fell to his knees in front of me.

I smiled at him, liking the dimple in his chin and the way his messy blond bangs brushed his lashes. He had such a sweet face. Then I came to my senses. "Uh. It's just that—"

"She wants me!" Cutie Face suddenly snarled, glaring at the men crowding around us. "It's me she wants to be with. Back off!"

"Stupid punk kid!" A construction worker pulled Cutie Face up from the floor by his collar and cocked his arm back as if to hit him.

"Stop!" I screamed.

Construction Guy dropped his prey onto the floor. "Anything for you, sweetheart."

In a flash, Cutie Face threw himself at the brawny older man and started swinging. Others joined in. Soon the whole male population was brawling, and it was spreading to the upper level of the store. Pink and black garments of all types rained down on us, and more men on the spiral staircase pushed and shoved, trying to get down to pay for it all.

"This is crazy!" Shar cowered against me as a pink nightie fluttered down from above. The female clerks and the few other customers were screaming. Shar had her hands over her ears.

Suddenly, my purse vibrated wildly—but it wasn't my cell. I dug around inside and pulled out the iPhone, its screen glowing scarlet. On it, I read:

To stop the thrall, just give a call:
Ase me isihi!

I passed it to Shar just as two guys slammed into the case next to us, shattering the glass. I gasped, and both of us jumped back and stared at them in horror. Now security guards were running toward us, but instead of grabbing the men on the floor, they started loading their arms with clothes and waving them at us.

"What does that mean, *ase me isihi*?" I hissed. The guy closest to us stopped short, a disoriented look in his eyes.

"Why am I here?" he asked. "I'm late for a meeting." He dropped his bundle, turned, and hurried off.

"Whatever it means, it stopped him," Shar said, excitement building in her voice. "Wait, that's it! We've used the gifts!"

"We have not!" I retorted sharply, stepping out of the way of two grappling Wall Street types. "All we did was—" I stopped, a nasty realization clawing at my brain.

"Talk to people and look at them," Shar said grimly. Then, reading the iPhone again, she nodded at me. I reread the words.

"One, two, three," she counted, and then together we shouted, "*Ase me isihi!*"

The store was suddenly quiet except for the steady hum of background music. Slowly, people started moving. Men got up from the floor, dusted themselves off, and headed for the doors.

"It worked!" I whispered, relieved.

"What's going on here?" one of the security guards barked. He looked suspiciously from person to person. Men shook their heads. When his gaze caught the tiger-print thong clutched in his own left hand, he blushed furiously and hastily dropped it.

"They just went insane!" Shar's saleswoman sobbed, coming out from her hiding place behind the counter. There were bits of broken glass in her hair.

The guard turned to us. "Tell me what happened."

"Uh…" Shar examined her shoes. "I…we…were over there getting ready to pay and they started grabbing and throwing everything in sight."

While he looked around, I whispered, "Let's buy something, it'll look less suspicious. Then we can leave." I grabbed a stack of black stuff. Shar did the same with a pink pile. I looked hopefully at the still-frazzled saleswoman, then jerked my head in the direction of an unsmashed counter. She nodded and made her way over, glass crunching under her feet as she went.

We followed at a quick pace; I wanted us out of there before someone called the police.

"Will that be cash or charge?" the woman asked.

"Charge." Without looking at her, Shar slipped Hades' shiny black Visa card out of her wallet and slid it across the counter. When the woman picked it up, I saw the image on the hologram sticker—Hades in a skimpy toga. Not something I needed or wanted to see. We ended up carrying out three bags each, and I didn't bother asking Shar what the bill came to. Hades' nasty ID was disturbing enough.

Once out in the fresh air, reality set in. This was going to be a lot harder than we thought, and I was starving.

"I need food," I said. It was nearly two o'clock, and so far we'd only had the almost-disastrous coffee.

"Me too," she said. "Hey, we're right by Red Velvet!" She all but clapped her hands.

"As in cake? Sorry, but I'm going to need something more substantial after that."

"They serve everything. Come on."

"I really don't want to deal with anyone else," I whined. "Can't we just go back to the apartment and get take-out?"

"I think I know how this works," Shar assured me. "We'll be smart about it. I'll talk but not look, you be charming but silent. And if we run into trouble, we'll say that *isihi* whatever."

Ignoring my protests, she ushered me down the street, keeping her eyes lowered. After a block or so, I spied Red Velvet's scarlet awning jutting out stiffly from the side of the building. When I stepped into the richly dark vestibule of the lobby, I found myself staring into a Victorian armoire. Its back-lit shelves were crammed with chocolate sculpted into Victorian winter-themed shapes; a furry boot with a curvy heel, cherubs surrounded by holly. *Let Them Eat Cake* snaked over the door in scripty gilt letters and the tantalizing scent of comfort food—roast turkey, mashed potatoes, fresh baked bread, and chocolate—filled the tiny space.

"You do all the talking," I reminded Shar.

She nodded, and laying a well manicured hand on the richly embossed brass door, swung it open and strolled inside.

A bird-sized woman stood behind a heavily carved and highly polished podium suitable for an archbishop, reading. Her black hair was drawn tightly away from her face and pulled her features into a haughty and unbecoming expression.

"Excuse me," Shar began. "A table for two, please."

"Do you have a reservation?" The hostess never looked up from her podium. Her voice matched her Kewpie-doll appearance—soft and squeaky.

"No, but there's room," Shar answered confidently, staring at the woman's face. *You're not supposed to do that! What if she looks up?* I poked her, but she waved me off behind her back.

Doll-face looked up and smiled smugly. "We're full up, I'm afraid. Unless you have a reservation."

Undeterred, Shar glanced at the dark and sparsely populated dining area. Only two tables were occupied.

"There are several empty tables and there doesn't seem..."

Now Doll-face looked very irritated. "We have nothing available. I suggest you call and make a reservation for another afternoon. We require at least 24 hours notice." She gave Shar a snide smile and resumed reading.

She was finished with us, but Shar wasn't done. She pulled me forward, her long fingers digging into my arm, a commanding look in her eye: she wanted me to try.

I coughed, and Dolly raised her head, and I said slowly, "Are you sure you can't seat us?"

"No," she replied coldly. "Is there anything else?"

"And there you have it," I said to Shar, and turned to leave.

"But—" Shar started.

"The manager can explain our policy if you need further clarification," Dolly said icily.

"That won't be necessary." I grabbed Shar's hand and steered her to the door. This time she complied.

"What happened back there?" she seethed fifteen minutes later when we were safely tucked into a booth at a quiet burger place. She'd managed to avoid eye contact while she ordered for both of us. There are times when only greasy fast food will kill the gall of being snubbed, especially by a half-starved, doll-faced tart.

I shrugged. "I don't know. She loved us not?"

"That's not supposed to happen. All those guys were ready to throw themselves off buildings for us."

I pointed at her with a French fry. "But not the hostess *girl*. Think about it. The barista wasn't affected by us, and neither was the saleswoman at Bendel's."

"You're right!" Shar lit up. "Great! I can still get my bikini wax! Oh … wait." She slammed down her diet soda. "Meg, we have to interact with guys."

I nodded thoughtfully, then brightened. "You can wear sunglasses—then no one will be able to see your eyes!"

Shar beamed at me, but her smile faded quickly. "But what about you? How are you going to get out of talking?"

"Learn sign language?"

"Cute. No time."

A guy jived by our table, headphones in his ears. I dug in my purse and pulled out my iPod.

"Look." I brandished the headphones. "I don't have to have it on, but if people see me with these in, they won't talk to me because they'll think I can't hear them."

"That's lame, Meg," Shar shook her head. "You can't have those things in your ears all the time! And what excuse could I have to wear sunglasses indoors?"

"You could say it's for medical reasons," I retorted. "Tell them you've developed glaucoma."

"Real funny, girlfriend. We'll have to think of something. Let's go."

Toting bags from Bendel's to Red Velvet to Burger World had been a chore, so we hailed a taxi. I made eye contact with the driver, nodding while Shar rattled off the address to the penthouse.

"All right," I said, once we were back in the apartment. "We have less than two weeks. What do we do?"

"I know what I'm going to do," Shar said, raising up a shopping bag. "I'm going to try some of this stuff on. I have no idea what we bought, or what sizes things are. Those guys were just throwing everything at us. At least they got the colors right." She dumped a bag onto a chair big enough to be a bed. "Here, take yours."

I poked at the black pile. I liked the black umbrella that some balmy guy had tossed to me, but I hated the idea of how much it all cost and the certainty that someone in some far-off third-world country was being exploited because of it. I fished out a sheer, antique-looking black blouse with faceted jet buttons. Shar was already heading to her room with an armful of pink fluff.

Cloistered in my bathroom—there were too many mirrors, I didn't need to see that much of myself—I took off my top, slipped the blouse on, and buttoned it. When I looked up, I squinted at the mirror. There was a small shadow behind me, but it didn't make any sense. I undid a few buttons and slipped the blouse off a little. Twisting around, I caught sight of what looked like a feather.

"Damn it," I muttered. Probably one of the pricey accessories in our stash had stuck to the blouse. I pulled at the feather and a twinge of pain shot up my spine. Frustrated, I closed my eyes, stopping myself from groping at the thing and making it worse. Some tag or pin must be caught in the fabric. Carefully, I got hold of it again and pulled slowly. I let out a squeak in spite of myself—that really hurt!

Then Shar screamed.

Topless except for my bra, I ran to her room. A new pair of jeans lay on her pink bed, ready to be tried on. She'd taken her shoes off, but that's as far as she'd gotten.

The toes on her left foot were fused together into three scaly ... talons.

"My foot!" She hopped around. "How am I going to wear my shoes?" When she saw me she stopped. "Oh ... Meg ..."

"What? What's wrong?"

She reached a slender arm over my shoulder and gently tugged on a long black feather, waving the top of it at me. Then she gave it a little tug. And sneezed.

"Ow!" I howled.

"It's *growing*!" she cried.

"Of course it is. You're becoming my Sirens." We both jumped. Hades was lounging on Shar's bed in a pose suggestive of a Harlequin romance, wearing a half-unbuttoned copper shirt and dark brown trousers. I blushed and swiftly covered my chest.

"Relax, Margaret." He snapped his fingers and I had my T-shirt on again. "Why so surprised? You know what Sirens look like. I do so love literal textbook interpretations! Every time you use your powers, you become a little more Siren-like. Naughty girls! I warned you only to use them on Mr. Romanov."

"You could have been more specific!" I spat. "And you should have told us it doesn't work on females!"

Shar stepped forward. "Now we can never look at or talk to any guys!"

"A minor detail, Margaret. And Sharisse, of course you can do both those things." Hades rose to his feet and pointed at us. "But you did more than simply talk to them and look at them today. You *engaged* those gentlemen in the coffee shop and in Bendel's with your eyes, didn't you Sharisse? You wanted their admiration—you were preening! And Margaret, you just had to tell them what to do. *Stop! Please save me from the weirdo convention!*" Hades mimicked my voice perfectly. "Sound familiar? Your looks and voice obeyed your intents."

"We didn't know!" Shar fumed.

"You should have. I told you, only use the powers on Mr. Romanov. Do you think those men would have followed you if you were just two teeny-girls out on a latte binge? Of course not. They heeded the Siren call because that's how you intentionally acted. Of course, you can access all this information on the iPhone. Didn't you check the apps?"

"No," I snapped. "Who's had time for that?"

"It's a handy little device. You should make time." Then he sent a suggestive look in Shar's direction. "*You* can always speed-dial me if you want me."

I turned away, disgusted.

Shar glared at him, then gestured angrily at her feet and my feathers. "Is this … permanent?"

"Only if you don't finish your assignment." Hades smirked. "But I'm sure you won't let that happen." He stood and stretched languidly, then disappeared.

Shar sneezed. "This is a problem. I'm allergic to feathers."

Shar

Chinese Fortune Cookie Say...

This is a disaster! Not even a good pedicure will disguise these!" I wailed. "No peek-a-boo pumps, no strappy sandals!"

"You're not alone in this Greek tragedy," said Meg derisively. "Look at me! What if someone sees this? Or maybe you know someone at your fancy salon who plucks chickens on the side?"

Okay, Meg was right. She had it worse. I could imagine the horror on people's faces if she wore a tank top. Back wax? Not going to cut it.

"Just don't get naked in front of anyone," I offered.

"Brilliant, Shar."

She turned around and around, trying to see her feathers in my full-length mirror.

I thought it was a good idea, I mused as I tried to shove my bird toes into a pair of bunny slippers.

No go.

"Oh for God's sake! Not only do I have ugly feet, but they're bigger!"

"Stop whining, Shar. It gives you an excuse to go shoe shopping." Meg was trying to tuck a stray feather back down into her shirt. It refused to stay put. "Grrr! Let's order some pizza while we figure out how to deal with this." She stomped off to the kitchen. I followed.

"No pizza!" I shouted after her. "Remember what happened last time?"

She tapped her cute little size nine-and-a-halves impatiently. "We can do Chinese—but only if it's vegetarian."

I jammed my fists onto my hips. "I'm a carnivore, and I want barbecued ribs and pork fried rice."

Meg huffed, blowing up her bangs. "Fine. I'll order." She muttered something under her breath about vultures.

"Top of the food chain, baby," I replied sweetly. She didn't respond. I returned to my room to find footwear that fit.

"About twenty minutes," she said a few moments later.

I was trying on all my boots. No dice. My former feet were narrow. All I could get into were my Uggs and some ratty old sneakers. My talon clicked on the marble floors as I dejectedly went to set the table with the Limoges china I'd seen in the dining room cabinet; leave the paper plates and plastic cutlery for the school cafeteria. When the doorbell rang, I reached for my glasses—no need to entrance the delivery guy—but I couldn't find them. I'd have to make do. When I opened the door, a rich aroma of garlic and roasted meat escaped from the boxes he carried.

"Meg! Food's here!" I yelled, averting my eyes. I grabbed the packages out of his hands. "Here's a fifty. Keep the change. Bye."

I thrust the bill into his hand and slammed the door. Two seconds later I heard the ding of the elevator, but just to be sure, I looked through the peephole. He was gone.

"Miss Manners would not approve," drawled Meg.

I made a face. "The Siren mojo. Didn't want him drooling all over the doorstep."

She threw up her hands. "Half the world's population is at risk. What's next?"

She followed me into the kitchen and I opened the boxes. Finding her dinner, she took a fork from the drawer and headed over to the couch.

"Aren't we going to eat in the dining room, with the china?"

Meg looked at me defiantly. "I'm watching *Judge Judy* while I eat."

"We have to attract a sophisticated man who's dined with world leaders and the ultra rich. Even with our new talents, we might not get past the front door if we act like pigs. Learn some manners. After we get rid of Arkady, you can go back to eating off trays."

Grumbling, she clicked off the TV, plopped her veggies into a bowl, and slumped at the table.

"Thank you," I replied primly, my back straight. We ate in silence for a bit before Meg grew restless.

"I can't just sit here and eat."

I put my fork down. "I know. I want to be done with this too. I'll Google Arkady's name and see what comes up. You check the iPhone apps. See if you can find one for portals. Hopefully there'll be at least one or two places close to where he works or parties. But you're not excused until you eat your vegetables." I caught her trying to suppress a smile.

After dinner, we hit the electronics.

I couldn't find much on Arkady. There were barely any records of him appearing in public at all. I clicked through my meager list hoping Meg would have more luck. But she wasn't saying much. I knew that whenever Meg was quiet, it either meant it wasn't good, or it was worse than I thought.

"Well, I found an app for the portals … " Her fingers skimmed over the iPhone. "And a bunch of other stuff too. Listen to this: *Abacus. Sundial. Don't be a Creten*"—she peered over the iPhone at me—"for those who want to know about godly etiquette. But wait, there's more: Lost? Try the *Go Homer* GPS." She paused, and curled her lip into a disgusted sneer. "*Feeling Illiad?* At least he has Pandora."

"Meg, the portals? Where are they?"

"The men's room in Madison Square Garden, near level G," she said finally.

"Gross."

"The locker room at the 34th Precinct."

"Not going there."

"The Wonder Wheel at Coney Island."

"Useless."

"The Botanical Gardens, next to the huge cactus."

"Unlikely."

"The city morgue."

"No way."

"I'll take the men's room over the morgue any day," she volunteered, to my surprise. "This list doesn't get any better. What have you found so far?"

"Hardly anything. Arkady's boutique and executive offices are on Fifth Avenue. That's basically it. He's become a recluse. Never seems to go anywhere public anymore."

"Not surprising." Meg nibbled an almond biscuit. "But we don't have to know his life story. What does he look like?"

"I couldn't find any pics of him online except this. Look."

She leaned over my shoulder. "He's wearing gloves and a hat pulled down to his chin. You can't see anything! We won't know him even if we're standing next to him!" Walking over to the counter to the food bag, she rummaged around inside. "Here, catch!"

She threw a fortune cookie to me. I caught it midair. If only I was this coordinated in gym. I snapped the cookie open, pulled out the message, and choked.

"You okay?" Meg asked, alarmed.

"It says, *He's hiring interns. Go apply. XOXOXOX Hades.*"
Meg looked fearfully at her cookie.

I frowned. "Open it. Apparently he's giving us help."

"That's what I'm afraid of. Look at all the *help* he's given us so far." With great reluctance, she crumbled her cookie and read the message. Her face turned bright red. "*Wear a turtleneck sweater and keep your mouth shut. H.*"

Ouch! Oh well, hopefully there'd be no more nasty surprises or omitted details.

Over breakfast the next day we went over our plan.

"If we have to deal with guys, you do all the talking. It worked with the cab and delivery guy," Meg said as she handed me my sunglasses. "And we'll both try to get as much information as we can from females. That way we can both talk."

"We'd better get moving," I said. I slapped on my fave shades—Dolce and Gabbanas—and we headed out. We'd decided that it probably wouldn't be a good idea for Meg to go to an interview with buds in her ears. This was not going to be easy for her.

"If you have to talk to a guy, just watch your words," I told her. "Don't get bossy." She gave me a curt nod.

We started walking toward Fifth Avenue. I decided it was better to burn off some nervous energy so I didn't mention getting a cab, although the wind was starting to pick up and I could feel my nose getting red and runny. Or was that from her feathers? She only had one or two. What would I do if she really started sprouting them?

I recognized the building as soon as I saw it. *House of*

Romanov glittered in crystals embedded into the stone. We gave our names to the—thankfully!—female concierge at the desk, who sent us to the executive offices on the tenth floor. Riding the elevator in silence, we ignored the friendly gaze of the FedEx man. We pushed through double glass doors to the receptionist's desk and got in line behind another girl about our age.

"Please, please, *please*, can't I take my resume to his office? How about to his secretary?"

The receptionist, a voluptuous woman with red hair and piercing green eyes, puffed with indignation. "No. Resume here." She pointed to a black tray where other papers lay.

At that moment, a door flew open and a fake-baked, super-slim man burst out. His black hair was smoothly plastered to his head and matched his fitted slacks and silk shirt. He was sweating big time, and it was making his eyeliner run.

"Mr. Arkady is not happy!" he squeaked, in a slightly Spanish accent. He whipped out a silky handkerchief and dabbed his forehead.

From the offices beyond, we heard unintelligible yelling.

"*Dios mio!*" he squealed, then crossed himself and sashayed away.

"On second thought," said the girl, picking up her resume from the tray, "maybe I'll apply at Betsy Johnson."

"Goodbye." The receptionist wagged a finger toward the door. The girl scurried away.

Arkady Romanov was not going to be easy to deal

with. If that was him shouting back there, he sounded deranged and dangerous. Super-fab!

The receptionist turned to us. I gulped and heard Meg do the same. *No way are we getting past Ms. T-Rex.* And we didn't even bring resumes. I started to push the glasses off my face and got ready to plead our case.

"Demi, where's the schedule for the show?" said a svelty male voice.

Quickly, I slid my glasses back on. We turned around. Another guy had walked into the reception area. A lock of wavy dark hair caressed his forehead and his mouth crooked up higher on one side, with a dimple. Black jeans and an open-collared white silk shirt clung to a bootyli-cious body. He didn't have eyeliner on, but his blue eyes were just as mesmerizing.

It was *him*! Sweet Jeans! *Oh mama.* When Meg inhaled sharply, I knew he was having the same effect on her.

"Hey, it's you two! What are you doing here? Come to hunt me down?"

Would you surrender?

"Uh, we're here to apply for the internships," I stam-mered after Meg nudged me.

"Get out! I'm Mr. Romanov's personal assistant. If you two feel as passionate about clothes as you do shoes, you'll be a great fit." He held out his hand. "By the way, I'm Jeremy Jamison." He gave us both a disarming smile that made my knees weak.

"I'm Sharisse."

He nodded and turned to Meg. "And you are?"

She was afraid to answer, I could tell. Unintentionally using her powers on Sweet Jeans and sprouting new feathers had to be her biggest worry. Well, at least she wouldn't be able to talk her way into going out to some club with him. Then the horror dawned. I wouldn't be able to bat my eyes into a date either!

Finally, she spoke.

"Meg," she answered timidly. She smiled prettily—scary pretty—and stuck out her hand for him to shake.

Total foul! That's my approach! But before he could say anything else, Demi the receptionist interrupted him.

"Not so fast, Jeremy. They have to fill out applications."

We'd forgotten about Ms. T-Rexy.

"I do the preliminary approvals." She curled a mauve lip. "And it's not looking good for these two. Resumes?" She crooked a long and forceful index finger, its nail polished to match her lipstick.

Meg fidgeted.

"Oh, ahem," I stuttered. "We could drop them off tomorrow. Or email them tonight." *Hades said go, so we went. Why couldn't he just get us the jobs? It probably amused him to watch us squirm.*

Jeremy leaned on a corner of the bare and gleaming silver desk. "Look, I'm desperate for help. Give them the forms, Demi. If you two can start work tomorrow, you're hired. Unless"—and he turned the charm full blast on us—"I find out you're spies for another house."

We both shook our heads vigorously.

If Demi could refuse him, she simply wasn't human. But why was he doing this for us? Was it our Siren powers at work? Meg had only said one word and I'd made no direct eye contact. Nervously, I wiggled my remaining toes. They didn't feel different. The last thing I needed was to grow another talon. I'd have to get custom-made shoes. How fun would it be to explain those ugly feet? I forced my concentration back on Demi.

She quirked an auburn brow. "I don't think so. There are to be no exceptions. For anyone. Mr. Romanov depends on us to protect him from..." She gave us a scornful look. "Undesirables."

"We're both seniors on scholarship at the Academically Independent High School, and I've been accepted to FIT and Meg to NYU," I blurted. Meg nodded and grinned at Jeremy.

He smiled back.

No fair!

"And they love to fight over shoes. I'll clear it with Mr. Romanov myself," Jeremy said. Demi huffed and gave us both a look that promised retribution, while Meg blushed. When Meg turned her head and our eyes locked, it was clear. *We both want him. It's going to be war.*

War it would be. And may the better-looking, better-dressed, nicer girl—namely, me—win.

Meg

Bad Kitty

I'd always pictured my first real job as championing some underdog, not-for-profit charity project, or maybe interning at a record label—not this.

Not wanting to waste any time, Shar insisted we call our parents and tell them we'd be spending the rest of our winter break with the other one's family. This way, she reasoned, we'd be close to Arkady, the job, and the portals with as few distractions as possible. Even as task-oriented as Shar was, I knew she had ulterior motives. Not only was being at the center of a fashion three-ring circus a dream come true for her, but there were the countless potential opportunities she'd get to corner and—drat her—*talk* to Jeremy.

"We need to get to work early," she bubbled. "Show some initiative. We'll win that Demi woman over. And we need to get close to Arkady. It would be better to see him without his hat and glasses just so we're sure when we voodoo him. We should plan on staying there late."

I didn't want to stay at the House of Romanov a minute longer than I had to, but Shar had a point. Demi clearly didn't like us, but she was only a receptionist, or at best some sort of office manager. Still, the last thing we needed was anyone blocking access to Arkady. I dreaded seeing Demi, but at least I knew I could speak to her without sprouting more feathers. I would, however, have to control myself, especially around Jeremy.

It was barely light when we left the apartment the next day; I wasn't on the street this early for school.

"It's not seven yet," I said, pulling out my pocket watch. "Will the building even be open?"

"Relax," Shar said smoothly. It was overcast, but she wore pitch-black sunglasses to make sure no one could see her eyes. "There's always twenty-four-seven security in big buildings like that. If we're lucky, we'll be the first ones in the office and we can poke around. Maybe we can even see what House of Romanov has planned for their fall collections. I read that they made some deals with a few different celebrities to—"

I stopped walking. "So *that's* what this is about? You want to get a leg up on the latest trends so you're dragging us to the House of Decadence extra early to spy them out? Fantastic, Shar. Do you realize that by the end of the day I could sport a tail peacocks would envy? And let's say I keep mum—how am I supposed to impress anyone, much less do a job?"

Halting, Shar spun around, looking at me as if she was doing me a favor by answering me. "You didn't need to talk too much yesterday and you made a good impression. Especially on Jeremy. You're clever. You'll adapt."

"I said my name—not too impressive. Now he probably thinks I have the mental capacity of an egg timer."

I'd resigned myself to the fact that I had no chance with Jeremy whatsoever. Even though Hades said I *could* talk to guys without enchanting them, I still had doubts. Before bed, I'd spent an hour scrolling through the various apps on the iPhone. Some were ridiculous and absolutely useless: *Ancient Greek Pronunciation Guide* and *Are You Epicurious (food of the gods)* and *Odyssey Underworld Tours*. But what Hades told us was all there, word for word, in an app called *Sirenz—A Beginner's Guide*, which said: *"Your looks and voice obey your intent. If you desire it, the Siren call will beckon."*

I didn't trust myself not to use the power by accident. Not that I would outright order Jeremy to like me; it was the intent of my feelings that might be dangerous. I just didn't know, and I didn't want to take the risk. Shar had to know I was at a disadvantage, and I'm sure she didn't mind that one bit. I crossed my arms against my chest and glowered at her.

She flashed her palm at my face. "Think what you want about my motives. At least *I* came up with a plan: get in early before there are too many people asking questions, and scope the place out. What have you done?"

I brightened a bit and held up my bag, which I'd made from recycling an old pair of jeans.

"You brought your purse. Bravo, Meg."

"Look past the purse." I picked up the metallic black cat fastened to one of the handles and shook it at her. The little bell inside it jingled.

"Okay." She looked at me like I was completely insane. "You have your purse, and you have a cat bell. Very smart, Meg. You're totally prepared to face the day."

"It's an ancient Japanese talisman for good fortune," I snapped, pushing the bag into her hands. She held the cat close to her face so she could see through her dark glasses.

"You're supposed to be smart, and you believe in this kooky stuff? And aren't black cats bad luck?" Shar flicked an annoyed glance at me. "Well, I think going into the office early will probably help us a little more than kitty cat here, even if it is cute." She pulled a lipstick from her purse and touched up perfect lips.

"Black is protective. I got one for you too."

Her head jerked up as she returned the tube to her bag. "Huh?"

I dug in my purse and pulled out a crumpled paper bag and handed it to her.

"It's pink!" she squealed when she pulled out an identical cat with paws upraised.

"Indeed it is."

"Where did you—"

"—the counter at Burger World when I paid the bill."

"Adorable!" Shar grinned, and wrinkled her nose in delight.

"It matches your outfit, too," I chirped, looking her up and down; she was a walking rose, dressed head to foot in pink.

"You're right," she laughed, and fastened the kitty to the strap of her bag. "Let's hope these bring good luck— we need it!"

Shar gave the security guard our names, and he let us up.

The sleek glass doors to the reception area were unlocked, so in we went and stood listening, but it was silent. I took a minute to survey our surroundings; a semi-circle of leather chairs bordered a glass table piled with slick magazines. It was almost like our latte-esque living room—beige and chrome, and more beige and chrome. I wondered if Hades had decorated this place too.

"Perfect!" Shar whispered. She pushed her glasses onto her forehead, her hazel eyes glowing with excitement. "Let's have a look around, and—"

She was interrupted by footfalls in the adjacent hall-way; we weren't the only early risers. If it was Demi, then she'd have to acknowledge that we were eager to please, and maybe that would get us a gold star. Hastily, Shar plunked the sunglasses back down over her nose.

A door opened, and out stepped Jeremy. I caught my breath. His hair was loose and hung over his cheek, brush-ing his chin and the collar of his slightly rumpled shirt.

He halted at the sight of us. "You two here already?"

Shar beamed. "Yes sir, bright and early and ready to work."

He looked at his watch, then pulled a band out of a pocket to tie his hair back. "Okay. Actually, this works out great because things will start to get busy fast around here once people start coming in, and that'll be in about ten minutes. I'll show you around."

He winked at me as he opened the door. The other side of the reception area was a different world. It was like stepping into Oz—there was no taupe or tan anywhere. Our feet bounced on a plush royal purple carpet as we walked, and I could see a distorted shadow of myself in the silvery foil pattern of the wallpaper. Every few yards, a glass case stood sentinel against the wall. Inside each one was a Fabergé egg.

"They're fakes," Jeremy whispered. "He keeps the real ones locked up somewhere. Hey, I have one of those!" He touched the cat hanging from my purse. "I'm always looking for good luck." He started down the main hallway.

I nodded and smiled vindictively at Shar, who scowled angrily while I tried not to gloat.

Jeremy walked briskly, speaking rapidly as if there wasn't enough time to tell us everything we had to know.

"It's a real hive in here. Mr. Romanov is already in his office and he's booked with appointments until eight or nine p.m., long after you're gone."

Shar piped up. "We want to be as helpful as we can. If you need us to stay late, we're good with that. Anything we can do for Ark—I mean, Mr. Romanov, we're there." Then she tripped over a lump in the fluffy rug and stumbled into the wall. We all stopped.

Jeremy looked back and frowned. "Are you okay? Don't you want to take your glasses off?"

Shar looked panicked. She didn't take off her shades—she didn't dare—and she didn't offer an explanation.

"Lasik," I blurted, before I could stop myself. For a few horrible seconds, I mentally searched my body, waiting to feel something sprout or puff...but nothing. Then I calmed down, remembering what Hades had said. I hadn't given any suggestions or orders, nor wanted to. I'd just offered an explanation. Perhaps this wasn't going to be mission impossible, just mission very, very, very careful. "Shar had Lasik surgery," I repeated, in as low and monotone a voice as I could.

"Oh," he began. I couldn't tell whether he accepted it or not, but thankfully, Shar joined in.

"Yeah, no more contacts for me. But I have to wear these for a while—inside and out." She tapped her glasses.

"Just take it slow then, okay? Mr. Romanov doesn't like to deal with workmen's comp." He patted her on the shoulder and I couldn't help but notice that his hand didn't linger there. We continued our tour of the office.

"Here's the Yellow Salon, the Purple Salon, the fitting rooms, and the Gold Salon. Admin is on the other side—Reynaldo, the Collection Coordinator, is there, and so is Callie, our IT person. Mr. Romanov's office is down the hall to the end, behind the huge double doors. I don't know if you'll actually be able to meet him, not many of the staff have. He's a very private person, and extremely busy."

Was this another of Hades' ironic manipulations? We'd be in the same building, on the same floor, and probably within feet of Arkady Romanov, but we'd never get close enough to him to get him to a portal. The nearest one was four blocks away at the city morgue, and I doubted we'd be able to convince him to go there without morphing ourselves into poultry. I nudged Shar hard in the ribs, and she looked at me and glared angrily. She had to be thinking the same thing as I was; that we should just toddle on down to the morgue, open a fridge door, and go to Tartarus ourselves. How could we ever do this assignment?

"Anyway," Jeremy continued, "you'll be playing a very important role. With our New Year's Eve showing, it's hectic. If someone needs something around here, you two are the ones to take care of it. If they need coffee, office supplies, TP, anything, you get it." He stopped and looked from Shar to me. "Do you understand?"

I tried to crack a smile and forced myself to nod.

"Totally." Shar answered. "We're here to pamper and please."

"That's what I like to hear. Now, the pay isn't exactly the greatest..."

Jeremy kept talking and walking, but I didn't want to hear any more about our duties. There had to be some redeeming qualities to this place—other than his perfect face.

From where we were standing, I heard someone come in, then the barking of several dogs.

Jeremy raised his eyebrows and put a hand on each of our shoulders. "Here we go!" He ran his hand lightly down my arm and I felt my face get hot. Redeeming quality found—physical contact!

We returned to the lobby area to find Demi, the amazon receptionist who'd almost made toast out of us on our last visit, dressed down in jeans and a brilliant spring-green sweater. She had a voluminous, daffodil-yellow shawl draped across her broad shoulders, and she was holding leashes attached to three super-sized dogs. The largest one looked a little too much like a wolf. They sat calmly at her side panting happily as she bent over the only desk in the area and sorted through a stack of papers.

"Demi!" Jeremy called.

She turned around and smiled coyly at us. "I see our interns are here." She checked her watch. "And early."

"Told you they'd work out." Jeremy grinned. "I'll leave them in your capable hands. I'm sure you have some things they can start with? Or ask Callie or Reynaldo if they need help with anything."

Demi reached down and patted the top of the wolf's head. "Oh, most definitely."

Jeremy turned and left, and the three of us stood there staring at each other. One of the dogs growled.

"So," Shar began, breaking the silence. I didn't like the way Demi was checking us out. "Um, you, uh, do a lot of…different things around here."

"Really, Sharisse, you're more dense than a petrified tree. Take those ridiculous things off. Lasik surgery indeed."

Wait—*how did she know about our little lie?*

"And you, Margaret," she said, turning to me. "Please, don't bother to mince words. You won't turn into a carrion bird talking to me."

Shar took off her glasses. "Do you know Hades?" she whispered.

Demi glared at her. "Do not speak *his* name in my presence."

"Who are you?" I asked.

"I'm someone who doesn't like being robbed of what is most precious to me."

"You're from the same circles as Had—I mean, our mutual acquaintance?" I asked.

She nodded.

"Who *are* you?" Shar repeated, at a loss. I was stumped too. Demi knew about us, and she knew about Hades. Apparently she didn't like him—that was something we had in common—but still, that told me nothing. Last night's flip through *The Encyclopedia of Myth* revealed that he had a long list of enemies.

Demi took a long, slow deep breath, like she was at the end of her patience.

"I don't mean to be rude," Shar stammered. "But since you seem know about our situation, we're ... a little nervous. With all these myths and ancient histories popping to life in front of us, and everything."

"Well said," I muttered, and nodded my head.

"I'm Demeter." She sighed. "Think you can figure it out now?"

Demeter ... I thought hard. Demeter was Hades' mother-in-law, and the goddess akin to Mother Nature. In her grief about having her daughter, Persephone, spend half the year in Tartarus, she made the earth hibernate each winter.

But what was she doing here, at the House of Romanov? Whatever the reason, it couldn't be good—for us.

"I'll make it a bit clearer for you," Demi continued. "That repugnant pig you're working for stole my baby. I've never been able to get her back. She deserves far better than him. Oh, my poor darling Persephone, spending half the year in that horrible place ... down there!"

"I'm sorry," Shar said. "But we have nothing to do with—"

Demeter waved at hand at us. "How could I ever expect *you* to understand? You're mortals. Simple, stupid, inferior mortals."

Pardon me?

"But maybe even you two can comprehend this: I *loathe* him. If I can throw his schemes askew, it gives a small bit of satisfaction."

"But if we don't get Arkady, then—" Shar began.

I elbowed her in the arm to stop her. "Nondisclosure?" I mouthed, wide-eyed. We probably already said more than we should have.

Demeter stared menacingly at us, and the halogen

lights over our heads flickered and buzzed. "I really don't care about your little arrangement with him. I want my Persephone back. *That* is my only concern." She crossed her arms and turned away from us, but I could feel the anger rippling off her. The dogs whimpered.

"Soooo, you know about..." Shar started cautiously, then pointed at herself and me. "You know. Our arrangement."

Demi's chin inched up. "I'm a goddess. There's not much I'm unaware of."

"If you're a goddess, then you have to know a way to get Persephone back," Shar argued.

Demeter seemed to grow even bigger, if that was possible, and together, Shar and I shrank and backed up into the wall.

"Impertinence! If there was a way, don't you think I would've done it?" she boomed. "We all have rules to follow, otherwise it would always be forever-summer because she'd be with me instead of him!"

Demeter was not to be trifled with. We seemed to be stuck in the middle, though, so we needed to make peace with her. Or at the very least, get her to see us as unwilling victims of Hades' plan.

I drew myself up to my full height—all five foot three inches—and stepped in front of Shar. Trying to appear conciliatory, I said, "I wish we could help you with that—"

"We'll try and stay out of your way," Shar added, nodding very hard. "We don't want any trouble."

Demeter spun around and regarded us with a specula-tive gleam in her eye that unnerved me. I felt Shar inching closer to me.

"There is … one possibility," she murmured, mov-ing closer to me. "I think I want to keep both of you in my sights." She smelled like a field of flowers; if I closed my eyes, I'd swear I was standing in an open meadow in springtime. I fought the urge to relax my guard and kept my eyes on her. She reached out an elegant finger and poked at the black cat hanging on my purse handle. "Tell me, do you really think these things work?"

"Absolutely," I answered, with as much confidence as I could muster. "I think it's more of a psychological thing. You know, it makes me think I can do what I need to do."

Demi nodded thoughtfully. "Charms are all very well, I suppose. But you can't depend on them. You and Sharisse should concentrate on using your talents."

"That's a little difficult," Shar said, "considering that every time we use them, we grow feathers and claws. I don't want to add a beak to match my feet!"

Demeter waved a dismissive hand. "The power you have goes far beyond the uses he's divulged. You two haven't even begun to realize what you're capable of."

I didn't understand. I'd scrolled through the iPhone a few times, and the rules seemed to be in line with every-thing Hades told us. Our powers—the enthralling look and the compelling speech—were always in effect; they only worked on males—we'd discovered that tidbit on our own; and they were more potent when we were in close proximity to each other. Once we'd enthralled someone, we could leave them and wait for the effects to wear off naturally; the duration was determined by how intensely we'd used the gift on them. Or, we could release them immediately by saying *ase me isihi*, which Hades thoughtfully footnoted was Greek for "leave me alone." It also reminded us that we took on more physical Siren traits every time we used the gifts. I couldn't find any mention of additional powers, which made me suspicious...of Demeter, but also of Hades and the iPhone. What was the truth?

Demi fixed her eyes on us. "Pay attention. I'm only going to say this *once*." She leaned in confidentially. "Your wiles don't just affect mortal males, you know. Even a god would be susceptible to you if you tried hard enough. Sharisse could have *him* under that well-pedicured size-ten foot of hers." She stroked the wolf dog. His eyes were far too intelligent and he seemed to be grinning.

"But—" Shar protested.

Demeter slapped a hand on one hip and stared at us with a bored expression.

"How do you know this?" I couldn't help asking. "What would Shar have to do?"

Shar pinched me. I guess I deserved it, but I was curious. Why would Demeter be encouraging Shar to play the role of seductress? It didn't make sense, because wouldn't it hurt Persephone? Or did Demeter think that if Hades focused his interest on someone else...*Shar*? I shut the thought out. It was too gross to consider, not to mention impossible. Persephone was a *goddess*. Hottie though Shar was, wouldn't Hades consider going from divine to mortal as trading down?

Demeter stared at us both as if we were stupid, and I was beginning to feel that way.

"Do I need to repeat myself, Margaret?" she snapped. "There's little about the gods that I don't know. Sharisse." She turned to my roomie. "Don't pass up an opportunity like this to use your gifts to *your* advantage. I'm practically giving you everything you want."

"Wait a sec," Shar interrupted, voicing what I'd just been thinking. "You want me and *Hades*—"

Demi raised an imperious hand, twisting her head away from us. After a moment, she turned back with a snarl.

"How many times do I have to tell you *not to say his name*? Think about the valuable advice I've just imparted to you."

One of the dogs howled. "That's right, Gorby," she said, patting its head. She turned to us. "Time to take Arkady's babies for their walkies." She threw the leashes at us. "You two do it. You might need the practice."

She snapped her fingers, and we were standing in the Central Park dog walk.

"What the—" I yelped, whirling around and tangling my foot in a dog leash. Shar held two leashes and I held one—the one with the wolf attached to it. How thoughtful of Demeter to pop us into our coats, and to tuck the pooper-scooper under my arm and the collection bag under Shar's.

"Maybe this isn't a good time to bring this up," Shar said to me as Gorby and friends started to drag us along. "You know those little cat charms? They don't work! That goddess is bad luck personified!"

Somewhere in the depths of my purse, something buzzed. Keeping my arm tight to my side so I wouldn't lose the scooper, I dug with my free hand. Was it the iPhone? It wouldn't surprise me if Hades was on the line, ready to deliver an acerbic comment—but for once I actually hoped it was him. I wanted to know why he didn't warn us about Demeter or anyone else who might pop up.

My fingers finally found the buzzing thing. Not the iPhone, but my own cell. I'd gotten a text. Flipping it open, I read:

So glad u came in. Fate likes me. J.

Jeremy?! I felt my knees get wobbly but managed to tap out a slow reply with my thumb.

Me 2 but where'd u get my #?

We hadn't traded. I hit send. About three seconds later, another text came through.

Cheated & took from ur app. U mad?

Not likely! I looked over at Shar, being dragged by the dogs a few yards in front of me. She was scolding them to slow down. I typed back.

Nooo.

I hit send and waited. A new message popped up:

☺

The wolf must have decided to surge ahead and catch up with his comrades, because he tugged so hard I almost lost my balance.

"Whoa!" I yelled. "Heel!" Immediately, all the dogs halted, and I felt a twinge on my thigh.

Frantically, I patted my leg. I'd sprouted another feather—or three. Crouching, I took a peek under each of the dog's legs. All boys—and dogs are mortal. Hades hadn't specified *human*.

"What the heck are you doing?" Shar asked, a wary look on her face.

"Do yourself a favor and don't look at the dogs," I said. It took her a second, but she got it. "Next time Hades shows his face, I have a few questions. Let's start with why Demeter is our coworker. You know, you could call him—remember when he told you he was on speed-dial? He is—I checked."

"Not listening!"

But I could tell she heard me and was thinking about it. Demeter's presence could bring our progress to a grinding halt, and that seemed awfully convenient.

"*Ase me isihi,*" I muttered, and all the dogs took off again.

Please, please PLEASE help me get through this, kitty, I chanted silently. *I have to stay focused. I have to...* I groped along the handle of my purse with my free hand, but it clasped on air. Kitty's empty chain swung from the strap.

The cat was out of the bag.

Shar

Here's π In Your Face

*M*uscles bulged underneath Gustav's bright white tee, and his Lycra pants were so form-fitting I expected to see each hair follicle. And he wasn't the first masseuse or medical person to strut through here. Yesterday, dog walking for Demeter; today, watching a parade of health technicians. I counted two personal trainers, a yoga guru, an aroma therapist, and three herbalists marching through the office before ten a.m. Was this a house of fashion or a wellness center?

I lingered outside Jeremy's office hoping for a chance to chat him up. He was alone now, but continually on the phone booking medical appointments for Arkady. Some of the treatments he mentioned were downright creepy and weird, even for the Hollywood crowd. Sleeping in oxygen tanks? Too much like a coffin. Eating nothing but raw veggies? Too depriving.

What some people will do to look good.

"Hi!" I waved at him when he hung up the phone. He looked up and smiled.

"How are your eyes?" he asked.

"A little better." I tilted my head to the side. Now what to say? "Getting ready for this show is a lot of work."

Well duh! Won't he think you're clever!

He nodded. "Tell me about it." He sounded annoyed.

I frowned. "Don't you like it here?"

He leaned back in his chair. "It's okay. I guess."

"You guess? You're working at one of the most exclusive houses in the city and it's only *okay*?"

"Jeremy!" A deep, gravelly and sharp voice echoed from the intercom.

"There's that," he said, pointing at the phone with a grimace, "and the fact that fashion isn't exactly my thing. But it pays the bills. Keeps me in music. Hey." His eyes lit up. Was I making some progress with him? I smiled, but looked at the wall just in case my glasses weren't dark enough. "Is Meg okay?" he asked.

"Meg?" She wasn't part of this conversation!

"Yeah. She's been really quiet. I saw her in the copy room and she just waved and went right back to work. Like she didn't want to talk."

Opportunity!

"Oh, uh, I think she might be a little nervous about being here. Fashion isn't really her thing either."

No no no! Don't say that!

"Really?" He perked up. "I thought she really wanted those shoes you two were arguing over."

"Jeremy!" Arkady's scream saved me from having to respond about our shoe confrontation. He pushed his chair back and got up.

"I'd better go. You guys are doing great. Tell Meg not to be nervous, okay?" He patted me on the shoulder like I was his bud.

Grrr! I watched him zip into Arkady's office. When I turned around, I found myself face to face with Gustav, who gave me a toothy Colgate grin as he lumbered down the hall.

Reynaldo, the sweaty but perfectly styled man we'd seen that first day, hustled closely behind him, but then stopped in front of me. I'd just learned that Reynaldo supervised the runway shows. I squinted at him through my shades. He wore tight black pants and an unbuttoned, flowing pirate-type shirt showing off his anorexic chest. The diamonds in his ear lobe winked at me.

"Nice glasses, chica. Go and get your friend and clean up the Gold Salon. A verrry important client is coming in. Hurry." He flicked a pinkie to dismiss me.

"Who is it?" I asked, smoothing down my hair.

"No one that concerns you," he huffed in a falsetto. My voice hadn't been that girly since sixth grade. "Just get down there, clean up, and leave as quickly as possible. Try not to be seen!"

I hurried down the hall. "Meg!" She was still stuck in the copy room. It was a good place for her. In the offices, we had no excuse for her to wear headphones, but in here, everyone just dumped their copy jobs in a bin and left without expecting any response. She'd managed to stay out of trouble all day. Her head snapped up when I came in and I caught a scared look in her eye. Must be hard for her to play the strong silent type. Never talk? I sure couldn't do it.

"We've got to clean up the Gold Salon for some client." My voice sounded sharper than I wanted, but who could blame me? *I'm talking to him and he's talking about* her. *And now I'm a maid!*

She sighed in relief, not seeming to notice. "I'll go any place where I can move my tongue. I think the muscles are atrophying."

Of course the room was a mess. Clothes, fabric scraps, paper, boxes, and so much other junk cluttered the room.

"We don't have a lot of time," I said.

"Big surprise," Meg replied tersely as she started collecting the trash. I pushed the racks of designer clothes against a wall and snatched up an upright vacuum. It took less time than I'd expected.

Meg exhaled sharply, blowing aside her spiky bangs. "What slice of serfdom will Reynaldo be serving up next?"

I couldn't stop myself from giggling. We were given all the crappy jobs. Who knew that fashion was an ugly, degrading business? What would the cruel powers on high think of next? But before I could answer, I heard a velvety male voice above me say "Yo."

He looked like someone famous, but I couldn't think of a name. Extensive grillwork on his teeth, *with* diamonds, a ton of heavy gold jewelry, pants almost falling off what was probably a buff butt—he was some hip-hop dude, but which one?

He smiled at me and I saw my surprised reflection in his Gucci sunglasses; not the ones they sold to the overpaying public, but the private, one-of-a-kind custom-made line.

"Yeah, I'm QT π. Here's an autographed pic for you, shuga booty." He snapped his fingers and another similarly dressed but less bejeweled guy rushed forward, shoving a glossy 8×10 in my face. "And one for your friend." He snapped another photo at me. I took them both, then turned to roll my eyes at Meg as I handed them to her. The third person in the mini entourage, a woman whose angular face should have been on the cover of *Vogue*, minus the sneering lip, strutted up to QT. She was cradling one of those yippy teacup breeds of dog. It was wearing more diamonds on its collar than an Oscar-nominated actress. The gems spelled out "Shakur."

"Get Shakur's outfits. *Now!*"

She gave an imperious wave in our direction. I could feel how brittle my smile was. My tinted glasses were in place and hadn't failed me all day, so I wasn't worried about vamping the party boys. Thankfully, Meg was keeping her cool.

"Um, dog clothes?" I asked.

Ms. Vogue looked down the length of her long patrician nose at us. "Arkady created an exclusive line just for Shakur and named it after QT π." She smiled lovingly at the flea bag, scratching it under the chin.

"It's called 'I Love Pi,'" he said, showing us a sparkly smile.

Was I supposed to think that was clever? Fail.

"And he's making matching outfits for me, so that Shakur and I can be coordinated. I want the leather jackets first. You!" she snapped at Meg. "Move your fat ass and find them. Then call Arkady down here."

"Were you speaking to me?" Meg inquired, overly polite.

No! Not now!

"Meg! Shhh!"

Vogue glared at Meg. "Yeah, you shush, and get moving!"

I wanted to march up to Vogue and scratch her eyes out—see what she'd think of that. Instead, I said, "I'll get Jeremy to assist you." I didn't bother with a smile.

Vogue's eyes glittered dangerously. "Get ARKADY. I don't deal with little people."

Oh, Vogue, you've gone too far.

"Don't speak to us like that!" Meg snarled.

I slapped my forehead with my hand. *I wonder how often Cerberus poops. Could I convince Hades to get a kitty cat?*

"Yeah, you heard the pretty lady. Don't talk to them

like that," said QT, turning on Vogue with a sharp voice and grim set to his jaw. Her mouth dropped open in shock.

I looked at Meg, trying to give her a subtle *Shut up!* gesture, but she was too busy being pissed off and didn't see it.

"We demand . . . ouch! Respect! Ouch!" Meg quickly put her hands behind her back.

Uh oh. She's sprouting feathers! If she doesn't shut up soon, she's going to be wearing an emu skirt. I sneezed several times.

But Meg still couldn't let it go.

"Keep a leash on her! Ouch! Damn it!"

"She's right," said QT, wagging a finger at Vogue. "You a mean woman. You need to be leashed."

"I'll get Jeremy, he'll speak to Mr. Romanov, and this will all be settled," I said, trying to shoo Meg out of the salon.

No one was listening to me. I felt another sneeze building.

"QT, don't you listen to her! You can't treat me like that!" Vogue did that hand-on-hips, head-weaving move that made her look like an angry Egyptian dancer.

"Baby, if she say you need a leash, then you need one—bad!"

A really nasty fight was imminent. I grabbed Meg's wrist and pulled her out of the room as fast as I could, but not before she turned to the shove-a-picture-in-your-face guy. She crumpled the photo into a ball and tossed it back at him. "Take your self-serving pictures back! We're not impressed!" He scrambled to catch them. She gave him her snottiest, most condescending look.

I rushed her into the nearest office, where Reynaldo sat at a glass and chrome desk. I whipped off my glasses and ogled him.

"Out. Now."

"Ever hear the word 'please'? You two sort things out. I'll be back in five," he murmured, then glided away. He gave a little two-finger wave as he stepped out and closed the door. It clicked softly.

"Are you ... Ah-choo! Effin crazy ... Ah-choo! Meg?"

She growled, pointing toward the hall. "Everyone has their limit. They breached mine!"

"Yeah, but now you're paying the price," I snapped angrily. "You realize we might get fired, then we'd have to use our powers more just to get close to Arkady, which means more feathers and talons for us! We could be running from animal control before tomorrow's out!"

She paled and I was immediately sorry. "Are you okay? Here, let me see how bad. You have underwear on, right?"

"Oooh, yes, do let us see. I love a full-figured gal."

That voice of temptation, frustration, and damnation. Hades. He stood there, arms crossed, casually leaning against Reynaldo's desk. If Reynaldo saw him, he'd be in love. Hades wore black jeans, which left little to my sick imagination, and a danger-orange silk shirt, open at the neck. I refused to look directly at the intricate design of his belt buckle on the low-slung jeans. If only he wasn't

Hades, and we weren't indentured servants, and he didn't have bad intentions.

"Well, ladies, I see you've been using your gifts. Impish girls!" He displayed a playful grin.

Meg jumped up. "So glad you dropped in. Would you mind explaining why your mother-in-law is here?"

"She is?" he replied over-innocently.

I poked him in the chest. "Not buying it. Don't tell us that you had no—"

"Do that again," he purred, leaning forward.

Now it was my turn to jump back.

"Next time." Hades pouted, then straightened up. "Demeter's a goddess, I can't stop her comings and goings. But you should know that she and I don't get along."

"Really?" said Meg thickly.

"Pants a little tight, Margaret? Let me help you." He snapped, and she was dressed in a flowing skirt. She sighed blissfully, running a hand over the material which sported a small black-and-white pattern of geometric flowers.

"Nice diversion, Hades," I said tightly. "Spill it; is this another *oh didn't I mention it* kind of thing?" He gazed at me as if I'd stabbed him.

"*Cara mia*, so cruel, so cruel! I wouldn't deliberately deceive you. As I said, Demeter can appear wherever and whenever she desires. She must've gotten wind of my doings, and well…"

"And now we have to deal with her too," Meg groused. "Wonderful."

"I admit it is difficult, but it's not impossible." Hades leaned against the door.

"How so?" I snapped. "If she's a goddess, she can stop us from finishing this job."

He smiled slyly. "Oh no she can't. We have rules that we must abide by, just like you mortals."

"So she said," added Meg, giving her skirt a twirl. She'd better not be distracted. Since when did she care about skirts?

"Yes, Margaret. And once you entrance Mr. Romanov, she can't undo it. He'll be under *your* command."

"That would be great," I said, "but I'm pretty sure she'll see to it that we can't get within five feet of him."

"And she might not even have to do that, considering he's constantly enshrined in that office of his and surrounded by people all day and all night," Meg added.

"You two worry over the wrong things. Look at you!" Hades picked up a stray feather and brushed it against his cheek while staring intently at me. His bronzed skin was smooth and so soft looking. I blushed furiously and had to shake my head to force my mind to think about other things.

"I'm fine. I haven't been using my gift that much."

"No?" He stepped forward, gently took my hand and brought it to his lips. It was then I saw the long, fierce-looking talons.

"Eww!" I always hated long, curved nails, acrylic or otherwise. Too cruel looking, like a bird of prey. I ran around to the desk, yanked open the top drawer, and searched until

I found scissors. Quickly I snipped off the offending cartilage.

They grew back.

"No!" I shouted, clipping them again. They grew once more.

I threw the scissors back in the drawer, shut it, and dropped into Reynaldo's chair.

"I can't have you using your powers and then destroying the evidence." Hades' smile would melt the polar ice caps, but I felt as cold as absolute zero. "Don't worry, *cara mia*, you will always be beautiful no matter what form you take. However, you and Margaret are running out of time. More action, less fooling around. Unless you *want* to join me. I will return your beautiful appendages at once if you do."

I blushed but shouted, "No! I'll do the job!"

"Then don't waste your gifts on people like QT. He belongs to me already and I can't have him confused over who is his master. Tell me, you don't think his pathetic raps alone got him that famous, do you?" Hades gazed out the window to the busy street below. "I miss the days when language was as musical as the melody. You people listen to garbage. Rock, Rap, Country, Techno." He visibly shuddered. "Talk about small talent! Not a performer today can measure up to a Greek minstrel. But things change so quickly with mortals and it's not easy living with the same gods for all time. You humans are what make life interesting." He turned around to gift us with that killer smile again. "It's so much fun to play with you. We on Olympus almost never correctly guess what stupid things you're going to do next. It's invigorating watching you struggle and fail, only to get back up and do it again. Like watching a mouse in a maze, waiting for the snake at the other end to find you."

"Glad you find us so amusing," Meg quipped. I snorted behind my clawed hand.

"Laugh all you want ladies, but remember what that clever man Will said, 'He who laughs last...'" The door flung open and Reynaldo burst in, carrying a tray of gourmet brownies. Hades smirked at him, but Reynaldo didn't seem to notice.

Hades snapped his fingers. Reynaldo, with a perturbed look, and Meg with her mouth slightly open as if to say something, stood frozen. Hades moved closer to me, a hair's breadth away.

"By the way, *cara mia*, this Jeremy? He's not worth your time. You keep vying with Margaret for his attention and I might call myself... vexed."

I turned scarlet. Hades gave me a burning gaze and licked his lips.

"*Ciao, bella.*" He breezed by Reynaldo, tapping him on the forehead. Reynaldo sprang to life.

"*Ase me isihi,*" I said, taking the plate of brownies. "Are these for me? Thank you!" I needed a chocolate boost after that confrontation.

"What?" Reynaldo looked distracted. He turned just in time to see Hades turn around a sharp corner down the hall. "No! You don't need the extra calories! And who was that?" he breathed, fanning himself.

"Avoid him," ordered Meg. "Ouch!"

Another feather prick, a parting shot from Hades. She was going to need a muumuu before the end of the day if she kept that up.

Meg

Pluck You!

We caught QT before he left and unvamped him, but not before I "suggested" that he reconsider his choice of female companionship. Then Shar looked at him and told him to stop using such vulgar language in his music. If he was under Hades' wing, let the O-Great-Lord-of-the-Underworld make a billion-dollar seller out of a swear-free rap song. It was worth extra feathers and scaly skin.

The next morning, Jeremy was waiting for us when we walked in.

"What did you say to QT to make him drop the doggy fashions? Mr. Romanov never wanted to do it, but it was a mega deal. He's more than thrilled with QT's new plans."

Apparently, when he got home, QT "ditched the bitch" and spent the evening drawing up leatherwear designs for "booty-ful blondes" and "shortie-pies." Several six-digit orders were placed.

Jeremy looked at me expectantly, but even if I wasn't hesitant about talking, I wasn't sure what to say. *Hey, we used supernatural means to put your renegade rap star on the straight and narrow* didn't seem appropriate. Besides, after the previous days' revelations, what other minute details could cause problems?

"Aghhh," I rasped.

"I think Meg's coming down with something," Shar said, placing a cool hand on my forehead.

"Are you okay?" Jeremy asked, tender concern in his voice. "Do you want to go home and rest?"

"I can handle things here," Shar said, patting my shoulder. "You can go home."

There was no way I was going to leave her alone with him, so I smiled and shook my head firmly.

Jeremy's worried gaze lingered on my face. "Keep an eye on her, Shar. If she gets worse, let me know."

Shar didn't look thrilled with the directive, but nodded.

In the few days we'd been at House of Romanov, I'd noticed that Jeremy went out of his way to seek me out. It thrilled and terrified—and puzzled—me. Had I made *that* much of an impression on the fateful night of pizza, shoes, and train wrecks? I'd met a lot of guys at raves and concerts and clubs, but never someone like him. Friends I was always able to make easily, but not boyfriends. I never got the kind of admiring glances I'd seen guys throw at Shar, and I found it hard to believe that Jeremy was different. I knew my own feelings; the image of his face lingered in my mind since the night at the pizzeria, and the reconnection only intensified things. I couldn't get his eyes, his lips, his voice out of my mind.

Then Reynaldo burst into the reception area as if his trousers were on fire.

"There you are! You two, copy room. *Ándale*! I need the five hundred copies of the programs for tomorrow's runway show collated and folded, pronto. They've just been delivered by the printer. When you're done, let me know. Oh, there's just too much to do!" he cried, ushering us away. Jeremy smiled at me and gave a little wave. Shar pressed her lips together and said nothing as we trooped after Reynaldo to the copy room.

"Poor Margaret isn't feeling well. Laryngitis, I think, isn't that right, dear?" Demeter's voice chimed in the hallway behind us.

"Don't breathe on me, I can *not* get sick!" Reynaldo squealed and covered his mouth and nose. He thrust us into the copy room and scurried away, screaming, "Someone bring me antibacterial wipes!"

"You'd better get started," Demeter sang. She hung in the doorway and glanced at us haughtily. "It doesn't look like you'll be leaving here for quite a while."

We were surrounded by boxes of programs. Without giving her the satisfaction of a reply, I turned away and got to work. Two hours later, everything was collated, folded, and stacked.

"I need to stretch," Shar grumbled, flexing arms and legs.

"Me too. I want to get a latte before we get sent on some other petty errand."

I led the way to the kitchen. We had just stirred the sugar into our cups when Reynaldo burst in, his sharp, black-outlined eyes glaring at us.

"This is no time for a break! Did I say you could take a break? Oh!" He fanned his face like he was going to faint. "We have to move fast, ladies! Get yourselves straight to the Purple Salon. *Vámonos*!" He clapped his hands and hustled us out the door. He glanced at his watch and his face registered panic. "Come, come!"

Down we shuffled to the Purple Salon. When we were all in, he shut the door behind us. The room was a sty. Pins, paper, fabric scraps, pencils, and coffee cups were all over the floor, and the walls were lined with rolling racks of clothes, all sealed in plastic garment bags. In the center of the room was a dais with a drape around it.

"Behold House of Romanov's summer collection! Isn't it divine?" He didn't wait for an answer from us. "As you can see, this place is a mess! Jeremy is going to bring Mr. Arkady down to approve the accessories before tomorrow's runway show. I need you to clean up and get out before he comes in. Mr. Romanov does not like anyone around him. I'll pop in and give you a one-minute warning." He patted his chest like he was having heart palpitations and flew out the door, his hand still thumping. He needed to self-medicate.

We surveyed the room.

"What bomb went off in here?" Shar said, propping the glasses on her head. She started picking things up off the floor and throwing them in the garbage. "But did you hear what he said? Arkady is coming down here! We might actually see him!" She walked over to the dais and stared at it. "What do you think this is?"

She pushed the drape back, revealing a platform upon which stood a dress form draped in a silken sheath.

"Wow," Shar breathed. "This must be their anchor piece. It's amazing! It's ..."

"...a beige dress. Those glasses are really starting to affect your vision. And didn't you hear what Rrrrey-naldo said?" I trilled his name. "He wants us to clean up, and then he wants us out. We need to get moving." I stacked some papers and put them in a corner, then started to pick up the coffee cups scattered on tables, chairs, and the floor.

"Maybe we can hide somewhere in the room, let him think we left," Shar offered, finding her cup of chai and taking a sip before I could snag it for the trash. "We could sneak a peek at him."

I tapped my foot impatiently. "And then when he finds us, we'll have to entrance him, Jeremy, Reynaldo, and every other male we come across on our way out of here and to a portal. We won't get halfway there before we're completely transformed. We'll be *winging it* to Tartarus."

"One of us should stay," Shar insisted. "I'll follow Reynaldo out of the room and try to keep him away. You sneak back and hide behind the rack. *If* either one finds you, say a few words and entrance them. Maybe we can take Arkady to a portal late tonight when no one's around."

I tilted my head. "I have a better idea! Why don't you take off your glasses and tell Reynaldo to let us stay in the room? Or better yet, *you* put the Greek mojo on Arkady and Jeremy. Time for you to catch up with me—a few more feathers and I'll have a full wing!"

"I already have total bird feet! And look at my hands!" Shar thrust them out for me to see, but the one holding her tea lost its grip. We watched as the cup flew through the air, almost as if in slow motion, and slammed into the dress on the dais.

A dark stain streaked down the silk, continuing all the way down to the hem.

"Oh my god! Oh my god!" Shar could barely get the words out.

"How tragic!" Demeter's liquid voice rippled through the room. All the doors were closed, so she hadn't just walked in.

Whirling around, I faced her. "This is *not* funny, Demeter."

"I disagree." A vicious smile appeared.

I snapped my head around to gape at the ruined dress. There was no way it could be cleaned in time; not only for the show, but before Arkady and Jeremy got here. Arkady was to inspect it and the rest of the collection, then all of it would be moved immediately to the Met. The show was being held there tomorrow, New Year's Eve, in the Egyptian Temple.

I was actually looking forward to seeing it, or rather, hearing it. I'd seen the play list and it featured nearly all of my favorite bands, including Elysian Fields. Jeremy had to be in charge of the music. Back when we were folding programs, I'd been trying to think of ways I could somehow ask him about it, but now it looked like I wouldn't get the chance.

"It was my fault," Shar moaned. "I'll tell Reynaldo. What's another bird claw?" Her shoulders slumped.

"There is an easy way out of this," offered Demeter. I didn't like her too-soft tone. I probably wouldn't like whatever was on her mind, either, but at this point, it couldn't hurt to listen.

"Are you going to tell us, or are we going to wait for Reynaldo to come and join us?" Shar said tartly.

Demeter's eyes flared. "Watch the attitude, missy. You're lucky I deign to help you at all."

"Sorry." Shar didn't sound it.

"Give him a call. Kiss up to him. Cry a few tears, show some feminine vulnerability. Tell him something to stroke his ego and then ask him to cut you a break on the bird claws. What's the worst he could want?"

Shar looked horrified, and I didn't blame her. The three of us knew full well what Hades would desire.

"You don't have other options." Demeter examined her nails, blew on them, then buffed them against her skirt.

I picked up the offending cup and stuffed it into the trash can. The room was ready, with the exception of saving the dress.

"We have other options," I insisted. "We have our powers. Or, we'll think of something else."

"Doubtful, Margaret, but do as you wish. You'll fail together. I might beg Zeus to let me go to Tartarus just to visit you. It would be very amusing to see you in a gilded cage—when you're not walking the dogs."

"I *doubt* Hades will let you come visit," mumbled Shar.

Demeter vanished, but not before knocking over the garbage can.

"High class, that goddess," I said as I righted it and scooped up what had fallen onto the floor.

Shar looked around hopelessly. "The place is clean, but what good is that? Reynaldo will be here any second, and once he sees…" She pointed to the dress, which sported an irregular-shaped stain that curved to one side.

I stared at it, thinking that the tea stain made it look more interesting; before, it was so plain. It gave me an idea. "Let's do something with the stain to make it look not like a stain, but part of the dress," I suggested.

"How? And with what?"

I searched around frantically. "I saw some fabric scraps on the floor."

"There's not enough to do anything. The stain is too big. We're screwed!"

I bent down to scoop up the material on the floor

when an errant black feather floated to the ground. I started unbuttoning my top.

Shar leaned away with a wary expression. "What are you doing?"

"Preparing for the Rapture. What do you think?" I wrestled one arm out of a sleeve and with my free hand, grabbed a couple of feathers, and pulled. Hard.

"Ow!" I bit back tears and gave Shar a handful of fluff. "Here. Start from the bottom."

She sneezed several times as she ran to a nearby desk and grabbed a stapler.

I tossed her scraps of fabric and trim and feathers as I built up the nerve to pull them out, but our progress started to slow. I was trembling with pain and her nose was running.

"Here," she said, handing me the stapler. "You fix the dress, I'll pluck."

"No, you won't do it right!" I protested, but she forcibly maneuvered me to stand between her and the dress.

"We can go faster if I take them out and you attach them. Besides, I can barely see! The down...ah-choo!...is making my eyes water!" She yanked, and I felt like I was being stabbed by a thousand needles.

"Ouch! Ow! Not the little ones!"

"Ah-choo! Freaking allergies," Shar muttered, but she kept going. "Not bad," she sniffed between pullings, looking at my work. "You're pretty good at collage."

"It's a...ow! Hobby. Owww! Come on, you can be a little more gentle than that!"

She gave me an exasperated look. "Oh stop whining, it's like pulling off a Band-Aid. Better to do it fast! And you won't look like you've been tarred and feathered anymore." She sniffled, then sneezed, again, and I felt a spray of droplets on my back.

"Ugh! Cover your mouth, please!"

"Sorry!" she snapped. "But it's your fault I'm sneezing!"

By the time we heard the sound of Reynaldo's heels clicking up to the door, we'd made a meandering river of feathers, fabric scraps, and sequined trim from the shoulder of the dress down and across the body to the hem. I was no designer, but I thought it was an improvement—less beige, and it smelled like cardamon. That had to be good feng shui.

My arms and back were red and raw, but I jerked my blouse back on and buttoned it. The door flew open and Shar hastily shoved the stapler behind her back.

Apparently Reynaldo didn't share my opinion of our creation, unless the tortured rabbit sound he made was for joy.

"What ... happened ... here?" His mouth remained open, forming a perfect pink O, and for a few painful seconds, everything was silent. Reynaldo didn't move. Well, it was a valiant effort.

A triumphant Demeter slipped in behind him. "I want to be here when Arkady comes in. He'll rip you both apart. Think how dramatic, not to mention ironic, it will be for Arkady to be your downfall." She turned her gaze exclusively on me. "Oh, here he comes, and with the pretty boy in tow as well."

She stepped to the side, and Reynaldo breathed again. Then hyperventilated.

"The … dress … it …"

"Reynaldo?" Jeremy's voice came from the hallway. Reynaldo didn't budge until Jeremy tapped him on the shoulder, then moved aside like a robot.

Jeremy came through the door first, but he didn't look at our feathery creation. His attention was directed solely back at what was out in the hallway. He stepped out of the way, but offered an arm to someone outside the room. A second later, a hunched figure hobbled in, clinging to Jeremy with one arm and leaning on a cane with the other.

This shuffling old man was Arkady? He was swathed in white cloth from head to foot and wore dark glasses like Shar. Neither hair, if he had any, nor skin showed.

Suddenly Jeremy realized that he, Arkady, and Reynaldo weren't the only ones in the room. He looked at us, mouthing, "What are you doing here?" He jerked his head to the side, motioning for us to go away.

Arkady grunted fiercely and jerked his arm from Jeremy's. Moving slowly and using the cane, he made his way over to the dress. He stood in front of it silently for several seconds. No one said a word. Then he turned around.

"Who is responsible for this?" His voice was grating and broken, thick with a Russian accent, and loud even through his wrappings.

"Oh! Mr. Arkady!" Reynaldo found his high-pitched

voice. Of course our humiliation would have to be a soap opera. He pointed violently as us with both hands. "It was them! They did it!"

Arkady slashed a hand through the air for silence. Reynaldo clapped a palm over his mouth and looked ready to cry.

I thought I saw a smile from beneath the silk wrap that covered Arkady's mouth and nose; it reminded me of a movie I'd seen about a mummy come to life to wreak havoc on everyone.

Then he roared.

"Magnificent!"

Shar

Pretty Claws, Pretty Clothes, Pretty Close

It was magnificent? Our third grade art project? I knew fashion, like art, was subject to personal perspective, but he really had to be kidding. It pulled our butts out of the fire, though, so I wasn't going to complain and neither was Meg. I heard her slowly let out a breath of relief.

Arkady spoke slowly, like he was trying to whisper, but it came out a coarse shout. "Bring them to the show tomorrow. The short stubby one needs updating. Tell the tall one her feet look too big in flats. She should wear heels. Send both out to get cleaned up. Everyone except Reynaldo, *leave me.*" Arkady held out his arm and Reynaldo rushed forward to guide him to a chair. He pulled a rack of dresses forward, unzipping bags.

"Meg, Sharisse," said Jeremy, gesturing toward the door with his head. Before we could think to mojo anyone, we were dutifully following him, pausing only when he closed the door behind him. "You guys are on a roll, but the next time you want to show that kind of initiative, please, give me a hint!"

Opportunity lost!

"Of course," I assured him halfheartedly. "And we would've, but... there was no time."

Meg exhaled slowly.

Jeremy looked at her. "Are you sure you're okay? I know he can be harsh."

She smiled and nodded, then squeezed his hand. She was getting way too personal.

"What happens now?" I asked as I moved a tad closer, trying to draw his attention.

Jeremy rubbed a hand over his face. "Mr. Romanov needs to approve the accessories for each ensemble before it can be taken to the Met. He and Reynaldo will be busy for a while. And, since I need to be there, you two can take the rest of the afternoon off."

He looked at us critically. "You'll need to wear something more appropriate to the show. Here." He reached in his pants pocket and, from a gold clip with his initials and the House of Romanov design, slipped out a card and handed it to Meg. "Take the company credit card. Buy a few outfits." He turned to me. "Look sharp. Be at the Met by seven p.m. And be prepared to work. *Hard.* You're not his guests. He's doing you a great honor. He *never* lets anyone close to him." He gave us a rueful smile, although I noticed it lingered longer on Meg.

Okay. Not everyone preferred blondes. My revenge would be a whole makeover—on her.

"Then we need to get going," I said imperiously. "I need time to work my magic on Meg. Shopping is serious business. See you at seven tomorrow."

Using Jeremy's card and dropping a few hints about the show and what could be hot for the summer, we were ushered into the Red Door Salon like pop princesses. Meg complained, but I brushed it all aside.

"They're known for their discretion. With these hands"—I wiggled my ugly fingers at her, the nails thick and curving—"I need someone who won't laugh. Or take secret pictures and sell them to the tabloids with the caption *Secret Government Cloning Experiment Goes Horribly Wrong.*"

We were escorted immediately back to a semi-private room, having chosen to get worked on together. We lay back in the ergonomic red-leather chaises. An icy blonde sporting a surgical mask worked on Meg's feet, submerging them in a warm footbath. A stunningly beautiful Asian woman, also with surgical mask, held one of my hands.

"You have fungus?" she asked, examining my fingers Thank God I'd skipped the pedicure. How can you explain bird toes without people, no matter how professional, calling Guinness?

"Something I must have picked up in Taipei. Maybe you're familiar with it?"

Totally nasty, yes, but it hurt me to see my once-cute toes and fingers looking like something off the dino skeletons at the Museum of Natural History. For this alone I hated Hades. The deal we were forced into was an added incentive to despise him—his good looks, omnipotence, and tight butt notwithstanding.

The woman shook her head and got to work. Aromatherapy candles of nutmeg and oranges and a CD playing rain and thunderstorms soothed us. As the technician lathered up our faces for a scrub, I asked Meg, "How do you like it?"

"It's too weird having people play with my feet, and hands, and face."

"Sit back, relax, and enjoy the pampering. I doubt Had—" I cut myself short before I said his name. "I doubt he has these facilities where he lives." The technician was struggling to smooth my claws. "God, I *hate* long nails!"

Meg's voice was muffled as the woman scrubbed off dead facial skin. "Don't feel so bad. I'm waiting for someone in the office to tell me to go on a diet. That skirt that he arrayed me in yesterday was a whole size bigger than what I usually wear."

"Like these are attractive," I wiggled my claws at her. Dragon lady nails.

"You have the rest of the package." Meg sounded a little forlorn.

"Curvaceous body, sparkling blue eyes, and a quick

wit. Cry me a river. But by the time I'm finished with you, even you-know-who will be panting in your direction."

Meg narrowed her eyes. "What do you mean?"

I could feel the tension in her voice. I glanced down; she was gripping the chair arms tightly.

"You're here for the complete makeover, *ma Meg.* You're going to knock the breath right out of any guy and leave him begging for scraps of your attention."

Maybe Hades would come on to her for a change. Him, or someone at the show. That will leave me to comfort Jeremy. There's still a chance.

"Come on, Shar." Meg shook her head, "That's not going to happen."

"You have a lot going on for you. Ditch the mourning clothes and you might see it."

"Why are you doing this for me?" Her voice was whisper soft.

"Because (a) you're my roomie, and I have standards if you want to be seen with me, and (b) Arkady told us to 'clean up,' although I'm sure he was talking more about you. I'm *always* put together. And (c) one of us should find a Prince Charming. It might be you. So shut up and take it like a trouper."

"Thanks, Shar." Meg reached over, clasped my hand, and gave it a squeeze. I tried not to feel guilty about my ulterior motive.

"Let's see if you still feel that way after these ladies are done!" I smiled to myself. *Eyebrow wax!*

Three exhausting hours later, we stumbled out. Except

for where she'd feathered out, Meg had been buffed, scrubbed, exfoliated, and moisturized to within an inch of her life. Her short and razored haircut emphasized her blue eyes, and the makeup job made her skin glow. Maybe I'd been too thorough with her makeover; she looked unbelievable.

I felt pretty good myself. The nail technicians had made the claws less obvious with a dull skin-tone polish. They couldn't cut them because not only would they grow back, but now they'd hardened and were too tough. Hades' doing. But for now they were shaped and doable.

Squinting through my dark glasses now that we were out on the street, I said to Meg, "I'm tired, and it's too late for the boutiques. Let's head back to the apartment and go clothes shopping in the morning. Then we'll head over to the show."

Meg shrugged listlessly.

We hailed a cab, stuffed our bags of beauty and bath products into the back seat, and rode in silence back to the apartment. Once chic, the penthouse now felt cold and almost forbidding. We ordered the latest chick flick on pay TV and Thai from the restaurant across the street, then settled in for the night. Before bed, Meg handed me the iPhone.

"Look, way down at the bottom of the list—it says there's a portal in the Met. It's not in the main area, see, it's over by the back offices. We can get him there."

"You think? If our luck holds true, we'll be eating out of bowls with the hell hounds," I grumbled. But it was hard not to let her enthusiasm get to me. There was a portal on the same floor, in the same wing, where we were going to be.

The next day was a flurry of activity. By nine a.m. we were showered, dressed, made up, and out the door.

"So are they waterproof, like a duck's?" I asked while we stood outside waiting for a taxi. A light snow had fallen and the Christmas decorations felt almost depressing. It was the end of the holiday, one which I usually enjoyed, but too many unsettling things had happened. This was one vacation I would be glad to finish—if everything worked out successfully.

"What?"

"Are the feathers waterproof? Does water just slide off them, like with ducks and swans?"

Meg glared. "Do your talons keep your meat from running away? *What do you think*?"

So much for making light of the situation. Meg was her old self. "Well, if I knew, I wouldn't be asking, would I?"

"Sorry." She gave her head a shake. Her newly shaped tresses waved cutely. "I guess I'm a little anxious about this evening. I keep imagining every conceivable disaster."

"What happened to 'we can get him there'?" I reminded her. "But I understand; creepy old man, portals, eternal servitude. Oh, and a completely new look. It's a lot for one night."

A cab pulled up. "Where to?" asked the driver.

"Downtown, 9th and 14th please," I answered. I leaned closer to Meg. Her earth-friendly hair spray had a pretty vanilla scent and seemed to have a masking effect on the dander. I whispered, "I'm never setting foot in Henri Bendel again after what happened last time. We're probably on security tapes and posters."

She nodded grimly.

A few minutes later, the cabbie deposited us in front of a line of boutiques.

"I know we'll find you something good, even if it's black," I assured her as we walked into the first shop.

Of course I found a ton of things for myself. For the show I chose a long black skirt with a silver overblouse. I also had to get a sleek pair of gray pants that caught my eye, and a light blue button-down shirt and a long black jacket to go with it for the office. For something fun I chose flared jeans with a beautiful greenish-gray sweater. Fortunately, I'd managed to find good-looking black stiletto boots that actually fit at a store that carried larger, wider sizes. For transvestites. It was a relief to be out of the mangy sneakers I'd been sporting. I stocked up, buying a dozen pairs of shoes. I was almost in my happy place.

After that, I dragged Meg to some cute boutiques where we found a flowing black skirt with a sleek tailored jacket to cover her feathered areas. And of course I got something for myself too—a slinky, revealing turquoise halter dress. Her feet, damn her, were still normal, and I was surprised when she chose a pair of butter-soft Chie Mihara Victorian boots—in lavender. There was hope for her yet.

"Who's Mary Poppins now?" I teased as she twirled around.

Meg started to tear up. *Uh oh. Guess I went too far.* "I'm sorry! I just wanted to—"

Meg shook her head. "No, I've never had anyone do so much to make me feel special. All this"—she motioned to her new clothes—"and this whole situation ..." She sniffed, took a deep breath, and looked me in the eyes. She smiled. "Thanks."

I'd never seen Meg emotional. Or at a loss for words. She was the rock; I was the slobbery one. It added to the guilt I felt—since my goal had only been to get Jeremy to notice *me* if men or gods were all over *her*.

"Well," I said awkwardly, "not just *anybody* can be seen with me."

Meg laughed, breaking the tension.

I led her over to a glass case. "Okay, while we look at accessories, I'll cry over my ugly feet and you'll think how we can get Arkady to that portal." I had to get my mind off Jeremy and onto the task.

But neither of us came up with anything. Meg pointed out that we'd need to know where Arkady was in relation to the portal in order to figure out how to get him there.

"What if in the end he won't go?" Meg sighed.

I didn't want to think about that. Hades' interest in me wasn't innocent. I doubt I'd be the Tartarus dogsitter for long; more like dogmeat, and Hades the hungry puppy.

After we loaded up, thanks to Arkady's beneficence, on satin headbands, lacey gloves, and evening bags, we went back to the apartment and got dressed. At 6:45 p.m., we were standing in front of the Metropolitan Museum.

"Let's go," Meg said, striding forward. I could see the determination in her step. Jeremy was in the atrium directing models, makeup artists, and dressers to the staging area. I saw him look at Meg, do a double take, seem to forget what he was doing, and look again.

This was not how it was supposed to go down!

"Please tell me it was worth my suffering," I quipped, sliding up to him in front of Meg. The inevitable glasses were back on.

"*Your* suffering?" said Meg, pulling even with me. "Who had their eyebrows waxed, their face poked and squeezed, their—"

Jeremy started laughing. "I'm glad I'm a guy. Getting my hair cut and putting on eyeliner once in a while doesn't involve pain." He sobered and gazed at Meg. "But you look incredible."

"We thank you," I said, brushing past. I needed to find a crowd of admirers for her. "Where do we go?"

Jeremy nodded, still not taking his eyes off Meg. "Down to the Egyptian Temple. There's a work area set up behind the runway. I'll be down in a few, but Reynaldo's there and he'll get you working." He winked, and with reluctance went back to his clipboard.

And work we did. We lifted boxes, soothed cranky super models, fetched chilled water and snack bars for the technicians, and generally ran our butts off. I kept my head down, avoiding all eye contact with guys. I noted that

Meg was keeping her mouth shut, despite the looks she kept getting from all quarters. If she had a slip-up, I didn't see any evidence of it.

When Jeremy finally came down, he hustled over to Meg and whispered something in her ear that made her giggle. I approached them only to hear him say, "Meg, would you get the duffle with the extra accessories, please? It's somewhere in the mess in the hall."

She hopped to do his bidding—the perfect time for me to catch him alone. He was talking on his cell, giving last-minute instructions to the lighting crew. I snagged a bottle of cold water and a sandwich for him from a food table and waited patiently for him to finish his conversation. He stuffed the phone in his shirt pocket and turned to me.

"Here." I held out my humble offerings.

"Thanks, just the water." He twisted the bottle open and slugged down a good half. I returned the plastic-wrapped sandwich to the platter and gave him a bright smile.

"So is, um, everything going okay?" I didn't know what else to say. Hades was right; Meg was the glib one. She could hold a riveting conversation with a telephone pole. Me? I had trouble unlocking my tongue fast enough to keep up with my brain. If I'd been more erudite, Meg and I would have had our girl talk long before the ill-fated sample sale and I might have talked her into letting me have the red shoes. *And* my life would not include the very real possibility of chasing dog-slimed rubber balls and filing down talons.

Jeremy swiped his mouth on his black linen shirt sleeve and looked at me quizzically.

"Yeah, good so far, but the show hasn't begun and there's always at least one catastrophe. I think med students get more sleep than I do."

His elfin grin was too cute.

"I'll help you," I offered shyly, stepping toward him.

His look became guarded. "You and Meg are a big help." His head swiveled around as he moved away. "What's taking her so long?"

Not too subtle, Jeremy.

"I'll go help her," I said stiffly.

"Uh, thanks."

I flipped a careless wave that said *I don't care.* I would *not* tear up. It was hard to swallow; my throat felt tight. *Rejected! Why?*

I found Meg, and two minutes later, with minimal conversation, we located the duffel. She ran it to Jeremy. I stayed back, eyeing them coolly. I watched his eyes flicker over her. He touched her hand before he hastened away. I tried to put the image out of my mind. Meg went right back to work, apparently unaware that she'd just won the grand prize.

When the runway show was about to begin, Meg and I sat on a trunk, sipping water. There were to be no noises from backstage until the music started. Now more than ever, I wanted this over with. I didn't want any more close or semi-close encounters with Jeremy again if I could help it. And there was only one way to ensure that—get rid of Arkady.

"Where's Mr. Romanov?" I whispered to Reynaldo, who was winking and flirting with the hair stylist. "He did come, didn't he?" I poked him to get his attention. "Reynaldo?"

"What?!" he snapped, annoyed at the interruption.

"Mr. Romanov. He's here, right?"

"He's watching the show by live feed from an office."

"Won't he bow and wave at the end?"

Reynaldo looked horrified. "Never! Go into that room with all those people? Who knows what germs could be out there?" He turned back to smile at Andre. I doubt that was his real name—so Euro. I'll bet his real name was Myron. Or Charlie.

When Reynaldo walked away, Meg whispered to me, "The offices! This couldn't be more perfect! He's already back there!"

"Sure, but how are *we* going to get back there?" I snapped, a little unfairly. Jeremy's diss wasn't her fault. "We're supposed to stay here until we're needed."

"I'm sure we'll think of something." Meg didn't look too sure, but maybe inspiration would hit one of us.

Music suddenly blared, making everyone jump and signaling the start of the show. We were on call, to sit there until summoned. In the meantime, I enjoyed the chance to just sit. Surprisingly, my bird feet were holding up well.

But I'd trade them for two human feet loaded with blisters and boils and broken toes.

The Temple was the backdrop for the show, the theme being Egyptian Goddess. All the models were dressed in form-fitting bronze, deep lapis, and coral silk sheaths. The last dress, with Meg's feathers all over it, would be the climax. I couldn't help being excited. This was where I wanted to be—just under different circumstances. More specifically, not fresh off a rejection, or trying to eye up a mummy, or keeping temptation at arm's length. Suddenly, I thought, *I can't wait to start classes at FIT.* It would be a different life, a new start. If I survived this whole mess, maybe Jeremy would give me a reference—even if he wouldn't give me anything else.

I found myself tapping my feet to the heavy beat of the techno music that blared out of the backstage speakers. It was making the floor vibrate. Was this what Meg and Jeremy subjected themselves to at those club shows? No thanks.

I recognized the song. It was something Meg played in our dorm room. Glancing at her, I saw that her eyes were closed and her head swayed in perfect rhythm with the music. Her lips mouthed the words. I stopped staring at her and scanned the room. Jeremy was standing by the stage door, doing the exact same thing. The exact words, the exact same sway. It was almost eerie.

After a few moments, he opened his eyes and searched the room, stopping when his gaze found Meg still in her music-induced trance. Slender models with taut limbs and perfect faces passed in front of him, but he didn't notice them. He only saw Meg, and his eyes drank her in. I'd seen the look before. He *really* liked her. *They've only exchanged a handful of words since we reconnected…* I bit my lip and looked away.

The evening wore on, and the show seemed to be a success. Near midnight, Jeremy spoke to the audience and wrapped things up with a champagne toast, finger foods, and gift bags, and then Reynaldo came running over, out of breath. His makeup was starting to smudge.

"Jeremy sent me to tell you that Mr. Arkady needs ice, glasses, and two diet sodas brought to him. NOW. The Director's office, just down the hall. Don't tell anyone where you're going. I can't believe he hates the hair!" He moaned and sniffed as he screamed at Andre. Meg shot me an excited smile.

We hopped off the trunk, rounded up everything, and made our way through the backstage maze. We ran, as fast as a girl can run in stiletto-heeled boots carrying a bag of ice, to the office. Meg knocked on the door.

Jeremy answered. "Hey you two." He refused to look at me.

Wimp! I was the embarrassed one, the one who got rejected!

He stepped back to allow us in. Arkady was sitting at a massive oak desk, surrounded by TV monitors, his back to us. There was no sound except his raspy breathing.

"Put it all on the table, please," said Jeremy, reaching for the vibrating phone in his pocket.

"Let's do it now," said Meg's low voice in my ear. There was only Arkady and Jeremy. This would probably be our best chance. Maybe our only chance.

I nodded. I pointed to Arkady, then to myself. I'd handle him; I'd leave Jeremy to her. She nodded, regret etched in her eyes. It was a sneaky, mean thing to have to do, kind of like hypnotizing him against his will. But enthralling Jeremy seemed too intimate for me to do now. Besides, if he had a choice, it was too obvious he'd choose Meg to vamp him. And that left me with Arkady. I felt the bile rise in my throat. I was *not* touching him!

Jeremy grabbed the doorknob. "I've gotta run. Reynaldo's flipping out over the hair situation. You two set up the drinks and leave. Lock the door behind you." He shouted in Arkady's direction, "I'll be right back, Mr. Romanov." Mummy man didn't notice. Jeremy ran out.

Was our luck beginning to change? Meg looked at me and nodded almost imperceptibly. The TV monitor had a special screen which magnified the images immensely. With hesitant steps I walked around to the front of the desk so that I was facing Arkady. Even though he was alone and the room was warm, he was enveloped as usual in a fedora hat, Burberry scarf, and Italian leather gloves. But he wasn't wearing his thick, reflective glasses. I removed mine and gave him the full stare.

"Get up," I commanded. I wanted to say something nastier to him, considering he'd called Meg stubby and said I had big feet. But nothing came to mind.

Meg's voice was sultry, beguiling. "It's time to go. Hades is waiting." How could anyone resist her?

Arkady never flinched, although he did sway in his chair trying to see around me.

I leaned down so that when his gaze shifted, he'd see only me.

Meg leaned over the desk. "Come with us. Now!" she yelled.

"Eh?" His head bobbed up and he looked confused. I was so close to him now, I could see that his eyes were milky white. It brought back the horrifying images of when my cat died. Her eyes had glazed with the same opaqueness. With a palsied hand, he brushed us away.

He was deaf and practically blind.

"Hmmm. Having a bit of trouble, ladies?"

We jerked up.

Hades was looking at some Mayan artifacts. The disdain on his face was clear. "Primitive junk," he muttered before turning to us. "But you look stunning, *mon coeur*." His eyes flickered appreciatively over me. I felt chilled to the bone. "And Margaret. Good improvement."

He was so rude.

"Need a little help?" His smile was evil and slick.

"Our powers won't work on someone who can't hear or see us, Hades." Meg sounded only mildly perturbed. This meant she was ready to explode at any second.

"I must have forgotten to mention that. How remiss of me." Hades dragged a finger along the cases, grimaced at the light coating of dust, and conjured a wet cloth to wipe his hands. With a careless flick, it was gone.

"I thought you said that Arkady made a deal with you for longevity," I retorted. I gritted my teeth to keep myself from calling him the words my mother would disown me for.

His eyebrows raised. "He did. And I gave him longevity. Arkady is pushing 349 years old. It would be 350 next month." His grin was malevolent.

"But look at him!" said Meg, backing away a pace. "He looks like he's been dead for at least a hundred years!"

Hades' smile was expansive. "He asked for a long life. He got it. He didn't stipulate that he wanted to remain *youthful*. It's always the little details one must remember. Be careful what you wish for—that's our motto."

So all those strange treatments weren't for staying healthy—rather, Arkady was trying to turn back the clock. What a revelation *that* was.

Hades made a full circle of the office, barely glancing now at the books and objects on the shelves and tables. "You're not using your gifts to their full potential," he said softly. "Come, girls, surely your wiles and imagination and natural charm should make this easy."

Like anything connected to him or this whole deal could ever be easy. Meg and I remained silent.

"If you need my assistance, tell me. But it will cost you."

That last bit was directed at me.

I exhaled sharply. I was tired, I'd been rejected by Jeremy, and I didn't want to be played with anymore.

"You're here, just take him now," I snapped. "It's not like he'd notice. Then we all go home and everyone's happy."

Hades looked taken aback. "That would violate your contract. *You* have to do this. Or, are you conceding?" He held out a graceful hand like he wanted me to waltz with him. "Then we shall leave."

Meg screamed "No!" and slapped his hand away. "We'll do it! Just go away!"

His eyes narrowed and his mouth thinned.

Angry God plus Big Mouth Roomie equals Dire Consequences.

We were screwed yet again.

Meg

Under the Wonder Wheel

*W*hat a night," Jeremy said. He rubbed his slightly bloodshot eyes and ran his fingers through his hair, making the cowlick in back stand up.

I nodded sympathetically; the night had been dramatic for us too. After Hades left, Shar and I had talked about dragging Arkady to the portal; he couldn't hear us or see us, and maybe he wouldn't even know what was happening. But it seemed too complicated, not to mention violent. Shar was now busy relieving stress by arguing with one of the makeup artists over eye shadow.

Jeremy had seen Arkady home and then came back to help pack up the show. "I'm spent, but I'm too wound up to sleep," he said, smiling at me.

"Me too," I mouthed. I was glad I hadn't had to use the Siren power on him tonight, but still, I wondered if his attention was real ... or if my power was somehow at work. I knew I'd never used it on him deliberately, but I'd become wary of everything to do with Hades, the gifts, and the contract. Jeremy didn't act like this with Shar; if anything, he was a little remote with her. So, if I were to actually use my powers on him—and deep down I knew I would have to, eventually—would he still feel the same way about me when I released him? Everyone we'd done that to so far seemed to forget us and move on. I couldn't help but wonder if that would happen with Jeremy. Since it would amuse Hades, the answer was probably yes.

"I need time away from here. Do you want to go somewhere?" he asked.

I clapped my hands and smiled.

"This is gonna sound crazy, but let's go to Coney Island."

I needed breathing space; the apartment had been feeling oppressive lately, as if the walls and furnishings were taunting me. *Hades owns you both. He'll come for you ...*

I'd only been to Coney Island once. It was summer, and when I emerged from the subway onto Stillwell Avenue, the first thing that hit me was the smell of hot dogs, salt water, and fried foods, steeped by hot days and baked into the subway tiles and sidewalks. Being there would be as far removed from fashion and glamour and Hades and Arkady as I could get at this point.

"Go. Maybe you can find something out," Shar said

when I told her. She'd been pretty quiet most of the night. Jeremy and Reynaldo had kept us moving, but I could tell something was bothering her.

"Can't I be off duty for five minutes?" I sighed.

"I'm not saying to use the gift or anything, but our time is seriously running out," Shar reminded me. "Just keep your ears open, okay? And have fun."

I squeezed her hand. "Happy New Year."

"Let's hope so," she grumped.

The crash of the ocean was audible as Jeremy and I emerged onto the street from the subway station. At 6:30 a.m., the place was a virtual ghost town. We walked along the water toward the amusement area and looked out at the waves.

I watched light creep over the water, thinking, *How am I going to get through the next few hours without talking?*

"You know, I'm glad you wanted to come here. It's nice to feel free, even for just a little while." He jerked his head back in the direction of Manhattan. Its skyline was dimly visible from where we stood.

I nudged him so he would look at me. I nodded a *me too* at him.

"Yeah? It's been a heck of a start for you and Shar. First QT, then the dress and Mr. Romanov's personal interest. And you've been sick."

"Better now," I whispered cautiously, keeping my hushed tone bland and even.

"Not completely." He put his finger to my lips. "Hush." He took my hand and I shivered as a little jolt of excitement ran up my arm. We made our way over to the maze of shut-up concessions, forgotten games, and food stalls that still smelled strongly of stale cooking oil and potatoes.

I was tired of gestures and whispers. There was so much I wanted to say, to ask. I wanted to know if working in fashion was really what he wanted to do with his life. Not talking at least had one advantage—it gave me time to observe, and Jeremy didn't seem happy. I wanted to look into his eyes and brush his hair from his forehead, but that had nothing to do with words...

I don't want to risk telling him what to do, or let my intentions take over.

Then I had a flash of brilliance. Whipping out my cell phone, I brought up his number. I tapped buttons furiously and hit send. He grabbed for his phone, still in his shirt pocket, when it vibrated. With a flicker of annoyance he pulled it out, then broke into a smile when he realized it was me. He grinned and bent his head toward my face. His nose brushed my cheek for a moment.

"How long have you worked for Mr. Romanov?" he read out loud. I waited in suspense, but felt nothing sprout. Perfect! Texting didn't count, so there'd be no more feathers today. Plus, this would count as the information gathering Shar was talking about—I ♥ multitasking!

"Seems like forever," he mused. "A little over a year. And people are surprised I've lasted that long."

I raised my now artfully waxed eyebrows at him.

"Come on, you see what the office is like. There aren't

a lot of people there, and the few that are don't interact with Mr. Romanov that much. I'm his buffer."

Shar and I had noticed this too. I had to admit, if I looked like Arkady and had his secrets, I'd want to deal with as few people as possible, too. I nodded thoughtfully, puffing out a breath and watched it steam and curl into the nothingness of the now-blue sky and beach.

"I was actually at NYU—"

I squeezed his hand excitedly, and when he looked at me, I grinned goofily and poked myself in the chest before I could stop myself; it was something else we had in common.

"NYU? That's right, you'll be going there. It's a great school." His eyes, the same color as the sky, with their fluttering lashes, and his full lips slightly turned down, overwhelmed me. We walked for some minutes in silence.

"Not that you need this, but … " He looked away. "Would you mind if I gave you some advice?"

I bobbed my head, and my fingers tightened around his.

"I know working at the House of Romanov looks like the beginning of a great opportunity for you. And for your friend. But finish up your internship, put it on your transcript, and then go to school. Don't get stuck there."

So I was right. He wasn't happy—but still, it didn't look like he was ready to move on. Sure, the job was demanding, but if he was P.A. to the infamous Arkady Romanov, traveled in those elite circles, and was going to NYU, didn't he have it made?

"I left school to work for Mr. Romanov," Jeremy continued. "Got placed there through the school's work-study program. I requested a spot with the ACLU; instead, I became an intern at House of Romanov just like you." He laughed mirthlessly, "I'm good at what I do. I'm a juggler—it's how I managed to stay on top of my classes. At least at first."

I rubbed his arm, encouraging him to go on.

"But this is where I am. Shar told me this isn't your thing either."

Shar? It took a moment to sink in ... *Shar helped me* ...

"Anyway, one by one, people dropped out of the office. Demi started just before you did, and Reynaldo and Callie were there when I started, but there used to be more people than that. As they left, I took over the stuff they were doing. Callie hardly ever leaves her office," he continued, "and Demi and Reynaldo only see him occasionally. I'm the one who really interacts with him on a daily basis, apart from his appointments, but it's crazy! He wants the specialists' visits on a rotating schedule. They're the select best in the world. He hardly sees anyone twice in the span of six months."

I shivered, recalling my time in the chair at the salon. The end product was nice, but it wasn't something I wanted to do too often. I couldn't imagine that many people working on me or touching me on a regular basis. More disturbing was the thought that Demeter had joined the House of Romanov right before us, just when we were forced into our unholy deal. Mere coincidence?

"After my first year I dropped out. It was just too much—between work and studying I had no time for myself. I knew working and going to school were going to be tough, but it really started to weigh me down. And when I told Mr. Romanov that I was going to have to cut back my hours because of school, he gave me more money—more than I thought I could ever make, even when I graduated. I thought I'd have part of my life back." Jeremy laughed grimly. "God, that Elysian Fields concert you guys missed was the first thing I'd been to in months!"

The sun rose higher over the water and a misty light filtered through the bars and light bulbs of the Wonder Wheel. We'd walked to the base of it. It soared into the sky, dwarfing the little ticket booth that stood only a few paces away. I felt a pulse somewhere deep inside of me. I looked at Jeremy, whose gaze was directed at a densely packed area of buildings that lay beyond the beach.

"You know, I can see this from my apartment," he said, changing the subject. "At nighttime. In the summer when it's open." Reaching up a long arm, he ran his hand over the brightly painted iron girders and rivets.

"The Wonder Wheel," I whispered, half remembering that I'd just seen or heard about this. Had it been in the news recently? I thought I'd read somewhere that a big entity had bought Coney Island and was planning to tear some of it down. Whatever happened, the Wonder Wheel would stay; it was a National Landmark.

He chucked his finger under my chin and made me look up at him. I couldn't turn away, and didn't want to.

The pulse I'd sensed before grew stronger; was it my heart racing? I'd waited for this moment. He bent down, his breath in my ear, his cheek brushing mine, moving across my face. I felt very warm despite the sharp wind that blew in from the ocean, slipping through the hodgepodge of stalls and buildings and motionless rides. His finger was still under my chin, but his other hand moved quickly to the back of my head, drawing me closer. My head swam. Somewhere far away, a dog barked.

Suddenly I heard a muffled buzzing. It made me start, but I pulled back to look into Jeremy's eyes, not caring what it was.

"I've been thinking about doing this for a while," he whispered.

Really? I wanted to hold on to this instant for just one more second. The moment before—the exquisite anticipation. I felt the vibration again, and, coming out of my daydream, I realized something was vibrating in my bag. *The iPhone.* It was my turn to carry it. Ignoring it, I twined my arms around Jeremy's neck and started to pull him into a kiss.

But something wasn't right. There was no response. I unhooked my arms from his neck and backed up. He was frozen, staring down at the spot where I'd stood, his body bent slightly in.

"Did I interrupt?"

I whirled around. Standing in the back door to the Wonder Wheel ticket booth was Hades, tall, sinewy, well dressed in total white, and as chillingly perfect as ever. The area behind him was pitch black and a wind blew out of it, making his auburn locks flutter like tiny silken flags. The barking was louder now.

I dug in my purse, pulled out the iPhone, and held it aloft. "Nothing in the rules says you have control over my life yet, Hades. Why are you here, to annoy me?"

"Do you think I like coming here?" he asked, looking around in disgust. "Next time, answer when I call you."

"What do you want?"

"I'm making sure that you're focused. Since you lost your kitty charm, I figured I might help you out with a little motivation."

"Have you forgotten? I tried to get Arkady tonight. I need a break!" I snapped.

"Ah yes, you're with the Rave Romeo. I must say though, Margaret, that I'm glad this development has shown Sharisse the error of her ways. I was hoping that it wouldn't take her long to get over her little infatuation."

"Wha—?"

"Oh please, you were both drooling over this specimen. He's okay for a human, but he's human nonetheless. Since he's snubbed her, she'll be more receptive to an admirer. I picture Sharisse with a more divine companion."

Jeremy had snubbed her? Was that why she'd been so silent at the Met? A chill raced down my spine, but I squared my shoulders. "You wouldn't."

"Oh yes, Margaret." He leaned a forearm against the door jamb and peered down at me. His face was set with intensity. "I want her, and I will have her. Her resistance is surprising. That doesn't happen to me too often. Which adds to her allure."

"Welcome to Unpredictable Human Behavior 101. As ... tempting as you might look"—I weighed my words carefully—"Shar has some sense. Why her? She's human and it would only be a matter of time before you got tired of her and moved on to someone else. We both know how you immortals operate. Your Greek history is pretty grim, from our viewpoint. It's littered with the unhappy fates of too many mortals to count."

"That is inconsequential," Hades replied. "I get what I want, and I want Sharisse. And you're right. She's no fool. And if we should part ways at some point, she'll be well compensated."

"Just discarded like trash, without a second thought."

"Grow up, Margaret! It's the way of your pathetic world. And who's to say you wouldn't be able to elicit something good out of this arrangement too? Let's talk about your assignment. The clock is ticking. Tick, tock." Hades waved a hand, and an hourglass appeared. "What have you done so far? You've managed to bungle the perfect chance to finish your mission. Arkady still hasn't been sent to my realm, and both of you have taken on an alarming degree of the Siren form. You, maybe a little more." He chuckled. "You're not holding your tongue very well."

"How astute of you to remind me."

"At the rate you're going, you'll find yourself in a bird cage before ever getting Arkady to a portal."

"Oh yes, it really would have helped if you'd told us

earlier he's practically blind *and* deaf. What good are our Siren gifts on him? And would it have hurt for you to let us know that he lives a cloistered existence, apart from the army of wellness gurus that march in and out of his vault every day? You couldn't make a portal in a more convenient place—like his office? We don't even know what a portal looks like!"

"Pathetic. You don't even realize you're standing next to one. Here." He stepped away from the ticket booth door. "Take a look."

Under the Wonder Wheel. It was on the iPhone list, and I'd heard a dog barking. *Cerberus?*

The ground beneath my feet thrummed. Darkness blurred the edges of the doorway as I turned toward it, and a chill air, different from the sea breezes dancing off the waves, came out, sharp and biting. I thought I heard whispers. My heart thudded painfully and I held my breath—this yawning blackness was the last road. Arkady and anyone else unfortunate enough to travel this path would never come back. I felt a growing horror... but before I knew what I was doing, I found myself standing at the edge, leaning inward. I heard a low growl and jumped back.

"Don't be afraid of my pets, Margaret. I know you'll get used to each other—eventually."

I narrowed my eyes at him, rage replacing terror. Then the portal dissolved, leaving only the rundown booth behind him.

"What would you say if I told you that fulfilling your assignment could be so much easier?"

"I'd say beware of Greeks bearing gifts."

"So cliché, Margaret!" Hades' voice, though low, echoed in the mist that seeped out of the ticket booth. "How about a little quid pro quo?"

I eyed him warily. "I don't have anything you'd want."

He chuckled softly. "Of course you do. Everyone has something to offer." His glance was watchful, making me even more uneasy. "You have Sharisse's ear. I want you to put in a kind word for me. After all, I'm not such a bad sort."

"Talk to her yourself." I inched a fraction away. Power emanated from him and I didn't like it.

"I'm not asking for anything dramatic, like telling her to jump into a portal or wrap herself up in a big pink bow for my birthday."

I snorted. "Hmmm. Wouldn't you like that!"

He waved a dismissive hand. "All you have to do is get her to admit that she'd like to be with me. Just a few words..."

"You're kidding, right?"

Hades sighed and shook his head. "She seems to be unaware of my charms."

I burst out laughing. "She's aware, she's just not buying into it."

"Well that's interesting!" He smiled slowly. "Still, if you go home and put in a good word for me, I would do something for you. It'll be a win-win situation."

I was leery of what that something could be.

"If you speak to Sharisse for me," he continued, "I'll remove some of the obstacles you've been facing."

"Like what?" I couldn't believe I was entertaining this proposal.

"Let's see." He rubbed his chin. "Arkady will experience some improvement in his vision and hearing, allowing your gifts to work better. I might also be persuaded to have a word with Demeter on your behalf. You could be done in hours."

"I thought you two didn't get along," I said, pointing a finger at him.

"We don't," he said curtly. "Speaking to her will be unpleasant for me, of course, but I'm willing to do something distasteful to achieve my ends. What are you willing to do?" He ran his tongue across his Hollywood-perfect teeth. "You couldn't imagine how I'd reward you."

I mulled over the proposal in spite of myself. I could say something to Shar—and tack on a big fat warning. Once she knew what Hades was up to, she'd understand why I'd made the deal.

"Oh, and Margaret," Hades countered, giving me a knowing, shrewd smile. "No tricks. It would have to be a real endorsement—no disclaimers. And no telling Sharisse about our little chat."

So much for that.

But he would make it so that we could get this done fast.
I'd have my life back again...

Shar would do the same thing if she were in my place.

Wouldn't she?

I wavered, about to tell him yes, I would do it, but then my head started to clear. His words were deceptive, twisted. Shar trusted me. If she breathed that she would go with Hades for even a millisecond, it would be the beginning of a steep, slippery slope. Her guard would be down. I knew what that meant for her.

Clenching my fists, I drew myself up and looked him in the eye. "Not a chance."

He towered over me, his eyes burning like coals. A wind whipped up from the depths of the portal, carrying a pungent whiff of wet dog.

"You dare to say no to me?"

"I won't do that to Shar!" I shouted over the din. Sand blasted me in the face as I stumbled back. I threw up my hands to cover myself. Suddenly it all stopped and was quiet again.

Hades stood over me, a disturbing grin on his face. "You had your chance Margaret. I don't really need you. I'll make Sharisse a deal that's simply irresistible. Either way, I'll have you both."

Before I could say anything, he stepped into the portal and it disappeared. What was he going to do?

I turned back, and Jeremy was still there, standing at the base of the Wonder Wheel. He had no idea what happened; he just reanimated, like the kids in the subway that first, horrible night. He stretched and yawned, and came over to where I was.

"How'd you get over there?" He rolled his shoulders.

"You hungry?" he asked softly, wrapping an arm around me.

"Mmm hmm." I was famished, as if all my energy had been sapped.

"Let's head over to Brighton. I know a good place there that makes a great veggie breakfast burrito."

We walked along Surf Avenue, sometimes staring out at the sea. It was hard to think about anything other than Hades, what he wanted, and what he might do to get it. If only I could warn Shar, but if I called her, Jeremy would overhear. And this wasn't exactly something for texting—a lot could get lost in translation. It would have to wait.

We shared a burrito, nachos, and iced tea. I made talking impossible by stuffing food in my mouth every time he asked a question. I was still wary about saying too much, and, as much as it killed me, I wanted to get back to the apartment and Shar.

"Want to grab a coffee tomorrow?" he asked as my train pulled into the subway station. We had walked in silence, enjoying the morning even though the temperature was starting to drop. The sidewalks were starting to ice. The city had that air of depression that seemed to settle in right after the whirlwind of the holidays. I always hated this time of year. I should go home and help my mom take down the Christmas tree, but getting Arkady consumed me.

I tapped in a ☺ and hit send.

"I'll take that as a yes." Jeremy yawned and rubbed his eyes. I could see how tired he was.

"You and Shar take the rest of the day off. I need to go in and make sure the clothes are returned to the showroom, wrap up a few last-minute details." He leaned closer, his breath warming my ear as he whispered. "Text me later." His lips brushed my check. I forced myself away and withdrew onto the car. I had to get back to see what damage control needed to be done with Shar and Hades, and we needed to come up with a new plan. Through the window, I saw him watch the train depart.

"So, what happened? Spill!" Shar practically jumped on me when I got back to the apartment.

"Was Hades here?" I said, looking around for evidence of what Shar would find irresistible—first class tickets to Europe? A mink?

"Hades?" she asked, wincing.

"Who else? He's after you, in a big way. He wanted me to put in a good word for him. And when I refused, he said he was going to make you an irresistible offer. You have got to be on your guard all the time. If you admit that for even one second you'd like to be with him, you're his."

She pressed her fingers into her temples as if she was thinking hard about something.

"Why me? I mean, he's been flirtatious—"

"He's beyond that. He salivates over you. He tried to bribe me to persuade you to say you want to be with him. He told me he'd let Arkady see and hear us, and keep Demeter away. This morning everything was going so great, and then he showed up and ruined what would have been a perfect kiss—"

"Jeremy kissed you?" Her tone was indifferent—or was it? Was she still interested? Was Hades lying about Jeremy snubbing her?

I waved her off. "Almost." I looked at her with great seriousness. "Shar, this is more important. Promise me you'll try to stay away from Hades, and don't agree to go anywhere with him."

"He can't be serious." She wrinkled her nose at me. "He has a wife!"

"That means nothing to any of them. Your refusing him is fueling this obsession. I'm sure no one has ever turned him down, and even though he doesn't like it, it excites him. This is getting scary, Shar. Don't admit that you'd like to spend even a single second with him, or you'll have one foot in the land of slaves and shadows."

"Well, aren't you a bucket of sunshine!" she snipped.

"I'm serious!"

"Alright, alright!" She rolled her eyes and put up her hand like she was taking an oath. "I promise, I swear, I'll be careful."

I could tell she wasn't taking me seriously, and that was a problem. I put my head down, racking my brain for the most decadent possible temptations Shar might succumb to.

"You swear"—I paused, pointing a finger at her—"to turn him down even if he … jets you off to some exotic location … and offers you the shiniest, most expensive, exclusive excessive shoes you've ever seen—"

"Oh for God's sake, Meg!" Shar shook her head.

"What if he makes your hands *and feet* normal again?" I cut her off, watching her closely.

She hedged, but only for a second, then grinned evilly at me. "Oooh, that could be a problem!"

Shar

Diamonds Are Forever—Trouble

*W*e can't get together today," said Jeremy regretfully as he gazed into Meg's eyes the next day at the office.

I rolled mine.

"I have some things to take care of for Mr. Romanov. Another time?"

Meg gave him a shy grin and ducked her head.

Oh, please!

"Awesome." Jeremy rubbed his temple. "Okay, I need you two to go to Sam's, two blocks down, and pick up lunch for the office. Make sure you order the tomato and rice soup," he said, exclusively to Meg. "It's so good, and it'll help your throat." Then he looked at me. "You won't have to wait long—they're pretty fast about getting things together."

"Can't we just fax them the order and have them deliver it?" I asked casually. Any chance to avoid the public had to be seized upon.

Jeremy shook his head slowly. "The last intern we hired tried that and Reynaldo whined for a week. Sorry, going in person makes for fewer mistakes. I'll take an order of vegetable samosas and a strawberry smoothie."

Was *he* a veg-head too? God, I was surrounded by herbivore freaks. If there was a worldwide famine, they could be my food source. I knew who I'd snack on first.

"Mr. Romanov?" Meg queried. I was glad she wasn't so besotted she'd forgotten why we were here in the first place.

"Should we order something special for him?" I asked, trying to spare her a feather or two.

"Oh no," Jeremy laughed. "His macrobiotic chef will be bringing his meal by a little later. Mr. Romanov only eats meals specially prepared for him. I'll tell you all about it another time. Make sure you ask Reynaldo, Demi if she's here, and Callie what they want."

I tugged my Coach bag out of the drawer of the desk where Meg and I had been busy writing personal thank-you notes for Arkady to the rich and notorious who'd attended his show. I gave a little wave. "Later."

We made the rounds. Reynaldo ordered a salad with exact measurements of nuts, berries, beans, and a sliver of salmon. Not too thick. No dressing. And get him a whole lemon. He would do the rest himself. He was so anal he probably squeaked when he ran.

The nasty goddess was in residence.

"Problems yesterday?" she snickered.

"Lunch order?" asked Meg, ignoring the taunt. The silent thing was becoming a habit, and she was using it to her advantage.

Demi answered brusquely. "Why, ambrosia, of course."

"You mean, that icky marshmallow fruit salad?" I scrunched up my face in disgust.

"How retro," Meg drolled. "I hear that was really popular sixty years ago, but I've seen it in a lot of delis. One ambrosia—" She started to write it down when the pencil flew out of her hand.

"Ugh! I would never eat any of the slop you call food. I don't want anything, Margaret. I ... what's the phrase you use? Brown bag it." Demi poofed a golden goblet full of some steamy liquid. It made the reception area smell like a fruit stand.

"Oh Demi, you've brought in your special diet drink again!" Reynaldo sniffed as he breezed through. "When will I convince you to give me the recipe?"

"Not in your lifetime," she said pleasantly, without even looking at him. Reynaldo tittered as he pranced back through the doorway.

Demeter sniffed. "As if! The pest. Sharisse, have you seen or heard from our mutual acquaintance? How is the dear boy?"

"Don't know, don't care." I headed toward the door which Demeter slammed shut in our faces.

"Never turn your back on a goddess." I felt myself being spun around until once again we both faced her. *She likes to play games! Goody! Does she know Twister?*

"You might want to be careful who you insult," she warned. Her face softened. "You know, Sharisse, with my son-in-law's looks—that hard body, bronzed skin, and although I hate to admit it, his irreproachable good taste—do you really feel repulsed by the idea of spending time with him?" I let my silence speak for me and pointed to the door. It swung open. "Although I must say you seem to be giving him a bit of a challenge. Maybe he's losing his touch. Go a little crazy. I'm sure he'd show you a good time."

"Then *you* sleep with him," I muttered under my breath.

"Don't listen to her," said Meg as we passed through the hall. "I don't know how we'll manage it, but we're going to do this. It's either that or you're stuck with me for a long, looong time!"

"With your taste in clothes? Don't torture me." My jest got no laughs. It made me queasy to think that Meg was right. With the scheming of Hades and Demeter, I was stuck in a hard place between two divine rocks.

The next stop was Callie, House of Romanov's one-person computer department. I guessed with all he had to hide, Arkady wanted as few hands in his business as possible. But man, did this one have reality issues! Callie spent way too much time playing Final Fantasy and guzzling those god-awful energy drinks.

We found Callie under her desk, the back end of her khaki pants and her sensible walking shoes sticking out.

"Ahem." I cleared my throat and Callie crawled out, dust and bits of paper stuck in her long and tangled brown mop. She looked up, blinking at us with bright, darting eyes.

"Oh!" she grunted, bumped her head and hoisted herself up into her chair.

"We're doing lunch orders," Meg said blandly.

"Yeah," Callie answered, perking up. "Food!"

"Uh-huh," I replied. "What do you want from Sam's?"

"Don't they make those awesome jalapeno bean wraps?" she drooled. *Who got that excited about a sandwich?* "I want one of those," she continued, "with extra cheese and hot sauce. Tell them to dump it all on. And a bag of Doritos—the big one."

Beans and hot sauce? I am so avoiding you for the rest of the day! Out of the corner of my eye I saw Meg crinkle her nose. *Right—make that the rest of the week.*

"Jalapeno wrap, Doritos, big," I said as Meg jotted it down. "Gotcha. Anything else? Something to drink?"

"Get me another three of these." Callie picked up an energy drink can—one of the super-sized black ones with the slime-green streaks down the front—and shook it in our faces. Something sloshed around inside and a fly buzzed out. She finished it off.

"All righty then," I said. There was no way I'd ever sit at a table with this woman.

"We better go before it gets really crowded down there," said Meg. "Bye!"

"Finally!" I steered Meg out of the building and we headed downtown. That was after Callie came running out of her office with a spreadsheet of the extra food she wanted. It took up a whole page, and she insisted on going over it with us. Talk about OCD. Then Reynaldo caught us and added a brownie to his order.

"No nuts." He'd wagged a finger at us like we were naughty children.

"I hate this job," I fumed as we strode down the street a good fifteen minutes later. "I hate the assignment, I hate Demeter, I hate Hades, I hate—"

"Couldn't agree more," sighed Meg. "Listen, I've been thinking about our situation. This might be a 'burst in and haul him away' kind of thing."

"And how are we going to break into his office and take him? He doesn't admit anyone other than specialists or your sweet Jeremy, who's there most of the time—we'd have to entrance Jeremy and whoever else is in there. Then there'd be problems if Reynaldo sees us, or Callie. And there's nothing we can do about her." The complications were astronomical.

"Or Demeter," Meg added. "She'd meddle just because she can, but she's weaving her own web, and we're the flies caught up in it."

"Please," I said, holding my stomach at the memory of the fly-in-the-can. "Don't talk to me about bugs."

"We have to do it when no one's around," Meg went on. "You had the right idea before, I think—if that's what you really want to do."

"What's that?" I couldn't remember what splendid idea I had.

"Go to work when no one's around and do some digging. There's got to be a schedule or agenda that will give us a clue to Arkady's activities."

It sounded reasonable; if we knew where and when he'd be someplace, we could coordinate his kidnapping.

We arrived at the deli—Sammy's Sandwich Shop, a regular hole in the wall. I was expecting something more exotic and upscale, but when we opened the door I knew immediately why the meals for House of Romanov came from here. I was seduced by the scent of hot pastrami on rye with mustard, and the sweet enticements of gooey chocolate chip cookies still warm from the oven—yum yum yummo! But Callie and Reynaldo's extensive food orders had put us at the back of a long line of power-suited people who were too busy to figure out what they wanted until they got up to the counter.

"We're going to be here forever!" I sighed, adjusting my shades. I'd gotten quite used to wearing them, but when this was over, I wasn't going to wear glasses for a solid week. Sun exposure over that short a time couldn't give me wrinkles.

Crow's feet on my feet AND on my face. Wonder if I can pre-pay a future facelift, like people do for funerals?

I dutifully positioned myself behind the last person, a tall, pin-thin blond woman. A small dog with a terrified expression on its face peeked over her shoulder. Meg took the tiny space that was left next to me. The next person would have to wait outside in the cold.

Blondie shifted from side to side as if she was slow dancing, and every time her poor pooch whimpered she would impatiently shush it.

While we waited, I examined every aspect of her that I could see. She had to be a foot taller than me, but we were both built the same way, slender with long legs. Blondie's were encased in snug-fitting jeans a color somewhere between beige and gold; there was a metallic sheen to the fabric. Definitely Dolce and Gabbana. Her jacket, bag, jaunty fedora, and five-inch heels seemed to be made from the same material, or at least they were all the same shade. When she moved under an overhead light, I discovered I was right—her outfit shimmered. If she wasn't standing so close, she'd look like a statue. Even the dog had a matching gold-toned collar. *How Hollywood A-List.* At least she should've looked *better* than the dog.

A large group left the store and the line shuffled up several feet. Now there were only a couple of people, including Blondie, in front of us.

"List," I said.

"Here you are." Meg held up the pad. "I think I'll get the same as Jeremy. It sounds good." She smiled faintly. I knew where her thoughts were going, and I envied her. My naughty thoughts had nowhere to go.

Meg pulled out Jeremy's House of Romanov credit card just as I was about to search for Hades'.

I clicked my tongue. "Which one should we use?"

"Does it really matter?" she offered. "It's probably all coming from the same place."

"But what if he gets mad?"

Meg waved a hand. "Pffft! Come on Shar, he wants you so bad you could buy Rockefeller Center on his Visa and he wouldn't flinch. Besides, it's kind of like a business expense."

The line advanced and Blondie was up. She had turned slightly and I could see her profile. Her skin was golden and perfect, and her features were fashion-magazine quality. The guy behind the counter started talking to her, and I turned my attention back to Meg, who was picking at a hangnail. I reached into my purse to get my wallet. I so didn't want to use Hades' card; the hologram was too suggestive. Seeing any more of him might burn my retinas.

I choked.

"What's wrong?" Meg asked, her voice low.

"My purse shook." Slowly I pulled out a small blue box tied with a white ribbon.

"What's that?" she asked.

"The box is from Tiffany's, so it has to be good!"

Meg looked confused. "We didn't go there together. When did you manage to sneak out?"

"I didn't! It has to be a gift. From *you know who*. Oh, this is going to be so *awesome!*"

"You're not going to keep it, are you?"

"You bet I'm keeping it—it's from Tiffany's. Oh, don't give me that look, Meg, it's probably something small and tasteful."

"Greeks bearing gifts," she mumbled.

One tug on the thick satin bow freed the lid of the box. Slowly I peeled it off. Now we both gasped. A chunky, square-shaped, crystal-clear blue diamond winked at us from a white velvet cushion. I stopped breathing. It had to be over five carats.

"I think that falls into the category of big and ostentatious," she said acerbically.

"I didn't make any promises!" I blurted.

"Next!"

It was our turn at the counter. Blondie had stepped aside and was arranging her packages and dog while she waited for her order. As we stepped up, she gave us a piercing glance that for some reason made me shiver, despite the fact that it was hot and close in the crowded room.

"Nice ring," she drawled. The little dog whimpered and she gently tapped it on its nose.

"A gift," I said, shoving the box deep into my purse. Blondie's order came up and she left. It was our turn.

I read the list to the man in the grubby apron behind the counter, and told Meg, "Wait here for the food while I go get the drinks." I pushed the list into her hands and made my way through the line, which had grown to the back of the shop again, to the fridge case and started pulling out bottles.

Even through all the background noise, I heard the deli man. "You want these sandwiches toasted?"

Before I could run back and respond, Meg answered him.

"No, don't toast them, but cut them into quarters and—" The words had hardly left her lips when she jumped and rubbed her rear. I grabbed the drinks and hurried forward.

"Anything for you, Miss!" The guy behind the counter gave her a toothy grin. Then he took the sandwiches from the line worker standing next to him and started cutting them up himself.

"Can I get you anything else?" he fawned.

"*Ase me isihi*," said Meg under her breath, and slipped out. Once our order was ready, I quickly signed the credit receipt and met her on the street.

"I'm going to be a walking feather mattress," Meg said, stomping back to the office.

"I think I need another Claritin." My nose was running and my eyes were starting to water. It was very hard trying to wipe my eyes underneath the sunglasses. Meg's proliferating plumage made me doubly cautious about looking at people. I'd definitely gotten the easier gift to deal with, but it was getting harder to be around her.

As soon as we got back to the office, Reynaldo was waiting, impatiently tapping his foot.

"There's a priority client in the Yellow Salon. Go offer

her something." He took his salad and brownie. "I'll be in to assist her in a moment. I simply have to get some food before I pass out! Maybe I'm hypoglycemic! Oh!"

"Go wolf down that lump of chocolate," muttered Meg when he was out of earshot.

I shook my head. "He's such a drama queen. C'mon. We'll drop the lunch order in the kitchen, find out what the client wants, and hit a coffee shop if we have to. Neither of us can make coffee that's drinkable."

The Yellow Salon was empty.

Meg's head swiveled around. "There's no one here. Maybe they've already taken care of whoever it was?"

"Good. One less thing we have to do. Let's go."

"I'm not done with *you*." The voice slid like cold steel along my spine. Out from a dressing room came Blondie from the deli. And her little dog, too.

"What?!" I asked.

Her jaw clenched and her eyes hardened. "So, do you frequently seduce happily married men? Flirt and take advantage of their weakness? Wheedle gifts and who knows what else from them?"

"I don't chase after any married men!" I responded indignantly. "I'm only seventeen! I don't even have a boyfriend!"

Meg leaned closer. "Shar, *married* man, *gifts out of thin air*. Think!"

It was like a slap to the head.

Hades. And now the happy little wife. What was her name...

"Persephone! It's a regular family reunion," quipped Meg in my ear. "At least she's being forthright."

"Oh jeez," I gulped.

Persephone gave us a glacial look, then lounged seductively on a striped yellow satin chaise. "Why is *my* husband, Lord of the Underworld, brother to Zeus, giving *you*, a stinking, lowly mortal, gifts?"

"Uh…" *Sorry, Sharisse can't talk now, she's brain dead.*

Meg jumped. "Shar never asked for anything from him. She wants nothing to do with Had—your husband."

Well, it was mostly true, but I still couldn't speak. Thank God Meg defended me while I continued to stand there, drooling on the yellow and sage-green carpet.

Persephone was unimpressed. She sprang off the chaise and waved an identical Tiffany's ring in front of me.

Hades, you idiot! Giving two women the same ring! We both should slap him.

"Liar!" she screamed at Meg, then turned to me. "You're using your wiles and cheap charm on him. Why would he want *you* when he has *me*, immortal goddess and Daughter of Demeter? Who put you up to this? What god? I command you to tell me what your interest is in my Hades."

Those intense green eyes, so like her mother's, bored into me. I could hear myself sweat. Slowly, she stroked her dog, which whimpered when she paused for too long.

"It's a working relationship only. Nothing personal. On my part. And I avoid gods whenever I can. At all costs!

I swear!" I held up the scout's honor sign. She didn't have to know I was never a Girl Scout.

"It had best *stay* that way. Any step over that line and you will regret it for the next, oh, *eternity*. Am I clear?" Persephone's voice was shrill.

"Yes ma'am!"

"Margaret, get me champagne, chilled, with a strawberry, and a plate of fresh fruit. Have your friend get me spring water for my pet while we wait for Reynaldo. Go!"

We scuttled out of the room in different directions. I knew I had to get Persephone what she wanted quickly, but I also had to have a moment alone to stop shaking. Just a minute, and then I'd be able to function. I couldn't go to the kitchen, the water cooler, or the ladies' room; my only option was the supply closet. Fine. If that's what it took for a few seconds of peace and safety, then that's where I was headed.

For a closet, it was pretty big. There was actually room enough that I wouldn't feel claustrophobic. Plopping down on a carton of TP, I leaned back and inhaled deeply.

"Hiding, *ma Sharisse*?"

I jumped. If I couldn't find peace in a supply closet, then the world was doomed. I ran for the door, but it wouldn't open.

"No need to run away," said Hades smoothly. "I won't harm you."

I had to face him. There he stood, in his True Religion jeans like they were made for every curve of muscle, and a black silk shirt that set off his olive-toned god looks. It wasn't the least bit tempting. Okay, a little, until I heard the yip of Persephone's dog and my spit dried up.

"Hello, Hades. Nobody left to torture in Tartarus?"

He held a hand to his chest. "You wound me, Sharisse. I don't torture anyone because then they can't serve me. And I would *never* do that to you. I can think of much more pleasant things we can do together."

"I'm sure you can. Do you have Persephone's permission to play with mortals?" Daddy told me the best defense was a great offense. *Charge!*

His eyes grew cold.

"Just in case you didn't know, Mr. Omnipotence, she's in the next room. And she thinks I'm chasing you. When she saw I had the exact same ring you gave her, she had a *fit!* Bad timing, bad choice, and bad idea! She scares me, Hades. Let me go." I jammed my fists on my hips.

He smoothed his countenance and spread out his hands. "Sharisse, calm down. Persephone and I have an open relationship. When she leaves me every spring, I'm so lonely down in Tartarus. She understands I don't like to be alone." He made a little pout, which on a different person I'd want to taste.

"I'm sure you can find someone who doesn't mind sharing you with the missus," I retorted. "You haven't gone through the whole pantheon yet, have you? You could have one playmate here and another down there. As long as you're cheating on her, don't stop at one. But don't think to include me."

Hades stepped closer. "Now you're just being nasty.

You're safe here with me. Here and in Tartarus, Persephone and I are free to come and go as we please, but under the terms of the agreement Zeus worked out, Persephone and I cannot meet each other on the mortal plane. I can't go into the next room and placate her, but neither can she burst in here to confront me about you." He licked his lips, so slowly. "If you would simply consent to give me one night, I would give you anything you desire. I'll get you a different ring. A *bigger* one. A pink one."

We stared at each other for a moment.

He continued. "I can guarantee that no harm would befall you. Would that soften your heart, my sweet Sharisse? Or perhaps..." Suddenly Hades was dressed in blue-pinstriped superfine wool trousers, a white cashmere sweater, and Gucci loafers. A cream cashmere coat was draped casually over his shoulder. An errant lock of hair slipped down across his forehead. With a deft twist of his head, he flicked it back.

When I pulled my eyes away from his elegant attire, I noticed we stood outside a marble building.

"*Buon giorno*," said a man strolling by.

We were in...*Milan*. In front of Ferragamo's. The mecca for shoe worshippers, of which I was a devout subject. Was Meg psychic? Or had Hades eavesdropped? My palms sweated and my heart pounded. Was this fear, or temptation? I couldn't tell the difference, and I was afraid of both.

"Ooh," was all I could manage. Hades stepped in front of me and opened the door.

"Shall we?"

I just wanted to look. On my grandmother's grave, I swore I wasn't going to accept anything.

"*Ah, Signor! E Signorina! Come stai? Prego! Prego!*" The man in the shop bowed, gesturing for us to come farther in.

"Giuseppe, my friend, how are you? And that lovely wife? Your children?"

Oh, he was smoother than Swiss chocolate. Asking about the wife and kids! How underhanded! He was just weaving a spell around everyone!

"*Buono, buono.*" They conversed while I slipped away to admire the displays. There was gilt everywhere, and each seat was a cream-colored upholstered cloud. The floors were buffed ivory marble. Even Giuseppe was attired in a costly, custom-made suit. His midnight blue shirt, against his pewter suit and yellow tie, created a picture of noble elegance. Soft music, the enticing aroma of leather, and the personal pampering added to the luxurious decadence. All around me were one-of-a-kind shoes, some with fourteen-karat-gold buckles or buttons. The inventory in this place could probably feed a third-world nation for several days. Now I was starting to sound like Meg. But it was true.

Hades came up behind me. I knew he was there; I could feel him breathing down my neck. I ignored him, but he wouldn't allow it.

"See anything you like?"

"Well, that's a really stupid question. Ask if there's something I *don't* like." If I die, I want to go to shoe heaven.

A finger trailed down my arm. Since when was I dressed in a lovely emerald green silk sheath?

"You can have them all. Just say the words." His breath tickled my ear. I shifted away a bit.

"And those words are?"

"One night."

Here we go again.

"Will Persephone tap me to relieve her when it's my turn to go into the ring? I don't do tag team sheet wrestling, Hades. Much as I would love to slip my feet into one of these babies, your price tag is too high. But wait, I *can't* slide one on my foot because I have talons!" I gave him my dirtiest look. It didn't faze him, not that I thought it would. Meg's warning notwithstanding, even I knew when I was being led down the garden path.

The mention of his wife's name didn't bother him. Without looking away, Hades snapped his fingers and two sales clerks hurriedly brought over expensive uphol-stered armchairs. Right behind them was Giuseppe with a footstool. The clerks rushed away, only to return a few moments later with iced champagne and a platter of cheeses and fruits.

We sat. I gave Hades my *this won't work* disinterested look, but I was savoring every second and every detail. I wanted to remember it when I was home, crying over my ugly feet.

"*Signorina*, please." Giuseppe gently lifted my foot and before I could cry *fowl!*, he removed my shoe.

My foot was normal. My toes even had my favorite

color pink polish. I breathed a sigh of relief. Giuseppe measured and chatted in Italian with Hades. I would let them go through the motions, fully aware he was trying to seduce me through my feet. It was a plot worthy of James Bond, but I was onto him.

Giuseppe hurried away and I turned to Hades.

"Doesn't he get upset you're wearing Guccis in his store?"

Hades crossed his long legs as he sipped the last of his champagne, which was instantly refilled by a hovering sales clerk who then moved back a discreet distance.

"It reminds him that I share my friendship and wealth with others. He makes sure I get the best he can give. The fact that I am bringing you here is something he will brag about to his competitors, who then will do anything to curry my favor."

"What does Persephone like? I mean, I wouldn't want to be caught wearing the same shoes. We've already got the same ring. How gauche."

His laughter was rich and warm and deep. A number of women cast admiring glances in his direction. The threat from Persephone and warnings from Meg still bolstered my resistance to his charm, although the bribes were killing me.

"Her taste runs more to a less inhibited style." Hades pointed to a pair of long black leather boots, the kind that go up over the knee, with sharp studs on them. I think hookers wear them with black pantyhose, micro miniskirts, and bustiers. Or maybe it was tacky pirates.

"Not surprised."

Giuseppe returned carrying a shoe I would have worked the rest of my life to pay off. A sleek three-inch-heeled pump, in alligator, with black onyx buttoned buckles. I didn't care that the terrifying, man-eating beasts were endangered—they made beautiful shoes. And bags. *Sigh.* I had to get out of here. I jumped up and ran out the door ...

And landed in the supply closet again, in my own clothes and with talons digging into my transvestite shoes. With ragged breath, I sat back down on the carton. Hades didn't follow. I had to calm myself before anyone saw me. I looked at my watch; fifteen minutes had gone by. I stood, put my glasses back on, smoothed out the wrinkles in my pants, and peeked down the corridor. Cautiously, I scooted out while it was clear and snuck back to the Yellow Salon. There was no light under the door now, and it was very quiet. First, I put my ear to the door, and when I heard nothing, I carefully opened it. It looked like Persephone was gone. Wearily, I made my way to the copy room. Meg stood there, attacking a stack of paper almost as tall as she was. She looked me over.

"What happened to you? Luckily Reynaldo came in before she could really start interrogating me and whisked her off somewhere."

"I was hiding in the supply closet. It was only supposed to be for a minute. Meeting Persephone really rattled me. But then Hades found me and took me to Ferragamo's. Tried to buy my body with shoes."

Meg inhaled sharply, although she barely looked alarmed. "What did you do?"

I started to rub my face, then thought about smeared makeup. My hands dropped. "I'm still here, so obviously I refused. Even though he dangled custom-made alligator pumps in front of my nose. By Ferragamo. In *Milan*."

"Italy?! No!" She slapped a hand over her mouth.

I bobbed my head.

Fear crossed her face. "Persephone will kill you. You didn't…"

"Over shoes? Please." I laughed bitterly. "Nothing happened. If anything, I told Hades I was afraid of her and wanted no part of his offer. He said he could guarantee my safety. I didn't buy it, and I'm not interested. Even if he dangles the most darling alligator pumps, with real gold and onyx button buckles!"

Meg looked doubtful. "You and your shoes. It's an unholy obsession."

"Trust me, not even I love shoes that much. He's really starting to make me nervous."

"Good." Meg scratched and a pin feather popped out. I sneezed.

"Come on," she sighed, tucking it back in. "Let's grab our lunch and sneak out. You need some antihistamines."

My bird feet took me out the door behind her.

Meg

Stairwell to Heaven

Shar sat across from me at the vast obsidian-topped dining table that was positioned in front of the glass wall in the apartment. Outside, the morning was clear and probably cold. If we didn't have a deadline to deliver Arkady to Hades, I might have enjoyed the view a bit more.

She took a sip of chai out of a huge mug. We'd stopped going out for food or anything else; the apartment had everything we could need, including an industrial espresso machine. It didn't take us long to figure out how to operate the milk steamer. Soon we were pumping out hot chocolate and chai tea lattes like professionals.

"I'm so sick of all of this," Shar said, running a talon around the rim of her cup.

"Agreed." I put down my spoon. I'd developed a taste for cereal with nuts and berries, yet another sign that the Siren persona was taking hold. It crossed my mind that if my new look became permanent, I might be able to get a job handing out flyers for a greasy chicken restaurant. But it didn't matter. If I turned into a Siren, it would mean we'd failed the mission—and I could be the mascot for team Underworld. Go Cerberus! Rah!

"The thought that he can whisk you off anytime frightens me," I added.

"Try being on the receiving end," Shar muttered.

"You need to make him clearly understand the meaning of 'leave me alone.'"

"Hello? Him, all-powerful *god.* Me, mere *mortal.* I read in the mythology book that the gods pull pranks like this all the time, and it's not like I can call up his wife to complain. She's after me too."

Anxiety lined Shar's face as she pushed her tea away. She could say no as much as she wanted; it wouldn't matter if Hades was that determined.

"I know you're in a bad place," I soothed her, trying to offer what comfort I could. "Let's concentrate on our next move. It might help you get your mind off *him.*"

Shar looked up and nodded morosely, then stared at me.

"Are you all right?"

She didn't answer, but flicked her gaze back and forth, from my face to my cereal bowl and back, her lower lip starting to quiver.

"Hey, it's not that bad, not yet," I said, getting up and moving closer to her. "We can still do this."

"It's not that," she started. "Well, it's that, but there's something else."

"You didn't—"

"No way! No, nothing like that. This has nothing to do with Hades. It has to do with ... Jeremy."

My stomach did a flip. "What do you mean, with Jeremy? Did you use ... it ... on him?"

She shook her head. "No, no ... its just that, well, I admit it, I tried to get him to talk to me, I wanted him to, you know, like me. But instead—"

"He liked me." I finished the thought for her. "Shar, I didn't try—"

"I realize that. It was a shock. I mean—" Shar faltered. "When it comes to that, I ... usually win."

"This wasn't a contest."

"I know, and everything that's been going on with Hades, I can accept it, sort of. But still, I'm confused."

I stiffened. "Why, because someone like Jeremy would want someone like me?"

"No!" she protested. "You two seem made for each other. You have the same interests ..." She trailed off.

"But you don't understand how he could be attracted to someone like me," I pressed.

Shar looked at me intently. "Meg, I don't know why you're so down on yourself. You look amazing, at least when you're not half bird." She patted my feathers, then sneezed. "Ugh! I thought I could go five minutes without doing that! Anyway, you turned lots of heads the night at the Met. Didn't you notice?"

I laughed and shook my head. "No."

"You should pay more attention."

"I guess I'll take your word for it," I said. "But Jeremy can't get between us, not now. Are you mad? Tell me the truth."

"I was at first, not so much anymore. Only—" Shar turned away.

I touched her shoulder. "Tell me what's bothering you, get it off your conscience. I'm sure it's not that bad."

She heaved a sob. "I'm sorry, Meg!"

"For what? You said you didn't do anything!"

"Well, I did. I got you all made up and everything, but it wasn't for you. It was ... for me. I hoped maybe you'd hook up with someone else and that I would get a chance with Jeremy. It wasn't because I was being nice."

"But it was nice." I put a hand over her talons. "And I understand. I knew you liked him too." I laughed, low and mirthlessly. "That day when we went to the office to actually start working, I just figured he would go after you. When he started talking to *me*, well, I was waiting for him to start asking me where you were and how you were doing."

"Like he did with me about you."

"He did?" I brightened.

"Oh yes," Shar huffed. "Then he moved away like I was contagious. Are you mad at me?"

"Not in this lifetime." I grinned at her. "Sirens have to stick together."

"Good." She took a deep breath and wiped her eyes. "That was bothering me more than anything, except for maybe getting Arkady to the portal."

"And the wrath of Persephone and her mother, and Hades stalking you."

"Thanks for reminding me. All right. Our next move—what is it, getting to work early?"

"Yes, we should get a look at Arkady's schedule. When he has appointments out of the office, Jeremy goes with him. When they're out, we can slip into his office or maybe Jeremy's."

"Sounds like you're on a roll." Shar waved a hand for me to continue.

"We'll look for his schedule, then figure out where he's going to be and where the nearest portals are. There are lots of them all over the city. I figured out how to map them out on the iPhone."

"Impressive, young padawan!" Then Shar's face sobered. "You do remember that the next time we try to get Arkady to a portal, we'll have to use the Siren gifts. On *other* people. Maybe lots of them, including Jeremy."

"I know." I didn't want to use the gift on Jeremy, but there would be no choice if he was at Arkady's side, and that looked like the one thing we could count on. Or else I could try to explain what was going on: *Jeremy, I realize this might sound… odd, but, Mr. Romanov? He made a deal with Hades, the Greek god of the Underworld. No, it's not a myth. No, I'm not on any kind of medication* ... No. And I couldn't do it anyway due to the nondisclosure thing. So Jeremy would hear my Siren voice, then hopefully, after I released him, we could both return to being absolutely human.

I went to my bedroom suite to get ready. I dressed as quickly as I could, but it wasn't easy. My thighs, torso, and upper arms were completely covered in feathers, and dressing usually resulted in them getting ruffled and tangled. Pulling on them smarted.

So far, the gift had left my feet, hands, and face alone, which was pretty much the opposite of what was happening to Shar. Our transformations had to halt here, or Shar wouldn't be able to be in the same room with me, and she might sprout a beak. I wound a long scarf around my neck. I'd keep it on all day and say I was in the midst of a relapse. That would keep Reynaldo away, and with any luck, Jeremy wouldn't mind playing text messenger a bit longer.

When we clocked in, Reynaldo put us to work finishing the thank-you notes for the runway show.

"How long does it take you?" He poked at a towering stack of envelopes. "You don't want Mr. Arkady to look ungracious! You could have been working on these before the show started, and then at the show!"

You mean, while we were busy redesigning the star dress, then trying to send Mr. Arkady down a rabbit hole?

Reynaldo shook his head and clucked his tongue as he cat-walked away. I picked up a pen and started to address an envelope when my phone vibrated. I flipped it open and read:

What r u doing now?

Jeremy. I texted back:

T-Y's for the show, Reynaldo cracks whip!

I kept the phone open and set it to silent. Another message popped up two seconds later:

Haha. Feeling better?

I looked at Shar, who was busy addressing envelopes. I typed:

Still no voice. But not contagious.

His next message came up almost instantly.

Cool. Think u can get away 4 a sec?

I snuck another peek at Shar. Was it fair to leave her? It would only be for a couple of minutes. I told him yes.

Come 2 the exit stairs 2 left of elevators :)

I snapped the phone shut and jumped up, startling Shar.

"Bathroom!" I yelped, and dashed out without looking at her; the guilt might make me reconsider.

I could feel my heartbeat speeding up as I walked past

the fake Fabergé eggs and into the beige reception area. Out the double doors. Down the hall. Past the elevators. No one was there to hinder me.

As I grasped the cool metallic handle of the stairwell door, visions of Jeremy and me on Coney Island zipped through my mind like a flickering slideshow. I'd been robbed of my moment—there had been no kiss, only the brush of his lips on my cheek, his breath in my ear, but no more. I had no idea what his experience had been; we'd never talked about it.

I pushed the stairwell door open with resolve and burst through. It was empty. I stepped into the stairs, my breathing shallow, my heart still racing. I closed my eyes as the door swung shut. Hearing the soft click of the latch, I shook my head; this was a Hades trick. *He's furious that I won't deliver Shar to him, and now he's going to mock me.*

Behind me, someone cleared their throat. *He's here; he actually had the nerve to come to confront me.* I spun around, ready for a fight.

"You—" I started, then stopped.

It wasn't Hades.

It was Jeremy.

In the half second that I turned to face him, his expression changed from a soft stubbly grin to wide-eyed confusion. I must've looked deranged.

"I'm sorry," he began to apologize, but I strode over to him, shaking my head. I put a finger to his mouth. His lips parted, letting out a short breath that tickled my finger. I moved my hand to his cheek; he felt real, warm.

"It's really you," I mouthed.

He quirked an eyebrow. "Expecting someone else?"

I blushed—nowadays I could never be sure.

"No." The word came out in a whisper.

He pushed himself away from the wall and, slipping an arm around my waist, spun me around so our positions were reversed. Brushing the hair away from my face with a finger, he bent down so that his face was mere inches from mine.

"I like your hair," he said. "I like your eyes. No, I think I love your eyes." His lips brushed my forehead, nose, then hovered above my mouth.

Here we were again—the moment, the *exquisite anticipation*. Never taking my eyes off his lips, mine parted. *No interruptions.*

Gently, he pressed me against the wall, his warm palms guiding my face closer. I could feel the feathers prickling against the skin of my back. He was still holding my face in his hands, but he pulled away slightly and stared at me for a long moment. *So close...*

"Is something wrong?" I whispered.

"No," he said, resting his forehead against mine. I inhaled deeply, losing myself in the mingled, spicy scents of patchouli and sandalwood—his scent. "It's just that...I feel like we've done this before...haven't we? I try to remember"—he squeezed his eyes shut—"but I can't."

I raised my right hand and smoothed his brow. His eyes fluttered open.

"We're here now," I said, my voice neutral. I lifted my

face closer to his and he descended toward mine. His lips were warm and soft, and his teeth tugged gently, teasingly, on my bottom lip. I closed my eyes. As the kiss deepened, he started to move his hands down to my neck, my shoulders. I shrank back, but not before he felt the weird padding on my arms. He didn't seem to notice. His hands moved up into my hair, drawing me closer to him.

The phone on his belt buzzed. Reluctantly, we parted. He closed his eyes and threw his head back in exasperation before looking at it.

"Reynaldo. I have to get back," he said morosely. "And Mr. Romanov changed his plans. I'll probably be gone the rest of the day. I'll text you as soon as I can."

I nodded, and reached up a hand to run it through his hair. He gazed at me for a moment before his lips reclaimed mine. I was torn between not wanting it to end and hustling him back to Arkady so Shar and I could ransack his office.

"I'll leave first," he said, pulling away reluctantly. "We really need to do this again."

I gave a little wave as he pushed through the stairwell door. Then I counted to sixty, replaying the last five or so minutes in my head, before leaving as well.

Demeter was at the reception desk when I went back in.

"Margaret, a word."

"Sorry," I whispered, patting my scarf. "I'm not feeling well."

"Save it, dearie. We both know you're perfectly capable of talking. Don't worry. I'll make sure no one interrupts us." I heard the doors bolt.

"What do you want, Demeter?"

Her look was disapproving. "What kind of friend are you? Leaving Sharisse to toil away while you have a rendez-vous. She hasn't had much fun since you've been saddled with your mission. You got Jeremy—what did she get?"

I knew where this was going and I didn't answer.

"She could find happiness like you—and you'd both be free."

"With Hades?" I retorted. "I don't think your daughter wants Shar anywhere near him, and I *know* Shar doesn't want his attention."

"Persephone is young and rebellious."

"She's a big goddess. I think she can take care of her-self."

"I liked it better when you minced your words, Marga-ret. Those who go toe to toe with the gods stumble and eat dirt. Some become dirt."

Demi raised her hands and all the doors opened—I'd been dismissed.

I found Shar finishing up the thank-yous.

"That's it, the last of them," she sighed, leaning back after she'd rubber-banded the last stack. "Make it to the bathroom okay?"

"Yeah," I said, and left it at that. She didn't need to be enlightened on current events—my interlude with Jeremy might annoy her, and my conversation with Demeter would definitely depress her.

About an hour later, Jeremy left with Arkady. As soon as they got onto the elevator, Reynaldo grabbed his hat and scarf and dashed off toward the stairwell.

"Date with Andre," Shar explained. "He told me all about it while you were out. He was totally stressing over what to wear, what to say."

"He's always having a conniption," I grumbled. "But look, Jeremy told me that he and Arkady might be gone for the rest of the day, and if Reynaldo is on a long lunch…"

"Let's not waste any time." Shar got up. "So, when did Jeremy tell you this?"

When I didn't answer immediately she sighed loudly. "Bathroom?"

I turned three shades of red and nodded.

"Whatever." She flicked her hair and quickly strode away.

Down we went to Jeremy's office. Shar looked around cautiously before going in.

"We'll start here—you check the desk, I'll do the computer," she ordered after we'd slipped through the door and shut it behind us. I found nothing in the drawers, and had just shut the last one when the office door opened.

Callie stood in the entrance, her right hand still on the doorknob. A techie tool bag was slung over her shoulder, and in her free hand she clutched an extra-large bag of chips.

We froze, and she stopped dead, seeing us. Her dark, bug-like eyes narrowed as she looked from me to Shar.

"What are you two doing in here?" she demanded, in her high and grating voice.

"Trying to find Mr. Romanov's schedule, why?" said Shar, looking nonplussed. "What are *you* doing in here?"

Callie looked taken aback. "I, uh, always make my rounds when Mr. Romanov goes for his mud baths. I have to do the back-ups." She looked ready to bolt or scream for help.

"Well, we have to review his schedule for new treatment options. We couldn't do it while Jeremy was working, and this is the only computer we have access to, but I think the program froze. Can you help us?"

"Morons," Callie said. "Next time, call me when something like this happens."

Setting her chips and tool bag on a filing cabinet, she shooed Shar out of Jeremy's chair and plunked herself down on it, making the air-cushion seat hiss. We stood behind her as she peered at the monitor. Shar had gotten as far as the password screen, but of course neither of us knew Jeremy's, or anyone's, password. Still, Shar had tried typing in something; a string of black dots almost filled the code-box.

Callie grabbed a pencil off the desk and tapped the point against each dot in succession. When she got to the end, she sighed dramatically and shook her head. "Typical!" she spat, disgusted. "You spelled the password wrong! There's only nine letters in 'longevity,' not ten."

She deleted Shar's erroneous entry and typed in the password. After a few rapid mouse clicks, up popped Arkady's schedule.

"Thanks," I said, maneuvering myself toward the keyboard. "We're good from here. We just have to print it out..."

Callie raised a hand to stop me. "I'll do it for you. I don't need you two messing up my systems!"

A few seconds later, the printer whirred and a sheet slid out.

Shar snatched it up. "If we move the Botox up one hour, we can squeeze that new treatment in, don't you think?" she said smoothly. I was seeing shades of Hades—having to do all the talking was turning her into a silver-tongued Shar-latan.

I nodded with authority.

Callie eyed us suspiciously as she pushed up her black-framed glasses with a finger. "Are you sure you're supposed to be in here?"

"Do you think Jeremy can be in two places at once? He had to go out with Mr. Romanov, and he needs us to map out these appointments so he can schedule them when he gets back in tomorrow," Shar said. "I wouldn't want to be the one to explain to Mr. Romanov why he'll have to wait eight weeks for new hair follicles."

I could add to the conversation, but Shar was doing fine on her own. I gave Callie gave a menacing glare and she backed up a step.

"We have what we need. The room's all yours," said Shar. She turned to go, with me following close behind.

Callie watched us closely as we left.

"Mission Impossible?" Shar giggled, when we were safely away.

I wrinkled my nose and shook my head. "I don't think so!"

Shar

This Ain't No Bed of Roses

With a copy of Arkady's schedule safely tucked into the tight pocket of my jeans, the rest of the day seemed a breeze. Tonight we would look it over, pick the best spot, and voilà! We'd be back to hum-drum school, prom, and graduation. And my shoes! My two dozen pairs of beloveds were getting dusty waiting for me. I know Meg couldn't wait either. She was getting close to being completely covered with feathers. If it weren't winter, she'd be dying of heat stroke, covered in fluff and continually wearing long-sleeved, high-necked sweaters.

On the way back to the apartment, we stopped off at the post office to mail the thank-you cards. Meg stayed outside, iPod in place, while I went in.

Between the dim lighting and my shades, the post office was dark. I bumped into the metal detector by the door. Enough! Frustrated, I pulled off the glasses and made a beeline for the outgoing mail slot. I could see now, but thanks to my monstrous bird feet, I managed to trip over a non-slip rug that had bunched up near the door.

When a nice man grabbed my elbow to steady me, without thinking I smiled at him warmly and gushed, "Thank you so much, you didn't have to do that!"

He promptly let me go. My head twitched—it had never done that before.

The man was standing next to me, staring at me with glazed eyes. *He was enthralled.* Damn! My toes were already fused and I sported scaly skin up to my knees. My fingers were curving like those old ladies who tried to look hip with long nails that yellowed and twisted, just like mine were now. The skin around my elbows was scaly and it was working its way down. My head twitched again.

"*Ase me isihi!*" I said to him, and he turned and left. I dumped the cards in the box and hurried out, tripping over the stupid rug again.

"What's the matter with your head?" Meg asked.

"I don't know. It just started." My head jerked back and forth, sometimes up and down. I was getting seasick.

"Does anyone in your family have epilepsy?" Meg craned her head and frowned while she studied me. People passing moved over a little farther than they needed to.

"It's really weird," she added.

"Ya think?!"

"What you need is a cup of chai." Meg clasped my arm and led me, twitching away, several doors down to a Starbucks. She pushed me into a chair.

"I'll order," she said.

"Do you think you should? You're running out of bare skin," I warned.

"I can handle it. Sit there and don't look at anyone." She walked off.

As I watched her join the line, I caught the eye of a college kid. He smiled tentatively at me. Raising a hand to my mouth, I blushed daintily and…

What is wrong with you?? Do you want to grow a beak? I really was a bird brain! Frantically I groped for my shades. Finding them, I slapped them on my face, only to have them rocked off as my head twitched again.

Too little, too late. Here came College Boy, tongue hanging out.

Damn, damn, damn!

"Tell me what you want," he whispered throatily. *Ugh! Coffee breath!* Didn't people realize how stinky it was?

"Go home. Study hard. Ace all your exams."

"For you, anything!"

"And *ase me isihi!*" I dropped my gaze to my ugly hands, waiting to see if I'd lose a finger. Or two. No, but suddenly my shoes felt incredibly tight. There was a ripping sound as the talons on my feet cut through my boots. How can anyone explain boots with claws? My nose felt a little longer too. I whipped out my compact.

My nose *was* longer! Now I looked like Gerda Shumholz from eighth grade; that girl had a honker that would look too big on the Sphinx!

Meg returned, plopping two cups on the table. She opened her mouth to say something, but nothing came out.

"Stop staring! It's embarrassing enough!"

"I leave you for three minutes, only to find you looking like…like…" She searched for a description.

"Like Big Bird! I know!"

She dropped into the chair opposite me. "What happened?"

I gave her a mutinous look. "I accidentally enthralled some guy." I pointed subtly at University Dude behind her. She looked over her shoulder, then turned back to me.

"Only one guy, and *that's* what happened?"

I started to say yes, then remembered about the older man in the post office. I closed my mouth.

"*Two* guys? Please tell me it was only two!"

I nodded morosely. Meg sighed, her shoulders drooping. Then she started to giggle. I guess she couldn't help it, but it still pissed me off.

"Shut up!" I warned through clenched teeth. The more she tried to stop, the worse it got. People were glancing our way, some smiling, but I didn't know if it was because of Meg and her silvery Siren laughter or my horrible appearance. I assumed the worst. *Oh sure, laugh at the ugly girl*. It made me uncomfortable to realize that I myself had been guilty of that sin.

A tear slid down.

"Oh Shar, don't cry!" Meg looked suddenly stricken. "I didn't mean to. I just couldn't help myself."

With a sniffle and a swipe, I nodded. "I know. It's just that when you're as vain as me, this is the worst."

Meg pushed my cup toward me. "Have a sip."

"Thanks. *Ah-choo!*"

She leaned away. "Take another Claritin."

I tried to get the pill into my mouth, but I kept missing it because my head kept jerking. In frustration, I dumped the pill into the chai and waited for it to dissolve.

"You know, you look familiar."

"I'm your roommate. You live with me."

Meg waved a hand. "No, I mean the twitching." She rubbed her chin absently. "I know! Your head moves like a bird's!"

"Geez, the hits just keep on coming! If this doesn't end soon, I'll have whiplash." I walked over to the self-service bar and nabbed a straw. It was either that or finish wearing the rest of the cup. My beautiful, winter-white scarf was spotted with drops of chai. Hades was definitely going to buy me a new one.

"We'd better get you home," Meg said.

Thankfully, only an Asian tourist stopped to stare at my feet.

"Vivienne Westwood," I said, and kept walking.

At the apartment, Meg pulled out Arkady's schedule and looked over the entries while I peeled off the remnants of my boots.

Meg thumped the paper. "Here. He's going to be at the Brightwater Clinic for a graft tomorrow at two p.m. And there's a notation that says 'back door.' I guess he's trying to be discreet." She held up the iPhone. "There's a portal somewhere in the alley by the back exit. If we can just be there when he arrives…"

"Then we'll wing it. No pun intended."

Meg pulled back a bit of her sleeve. Her sleek black feathers, which under the light revealed a rainbow-like sheen, came down to her wrist. "I don't have much room left for mistakes."

"Tell me about it. What's next for me, the full yellow beak?"

Meg stretched and yawned. "I'm going to take a shower. At least my hair is still my own. Order something, will you? I'm starving!"

I was about to pick up the phone when I saw something lying on the counter—a strawberry, as fat as my fist and dipped in dark chocolate, sitting on a gold plate.

Hades. That guy just never lets up. I stared at it, then picked it up and took a huge bite.

"Mmm, delicious," I said with my mouth full. "But unoriginal." After polishing it off, I padded into my bedroom. A trail of red rose petals led the way.

"Cliché." I trampled them.

A sexy black lace chemise lay draped over my pillow.

"Dream on." I took off my jacket and opened the closet door. A couture-line Badgley Mischka creation hung there.

I yelled. "Okay, nice—not that I can go anywhere looking like this." I pushed the gown aside and took out my pink Victoria's Secret sweat-jammies. I paused.

"You're not going to watch, are you? Don't make me tell your wife." Coming out of the closet, I saw that the lingerie was gone. When I peeked down the hall, the petals had disappeared. Then the doorbell rang.

Hesitantly, I turned the knob, wondering who would be waiting on the other side. I opened the door—and stood toe to toe with a smirking Hades, dressed in a Papa John's uniform. He held up three pizza boxes. The smell wafted out: cheese, pepperoni, and onions. I lost my appetite.

"What, are you part-timing now? They say the economy is bad, but Olympians delivering pizza and answering phones?" I shook my head. "What a sad day. What's next, vacation cruises to Tartarus?"

"My services are free of charge," he said. His voice, like silk, slid over me like a warm breeze, leaving chills in its wake. Only he could make his cheesy outfit look good. I wished Persephone was able to come pick up her playmate. Although no doubt she'd find a way to blame me for his showing up unannounced in my doorway.

"We didn't order Papa John's. Or pepperoni. Sorry. Wrong address, wrong order." I went to slam the door in his face. I wouldn't have that satisfaction when I became his prisoner—unless a more powerful god showed up to free me.

The door started to reverse course. Hades snapped his fingers and the pizza—and silly uniform—were gone. And so was the apartment. Suddenly I realized that we were in a sumptuous bedroom; the dark paneled walls gleamed in the light of hundreds of candles. A massive round bed, with a thick mattress canopied in sheer white curtains, dominated the room. On the left was a steaming bath big enough for a swim team, complete with floating rose petals and bottles of scented oils. Two champagne flutes, the contents bubbling up merrily, waited beside a plate of succulent fruits.

"Welcome to my boudoir," he purred.

His place?! I felt panic settling in.

On the right was a table smothered with all manner of food: meats, vegetables, breads, and the most wondrous selection of desserts. Every temptation, and I'm sure more I couldn't even dream up, waited there.

He stood behind me. His breath was hot on my neck but I got goose bumps—his lips were too close to my skin. He moved in to kiss me and I dodged him, running toward the bed.

Bad move!

My heart pounded, fear making my blood rush through my body. When he moved closer, I held out my clammy *normal* hands to ward him off.

"I don't date married men. I have a job to finish. I think my mother's calling me. Your wife's gonna kill me!" What else could I add? Oh, yeah. "Take me back."

"I can give you so much more, *cara mia*. Give me just one night."

I shook my head in denial, but he merely laughed. "I can see the passion in you, Sharisse." He leaned dangerously close but I refused to cower, even if I did skirt around, away from that monstrous bed.

"Margaret has time for Jeremy. You can make time for me."

I turned on him angrily. "I don't think so!"

Against my will, he brought my hand to his lips. I tried to tug it away, but it was useless. He was more powerful, even without being a god. I'm such a girl. I should sign up for some strength training.

His tongue drew little circles around each of my knuckles, his full lips trailing lightly over my skin.

If only he were someone—anyone—else!

"Forget about Margaret. We'll make a new deal."

My head was spinning from breathing so fast. My knees wanted to buckle, and I think they actually started to shake. With one smooth motion, he captured my lips and body for a searing, stop-my-heart kiss. Ooh, temptation! I felt faint, but strangely alive. It took a few moments before I was able to turn my head aside, breaking contact.

"I will destroy the contract," he drawled. My fingers dug into his shoulders because I felt too weak to stand on my own. "We'll make a better one."

"No." My voice was breathy.

"Is it so much? One evening of your undivided and *willing* attention and you keep everything. A single night with me and the contract is gone, Arkady is someone else's problem, and I'll even free Margaret. Plus, you can retain the money, the apartment, and the Visa, with plenty more to follow. Anything you desire."

"What about Persephone?" I gasped as he leaned in to nip my shoulder. My legs were definitely trembling now. He held me closer, molding his body to mine. I was scared. Force was ugly, no matter how pretty the package.

"Don't worry about her. She'll never know."

"Trust me, she'll know. And whatever you say about protection, I'm sure I'm a dead woman. So the answer is *no*."

"Think about it, *cara mia*. To show you my good faith ... " He kissed my fingers. I could feel my feet! And wiggle individual toes. I could wear my shoes ... but Meg couldn't wear a tank top.

This isn't right! I started to struggle.

"You've taught me that nothing is that simple, Hades," I said. "It's not black or white, yes or no. I can't trust you. And more than that, I won't screw Meg." I shook my head. "You always have ulterior motives. I'm no saint, but I don't do betrayal. Take me back so I can do the job you assigned me."

"Do you realize what you're giving up?" Suddenly Hades wasn't wearing his tight jeans and tee anymore. Or anything but a blatant invitation.

He was made for sinning, but not with me.

I flinched when I felt my clothes dissolve. He'd probably spied on me in the shower and seen me naked already, so I didn't give him the satisfaction of recoiling. I stood there boldly, although I did peek at my legs. It might be the last time they ever looked human.

"No." I held out one hand, the other I slapped onto my naked hip. "Clothes, please. I need to go back. *Now*."

He stepped closer. I jumped back.

"I think you owe me, Sharisse," he purred. "So many little things I do for you. Little gifts, visits." I could feel the heat roll off his body as he moved closer. I ran and yanked the bed sheet off, wrapping it around me.

"No fair tormenting the lonely virgin! How many times do I have to say it? No deal negotiating, no abandoning Meg, and no sex! And I won't be in your debt. Take all the gifts and give me back the talons. I'd rather have them and do my job." I held up a hand and cocked my head. "Wait, I think the iPhone says—"

I hadn't even finished my bluff when I was back in the apartment. Frantically, I checked to see if Hades remembered my clothes. *I wouldn't put it past him to dump me here naked.* I was dressed—but without panties!

"We're not finished, *cara mia*. I will enjoy my souvenir." Hades' voice was a whisper next to my ear, sliding like a lick down my neck before it disappeared.

"Pig!" I shouted.

"I'll say," said Meg, walking in and eyeing the boxes. "Three pizzas? How hungry are you?"

Meg

Best-Laid Plans

*W*e have five measly days left to do this job, so let's not mess it up this afternoon," I said, poking the calendar on the refrigerator door. Every day since we'd come into this doomed paradise had a large X through it; we were on day eight. Shar walked over, a troubled set to her pouty pink lips. I didn't want to tell her that that shade drew the eye toward her beaky nose. I think she was holding on by a thread—bird toes, scaly skin, twitches, and now this.

"Let's hope that today turns out to be successful. Think positive," she said. "Isn't that what you've been studying with your magic and feng shui and all that stuff? That it's, like, 98 percent intention or something like that?"

"Sorry, my power of positive thinking is running a little low today," I said. "Let's just go over the plan."

"Right," Shar said, strutting up and down the living room, from the glass wall to the door and back again. "Arkady's appointment is at two p.m. We go into the office and tell Jeremy, Reynaldo, and whoever else will listen that I have a checkup appointment for my eyes and that we have to leave at noon. You're coming with me, because I won't be able to see once they poke me, put drops in, blah, blah, blah."

I gave her a thumbs-up.

"Before we leave, we double check that the appointment is still on, and then go to the clinic and find the portal."

"Check," I said.

"Then I go into the hospital and charm someone into giving me a wheelchair if I can't steal one first. We bring said chair to the portal and we wait."

"And when Arkady shows up, we entrance whoever's in the car with him—"

"Even if it's Jeremy," Shar reminded me.

"—even if it's Jeremy," I stated firmly. "Then we put Arkady into his wheelchair..."

"...we bring him to the brink of the portal," continued Shar.

"...and in he goes, *dosvedanya*," I concluded.

Shar's hazel eyes sparkled. "Sounds like a plan coming together. I can't wait to do this!"

Everything was going according to schedule. We got

to the office and Demeter was absent. Hopefully talking to squirrels, spring cleaning, getting ready for Persephone's arrival. We didn't run into Jeremy as we went about our usual duties cleaning up old paper coffee cups, putting files away, and sorting copy jobs, all while waiting to tell someone about Shar's fictitious eye appointment so we could escape. When the clock passed eleven, I started to worry.

Shar nudged me out of the way to dump a load of copy mistakes into the recycle bucket.

"I say if we don't see anyone in the next five minutes, we leave a note and go. We can always come back when we're done," I offered.

Before she could agree, Jeremy's voice echoed in the hallway. "Meg? Shar?"

"Finally!" Shar poked her head out of the copy room door. "In here!" She waved.

Jeremy came in, looking harried.

"I hope nothing's wrong," Shar said, adjusting her sunglasses.

He looked at me. "Demi's out, and Reynaldo's been on the phone all morning with the buyers for orders. I'm totally on my own, and I have so much to do. And when we get back from Mr. Romanov's appointment, he immediately needs to have his wheatgrass tea infusion, and I don't have time to get it beforehand. It's not pretty when he gets thrown off schedule."

I wondered what Arkady thought taking wheat grass would accomplish. At least we knew the appointment hadn't been changed.

"Anyway, I need you two to run some errands so that Mr. Romanov will have what he needs when he gets back."

Shar looked at me, and I could almost read her thoughts. *We'll go wherever you want. After we go to the clinic. Your boss has a date with destiny.*

"You have go to Chinatown, to these pharmacies," Jeremy continued, handing me a paper with five or six addresses on it. "At each one, give them this list." He took another paper from his clipboard and handed it to me. It was covered in Chinese characters. I looked up at him and curled my lip—I had no idea what they meant.

He must have figured out what I was thinking. "Don't worry," he said quickly. "They'll know what to give you. Just go, and get back here fast." He turned to go, but suddenly swore, threw his head back, and closed his eyes. "We have models coming in today! I forgot to order food— Reynaldo is going to freak!"

"We'll do it," I whispered. Shar's boot hit my ankle. It hurt, but I forgot it as Jeremy's smile lingered on me.

He looked relieved. "You guys are the best! I'm taking you both out to dinner this weekend."

I watched him hurry back down the hall, enjoying the view. When he was out of earshot, Shar turned on me.

"Are you crazy? We can't do a tour of Chinatown *and* go to the deli to get lunch, *then* come back here *and then* go to that clinic. And as for dinner, I don't want to be seen until I look normal again, even if it's at the most exclusive place in the city."

I grabbed my coat and bag. "Who says we're going to Chinatown?"

"You just did!"

"A certain *someone* won't be here to need wheatgrass tea, or whatever these things are." I waved the list at her. "We'll save Jeremy a headache. You go to the deli so I don't have to talk to anyone. Order whatever Reynaldo wants, and lots of veggies and low-fat foods for the models, and bring it back here, then meet me by the clinic. This doesn't change our original plan. I'll go there now and scope it out." I grimaced. "I hope I can find the portal. We can't lose any more time."

Shar looked thoughtful as she buttoned her coat and wound a scarf around her nose and mouth. Between the two of us, we had enough raw material to make one large and very ugly bird. I shrugged off that depressing thought as we got onto an empty elevator.

"Okey doke." Shar pulled on mittens. "I'll meet you near the back door of the clinic in about an hour—but if I run into any problems, I'm bailing on getting the lunch. It's not like the models will eat it anyway."

"We'll buy Reynaldo some make-up brownies later and tell the models they're too fat for next season's line." I giggled, waved to her, then headed over to the subway.

The biting winter chill that had hung in the air for days had melted away into a nip-laced warmth. Was spring coming early? If so, Hades would be sans wife, and thus have time on his hands for more mischief.

I'd had a growing feeling lately that there was more to

his dark desires than just snagging Arkady. His incessant pursuit of Shar disturbed me. Why would he interfere with the completion of his own deal? In our current situation, he'd win either way: either he got Arkady, or he got us—but was he angling for *both*? Shar had seemed a little quiet today and wasn't saying anything about him. As for Demeter, it was becoming obvious what her motives were—if Hades was distracted with Shar, he might forget about Persephone, for a little while anyway. Demeter would probably get to keep her daughter for a bit longer. If that happened, maybe she thought she could adjust the bargain permanently and we'd start having longer summers; global warming, à la goddess.

I looked at the subway map, trying to figure out which line to take. The Brightwater Clinic was at 8th and 65th. I thought I could take the R train over there, but I wasn't sure.

"Excuse me," said a voice next to me. "Do you know what train we can take to Ground Zero?"

"Sure," I said, never taking my eyes off the map. "Take the N line over to Chambers Street, then cross over and walk down about two blocks."

Twang!

I felt something prick my ankle and immediately looked at who was standing next to me.

Two tourists, a man and a woman. The woman, who had asked for the directions, turned to go. The man stayed rooted to the spot, smiling dumbly at me.

"Harold, let's go now," she said.

Why? WHY?! I didn't speak to him!

"You told *both* of them where to go," offered another voice. A tall, slender blond woman stepped out from behind Harold and smiled through black Wayfarers. Persephone. "You'd better release him," she suggested.

"*Ase me isihi.*" Harold coughed, looked around, and then followed his wife, who was looking at me like I had a disease.

"You have to be careful about who's within hearing distance," Persephone said simply.

"What's another feather," I grumbled. I looked Persephone up and down. She looked like she was on a mission to win the "most animals killed to make an outfit" prize: leather jacket, leather pants, leather boots, leather bag, and was that a leather tank top underneath it all? As the goddess of fields, flowers, and animals, Demeter must not be pleased.

"Thanks for the tip," I added, walking over to the subway's automatic ticket machine. "Hey, aren't you supposed to be stuck down in Tartarus? With him? It's not spring yet, and you've been up here two times!"

"I don't care what anyone says, you're sharp." Persephone smiled coolly, pointing a long finger at me and giving a haughty toss of her hair. "But I'm a goddess, not a prisoner."

"But the myth says…"

She pursed her lips. "Why do you think it's called a *myth*?"

I bit back a retort.

Persephone shifted her purse to her other arm, nearest me. "Why does everyone think they know my story? No one ever asks me."

"But your mom's trying to get you back, right? And Hades stole you away."

Persephone blushed. "Hades *is* devious, but he couldn't trick me into being with him if I didn't want to be."

When she said his name, her lips curled into a lascivious smile. I looked away. What was that phrase Shar always used? *TMI!*

"Don't you ever get tired of going back and forth between your mother and Hades?" I asked.

She laughed merrily. "It's like a vacation. When I get sick of Mother, I go to Hades, and when he angers me, I go back to her. Staying here in the summer suits me fine. If they both want to believe the other one keeps me a prisoner, why should I enlighten them? But let me make this simple for you." She flicked an unpleasant glance at my baggy black cargo pants and matching turtleneck, which Shar had picked out. "I knew what I was getting into when I swallowed those pomegranate seeds. I wanted to sleep with Hades, but it's always easier to let men and mothers think they're controlling the situation." She smiled slyly.

TMI! TMI!

"You *wanted* to be with him," I repeated doubtfully. *And he's cheating on you! Or trying to!*

"Absolutely!" she murmured throatily. "You're too human to see his appeal. Yes, he's unpredictable, unruly at times, and not to be trusted, but then, none of the gods are. Who do you think gave the Trojans the idea of the hollow horse? It's what makes him so enticing. He's *dangerous*." She chewed her bottom lip, examining me shrewdly with her stormy eyes. "I know about his little escapades. He's frustrated."

She leaned in confidentially. "Unfortunately, Zeus made us agree that we can't see each other on the mortal plane, even when I take short trips up here in the winter. Whenever I sense Hades here, I have to avoid him. Few dare to disobey Daddy Zeus." She admired a Wall Street type walking by, talking on his Bluetooth. "Nice, but not as hot as my bad boy." She turned back to me. "So, as far as Hades is concerned, I allow a fling here and there."

I tried to control the churning in my stomach. If Persephone allowed Hades an occasional dalliance, why should the piteous mortal Shar—not that she was doing anything to get Hades' attention—bother her so much? Unless Hades had something else in mind for Shar. My brain raced through some potential scenarios, none of them good.

Persephone stopped talking for a moment to pull her dog, a tiny black Shih Tzu, out of her bag. She kissed it on its nose.

"Anyway, I know how hard it is when you only have your pets to keep you company. Sure, they're cute, but they can't compare. My poor Hades has only Cerberus. Isn't that right, Minty?"

"But your mother—" I started, intending to spill the

details about how Demeter had been trying to push Shar on Hades, but Persephone finished my sentence for me.

"Mother wants whatever makes me happy—as long as I stay with her." It seemed this wasn't the first time this subject had come up. "She doesn't like my husband, she doesn't like my clothes, and she wants to run my life. Does your mother do that to you?"

She didn't wait for a reply. "No one understands me," she said, shaking her head with a theatrical air and lifting up the little dog, its long hair tied up with a crystal studded ribbon, so that it faced in my direction. She spoke to it in a sickly sweet voice and waved one of its tiny paws at me.

"Hades and I have an understanding in one regard—our playmates. How else are we supposed to amuse ourselves while we're apart? Isn't that right, Minty?"

She settled the whining dog in her arms before turning her attention back to me.

"Tell me," she said, her tone still saccharine but now with an underlying sharpness. "Do you think Minty is a good name for her?"

I looked into the little dog's eyes. I had no idea why she named it what she did, and I didn't care, but I did feel sorry for it. Somehow I didn't get the feeling that this was a beloved pet, despite the crystal bow and manicured paws.

"Minty and I go way back, don't we, my pweshis?" Persephone prattled softly into its ear, never taking her eyes off me. "She isn't anything like she used to be. Do you know how I came by this little darling?"

I shook my head.

"I took her from Hades," Persephone said, her eyes darkening. "He saw her first, but back then, she wasn't a doggy."

She continued to stare at me and I squirmed in my lavender boots, not wanting to hear the gory details of Hades' fling with Minty. I already knew the outcome.

"His romps are all in fun. *Most* of them. When he gets too attached to a paramour, however, it becomes a problem—but not one that I can't resolve. I turned Minthe, excuse me, *Minty*, into a plant at first, but that was boring. She's much more fun this way, don't you think?"

She turned the dog around so that its nose touched hers. Its back legs shook violently.

"Stop that," she scolded gently, before putting it back into her voluminous purse. When she looked at me again, her eyes were the color of dark sea water. "Speaking to your Siren partner directly didn't seem to work. She never did come back with the water for Minty, and I'm sure she's seen Hades again."

"Look, Shar doesn't want anything to do with your hus—"

"I don't like having to fix things." Persephone glared at me. Then she peeked into the depths of her bag, where Minty was whimpering piteously. "Shhh!" The whimpering stopped. "I've watched you. You have sense. Make sure you complete your assignment and that certain *partners*, certain *roommates*, behave themselves."

"Hey wait!" I interrupted, her meaning suddenly clear.

I didn't want the responsibility of chaperoning Hades. "How am I supposed to—"

She raised a hand to silence me. Imperious, like her mother.

"Hades would never chase someone like Sharisse unless she gave him a reason."

"I don't know what he's been telling you, but Shar wants nothing to do with him—I swear!"

The face she made told me that she didn't believe me.

"Okay, well, you know about our assignment, right?"

"Of course," she said impatiently, tapping her fingers on her thigh.

"Then you know that if we don't succeed, we'll be going to Tartarus for a long time. Me *and Shar*."

She eyed me suspiciously. "And…"

"Well, if you want to believe that Hades is being manipulated by Shar, I guess I can't convince you otherwise. But…what do you think will happen if Shar is down there *all the time*?"

It was a dangerous card to play, but I was out of ideas. If I could motivate Persephone to help us—even out of self-interest—it would be one deity in our pocket. One more than we had before. Persephone's green eyes shifted back and forth; she was considering it.

"I don't need your roomie involving herself any further with my husband," she said finally, in a haughty tone. "Lucky for her, I can't touch her. *Yet.* Or she'd be gone already."

So Shar really had Hades' protection—for now. Apparently he was good for something besides money, bad contracts, and trouble. I moved closer to Persephone. "If Hades and Shar are kept away from each other, nothing will happen. The best way to make sure that's the case is for us to—"

"I'm not stupid, Margaret." Persephone gazed at me darkly. Whether she wanted to admit it or not, she had to know I was telling the truth.

"I never thought so," I said. "But—we're close to finishing our task. Shar and I are supposed to meet at a clinic later, where Arkady is going for an appointment. There's a portal by the back door."

Instantly, Persephone and I were standing in an alley. A red and white light-up sign that read *Brightwater Clinic* hung solidly over the door. A few papers blew around a dumpster that stood against the opposite wall. We were definitely in the right place—the thrumming under my feet told me that the portal was near.

"Outstanding," I said.

"Anything else?" Persephone asked as she stepped gingerly to a cleaner space on the cracked asphalt.

"We need a wheelchair," I said, looking around. "And I need to find out where the portal is. I can feel it, but I can't see it."

A few more careless waves, and there was the wheelchair. The black mouth of the portal now gaped wide, next to the side door that Arkady planned to enter.

"Here," Persephone said. Two sets of mint-green scrubs, folded and crisp with ID tags, and some clunky white nurse's clogs appeared in my outstretched arms. I suspected the twelve-and-a-half wides were for Shar. "To look official," she explained. "Humans are paranoid creatures. If they see you lurking in an alley they might suspect something foul. Don't screw up, Margaret."

She tossed her hair back and I was blasted by a cold wind. Persephone was gone, and Shar stood next to me in her place.

"Wait, come back!" I cried.

"What the—"

"Don't ask," I said, handing Shar a uniform. I wanted Persephone to stick around to make sure we didn't get any uninvited guests at Arkady's going-away party, but I figured that she probably didn't want to be anywhere near Shar.

"Just tell me that Reynaldo got his salad," I said wearily. "I can only deal with one hysterical person at a time."

Shar

What Fools These Mortals Be

o you really think Hades would let her morph me into a lower life form?" I demanded, jerking my head like someone with Tourette's syndrome. Meg had told me about her run-in with Persephone as we crouched behind the dumpster in the alley, hastily changing into the uniforms without being seen and trying not to get frostbite on our privates.

It was hard keeping my balance; it felt as though the ground was shaking. "Do you feel that?" I asked.

"The vibrations? That happens when you get close to a portal," Meg said. "I felt it at Coney Island, right under the Wonder Wheel. We didn't get close enough to the one at the Met."

"Spooky." I sneezed three times.

Being so close to Meg made my allergies worse. With the increasing amount of feathers, twitching, sneezing, molting, and sprouting, we were doing the chicken dance standing still.

"She turned that nymph into a plant, then into a dog!" Meg said, pulling the green scrubs over her feathery butt. "What do you think your fate will be—a stint as a potted palm and then maybe a few years as a Shar-Pei? She'd get vicious pleasure out of that!"

"I keep saying no, but Hades doesn't give up. No matter what I say or how nasty I am, he laps it up. He's a freak-o, let me tell you."

"And Persephone kept insisting that Hades would never be chasing you if you weren't encouraging him."

"Do you think I *want* his attention?"

Meg hesitated just a little too long.

"Oh come on, Meg! I swear I don't!" I told her about the visit to his place and my refusal. She looked troubled. I pulled on my drawstring pants and tied them. "Okay, I was flattered at first—who wouldn't be, with a god coming on to them? Even you have to admit he's hot. But I never did *anything*. I don't *want* to do anything with him. That last trip completely terrified me; I was in *Tartarus*! Suppose he'd kept me there? Being gorgeous won't do me any good if I'm a slave to slobbering demon dogs, the target of a vengeful goddess, and my friend thinks I'm a backstabber."

We got the shirts on next. Our nurse scrubs were way too small—yeah, Persephone was having fun. At least I'd only have a wedgie from the too-tight pants for as long as it took to dispatch Arkady the Relic. I pulled my hair into a bun, wiped off my lipstick, and put my sunglasses back on; no need to attract any more attention. Without a wig, that was the best disguise I could manage.

"Let's wait here until the car comes," Meg said, not responding to my defense.

"Sure. Uh, Meg?"

She turned her leg to the side, grunting with disgust at something she'd stepped in. The alley wasn't too bad, as far as run-down, filthy holes went, but there was a stench of rotting garbage coming from the dumpster and the slight stink of urine. The place must be horrendous on a sweltering day in July.

"Yeah?"

How to broach the subject of who would put the vamp on Jeremy? I took a deep breath.

"You want to do Jeremy, or should I?"

Meg's head snapped around so fast I was surprised she didn't break a vertebra.

"*Excuse me?*" Her eyes flashed dangerously.

I steeled myself to finish this conversation. "One of us has to siren Jeremy. You agreed to it. He's going to be here. Even if Arkady's not his favorite person, I don't think he's going to stand by and let us wheel his boss into the next dimension."

She ran her fingers through her cropped hair, exhaling heavily. "I know. It's just…"

"It's too personal for me to do it, yet you don't want to do it to him—it feels wrong."

She nodded morosely. "It didn't seem like that big of a deal before, but now that it's time…"

I squeezed her hand. "I'll do it for you, but only if you want me to. But you have to choose. And how bad can it be? It should just be for a few moments, max, then you can release him."

She hesitated before answering, not looking at me, just studying the grimy stone wall behind me.

"Meg?"

"I'm afraid that if I do it to him, he won't remember me at all after I release him," she blurted. "Like those other guys we entranced."

Meg looked truly worried. I thought about it for a few moments before I replied.

"But we didn't know those other guys; they were strangers. You *know* Jeremy already—you knew him before any of this started. You talked in the pizzeria, remember?"

"I know, but…" Meg stared at me, almost pleading.

"You'll get another chance to make a first impression!" I smiled brightly, wondering if my suggestion sounded valid. I thought it did. Hopefully Meg did, too. Now that she and Jeremy seemed to be a duo, my bewitching him would be kind of perverted. Didn't I have enough problems without getting caught in a love triangle? Oh, wait—in there, doing that.

"Maybe," Meg murmured, a troubled smile lingering on her pixie face.

Whether she thought it would work or not, the time had come to test my theory. A sleek black Lincoln Continental pulled up, Jeremy at the wheel. He slowed the car to a stop. Leaving the engine idling, he hopped out.

I removed my sunglasses. Meg stood still.

"Go on," I whispered. "Now, Meg. We'll only be able to do this if Jeremy's entranced." She nodded shakily, then, with faltering steps, moved forward. Jeremy recognized her, and at first he looked happy—then surprised—then confused. I couldn't see Meg's face.

"What're you doing here?" he asked, looking at the uniform.

She was panicking.

Say something! I willed silently. *Come on, Meg!* Before he could ask another question, I heard her stutter in her velvet Siren voice, "You will let us take Mr. Romanov."

I saw his handsome eyes glaze over and I felt a surge of guilt. I couldn't imagine what Meg was feeling, but we had to do this. Somehow, I'd figure a way to make it up to her.

"Yes, whatever you want."

I waited. *She'll get Jeremy to get Arkady out of the car,* I thought. But no one moved. Meg stood there, lost.

Jeez, Meg, this is a great time not to know what to say! I leaned closer to her. She was staring at Jeremy, her eyes filling.

"What's the problem?" I whispered. For a moment she didn't answer.

"What do I do with him?" She held back a sob. "Do I send him away? Where should he go? And then what?"

Damn. Sticky point. Then inspiration hit.

I whispered, "Give him the lists and let him do the shopping. It'll get him out of here for now."

Meg turned to me, forcing herself to smile. "Good idea." She took the slips of paper from me and handed them to Jeremy.

"Take these—" she started.

"What's taking so long out there?" screeched Arkady from inside the car.

"—and buy all the things listed. You wrote these; you know where to go. Then return to the office—"

"Jeremy!" Arkady's voice screeched, like Freddy Krueger nails on a chalkboard. I couldn't help cringing. I popped my head into the limo.

"Just a moment, sir, we're getting the wheelchair," I shouted. Without his glasses on, he couldn't see me. If he'd had them on, I would've tried ordering him into the portal, but no such luck. And my presence didn't pacify him. He kept yelling and pounding his cane on the car floor.

Meg still held Jeremy under her thrall. "Put everything in Mr. Romanov's office, then come back to get him. If anyone asks, Mr. Romanov told you to do this." She turned to me. "When Arkady disappears, they're going to call someone. All Jeremy's time will be accounted for now."

"Oh." I hadn't thought of that. There would be a lot of questions when a world-renowned fashion icon like Arkady Romanov disappeared. Even recluses were missed eventually.

"First, please get Mr. Romanov out of the car," Meg said.

I kept my eyes ready to enthrall anyone who might think of stopping us. So far, so good. Jeremy pulled the wheelchair closer to the door, then assisted Arkady into it. I turned slightly away and leaned toward Meg's ear.

"He doesn't have his glasses on, so he won't know us." She nodded.

"Let's go, you imbeciles! What are you waiting for, Lenin's resurrection?"

What a nasty piece of work. Why would Hades *want* this poor specimen of humanity? If I were Hades, this would be one deal I'd walk away from; keep at least one world between him and Arkady.

When Arkady was finally settled in the chair and wrapped in his lap robe, Meg lightly touched Jeremy's arm.

"Remember, go to Chinatown. You dropped Mr. Romanov at the clinic. You went to get his medicines and then you came back here to pick him up after his appointment. Okay?"

"Whatever you wish," Jeremy droned, enraptured. Meg tried to look away from him, but couldn't. The besotted look on his face was clearly painful for her to see.

"Let him go, Meg. The sooner he leaves, the sooner we get this over with."

Meg withdrew her hand from his arm. "Go," she said, her voice cracking.

Jeremy got back in the car and drove away.

"Let's do this," I said, as soon as he was out of sight.

Meg choked and wiped her eyes, then paused to scratch and tuck in a wad of feathers.

"What's taking so damn long!" Arkady began pounding on the arms of the chair. "Are you all incompetent? You're all fired! Where's Jeremy?"

"Filling out paperwork, sir," Meg shouted, running to an area next to the clinic door. "It's here, come on!" She touched the grimy wall and it darkened, like black watercolor spreading over a damp piece of paper.

"Jeremy!" thundered Arkady. "Take me to Jeremy!"

"Shut up!" I hissed, even knowing he couldn't hear me very well. "You're a vile, cheap, pickled"—I searched for the right word—"tapeworm!"

Meg, with her hands above her head leaning against the wall, snickered, then craned her head to gape at me.

"Tapeworm?"

"It's all I could think of. Give me some time, I'll come up with a hundred better ones."

I pushed the dinosaur toward the opening.

"You're out of time," said a cheerful voice.

Demeter.

Dressed in pastel scrubs identical to ours, she stood in the clinic door, holding it wide. I really wanted to hurt her. Ditto for her daughter.

"It's time for his herbal enema and face graft. I'll take him."

"I don't think so," said Meg, blocking her from Arkady and me. "We're pushing him through. This is the end." She crossed her arms, challenging the goddess to get physical.

Brave girl, Meg. Stupid, but brave...

Demeter's laughter was musical, like raindrops on silver bells. A tall Hispanic orderly came out of the clinic doors. He rushed over to us.

"*Señorita, por favor*, I help you." He reached for the wheelchair with his gigantic paws and tried to grab the handles.

I whipped off my glasses, smiled, and said, "No thank you, we can handle it. Why don't you see if you can help someone inside?"

He sighed dreamily. "*Sí, señorita bonita.*"

"And forget about us."

"*Sí.*" He turned and hurried inside the clinic.

"How amusing." Demeter snapped her fingers and two burly security guards appeared. "Ahmed, TaKwan, take Mr. Romanov inside." They flexed their muscles à la WWF wrestling. Meg and I took one look at them, then at each other, and laughed together. I stared at the one on the right while Meg spoke to the one on the left.

"Don't listen to her, and go away!"

The men dropped their arms, spun on their heels, and left.

I permitted myself a smug look and smoothed my hair. But the laughter died on my lips when I saw Demeter smirk.

"You two really are stupid."

She snapped her fingers again, and two even more burly *female* nurses stomped up.

It was Demeter's turn to enjoy the moment.

"We're finished," said Meg, a feather sprouting from her head.

"Big time!" I sighed. "Caw!"

"Bertha, Inga, please bring Mr. Romanov into the clinic. *I'll* deal with these two. It won't take long." The nurses clomped forward. Meg and I tried desperately to hold on to the chair's handle grips, but Bertha and Inga sneered and tossed us aside. We landed in a heap, and watched helplessly as Arkady, screaming and cursing, was pushed into the clinic.

With a snide glance over her shoulder, Demeter quipped, "You lose." She slammed the door in our faces.

Goddess trumps Siren.

So close!

Meg

Be the Bird

Without speaking a word, Shar and I stumbled out of the alley and waved down a cab. I was too tired to try to be environmentally friendly, and I wasn't feeling too compassionate toward Mother Nature—otherwise known as Demeter. In fact, I think I hated her.

Shar huddled into the back seat and swathed her scarf around her mouth and nose. She kept lifting her sunglasses to wipe her eyes, but then the twitching made it hard for her to get them back on. She poked herself in the eye at least once. I was clothed from head to foot, but it didn't seem to prevent my Siren dander from seeping through her scarf. We were both wretched.

Then an awful realization dawned. I felt my voice catch in my throat and I started sobbing.

"Oh no," I cried.

"What now?"

"I used the gift on Jeremy for nothing, and I didn't release him! How long does the enchantment last when you use it on purpose?" I searched frantically in my bag for the iPhone, but after a few moments, I gave up. I wanted to crawl into bed and never come out again.

Shar peered at me piteously from her burka-esque head wrap, not daring to loosen it even a little for fear of feathers. We rode the rest of the way in silence.

"God, I need sugar," she said when we got home. "Please tell me there's chocolate somewhere in this place."

I strutted into the kitchen and opened a few random cabinets. If there was one thing we could count on, it was the constant presence of distracting, sinful food. I took some gourmet hot cocoa down from a shelf and a chocolate torte from the refrigerator while she filled a kettle. Trying to ignore the clocklike tick-tick-tick of the gas stove as it tried to ignite, I fished dessert plates and forks from a drawer. Shar cut pieces of cake, definitely not the suggested serving size, then slapped a huge dollop of whipped cream on each slice.

The kettle whistled shrilly. I turned off the gas and poured the scalding water into two large mugs.

"I want an extra marshmallow!" Shar called as she carried the plates into the pristine living room. At this juncture, I didn't think a whole bag would help either of us.

I placed the two steaming mugs on a large tray and followed her. Shar took a cup, blowing on the hot cocoa, then twitched violently as if she was pecking at the floating marshmallow. She ended up with some on the tip of her nose, but wiped it off with her talon, foregoing the napkin. We drank quietly for a while, listening to the noises of the city below.

Eventually I let go a string of curses. "We were so SO close!" I wailed.

"Tell me about it," Shar said, digging into her cake. She seemed to have worked out the timing of the twitches so she could manage small bites and sips, but every once in a while she'd wear her food. She seemed beyond caring, an indication of how depressed she was.

"Have you noticed that this has happened *two* times?" I said crossly. "First, we couldn't get Arkady across a *hallway* because Hades *conveniently* forgot to tell us that we can't use our gifts on him because he can't see or hear us. And then *Demeter* shows up *just* as we're ready to send Arkady on his merry way. Do you know what this means?" I demanded.

"That we're doomed? Set up to fail?" Shar spit crumbs out, then cradled her head in her hands. "You know, I was trying to forget that doomed possibility. But you're right. They seem to know what we're doing. All the time. I always feel like Hades is watching us." She slapped the couch. "Such a beast!"

"Should we even bother to try again?" I asked.

"You know what they say, ladies—the third time's the charm."

Hades posed in the living room, decked out in black jeans and a shimmering black shirt, its collar open at the throat. He helped himself to my untouched hot chocolate. Was nothing sacred?

"Since you're just sitting around, why don't we watch a movie? How about *From Here to Eternity*? Mmm, this is quite decadent," he mused, taking another sip. The mug he was holding changed—it was still huge, but now it had his picture on it with the words "Kiss Me!" *Please,* I prayed, *don't let it be one of those trick mugs where the clothes disappear and we see what we shouldn't!* Thankfully, nothing changed. Hades poofed some whipped cream onto the top and took another sip.

I shot a tight-mouthed glance at Shar, and she angled her body away so as not to look in his direction.

Hades eased himself into a leather club chair next to her. "Another failure today, ladies. Really, I'm surprised—"

Shar jumped up and stuck a finger in his face. "You're *surprised*? Oh please, Hades. Everything would have been fine if your mother-in-law hadn't showed up and whisked Arkady away. But I suppose you had nothing to do with that!"

"I have as little interaction with *her* as possible," Hades said with distaste. "But even so, this is your deal. There were bound to be some problems. I never promised it would be easy."

"The words 'simple, no?' come to mind," retorted Shar.

He laughed. "The whole concept is simple—I never said a word about the execution of the concept. And why should I make it easier for you two? What have *you* done for me lately?"

Shar turned scarlet and looked away.

"First," I said, jumping to her defense, "we don't expect, and don't want, any help from you. But you left out some crucial details. It would have been nice to know that Demeter can ruin things at will. Doesn't she have any restrictions?"

"We all have rules to abide by, and if she breaks them, I can assure you that Zeus will have something to say about it. But I'm afraid I have no control over Demeter's doings—"

"Don't think we can't see where this is going," I interrupted. "Let's see—if we get Arkady, you collect on your contract, but if we don't, you get us. We knew that from the beginning. But this task is proving to be impossible because of 'divine intervention.' It seems you've got quite the operation going on."

"Demeter is hell-bent on us failing," Shar interjected. "She wants me in Tartarus because she thinks I'll be a distraction for you and then you'll forget about Persephone, but no way. Not happening!"

"Margaret, I'm a man of good business," Hades said to me with a wink, before turning to Shar. "Sharisse, you have no idea how I suffer. I'm not one to sit on a dark throne, brooding. I want excitement, a challenge. For six months, I'm devoid of feminine charms, so I'm—"

"Lonely, I know," Shar rolled her eyes. "Heard it before."

He rose slowly, like a sleek panther ready to strike.

"Don't mistake my attraction for permission to indulge in disrespect," he said through pursed lips. "You try my patience, Sharisse. It's about time you learned you shouldn't interrupt a deity. Especially one who's done so much for you. I saved you from incarceration and gave you all the material things you could wish for."

Shar inhaled deeply to argue, but suddenly sneezed several times.

Hades chuckled. "Perhaps you should invest in one of those flu masks. And you, Margaret—pick up some pet dander shampoo at the vet's."

A mirror hovered before her and Shar shrieked. Then she turned to me. Her lips had puckered, pointed and paled, and had fused to her now pointier nose; a beak! I looked at my hands; they matched Shar's, and my shoes felt tight.

"Oh my God, oh, caw!" I clasped my wing over my mouth.

"You two have been very busy with your gifts," Hades said smoothly. "I guess you're realizing now that sometimes the changes take a while to manifest." He rose and carelessly tossed his cup into the air. It vanished. "Now I'll give you another piece of advice; I'm simply too kind to you. I warned you before to only use your gifts on Mr. Romanov.

The more you use them, the more you hasten the trans-formation"—he looked pointedly at our trembling bod-ies—"and bring other attention. The Divine knows when its power is being used. You don't have much time. If you keep using your powers indiscriminately, you two can expect to be completely avian within a day or two. How-ever, maybe this little eye-opener will increase your moti-vation. I'm sure you'll be able to get Mr. Romanov near a portal again."

"How?" I squawked.

"Y-yes!" Shar chirped. "The gifts don't work on him. He won't wear his glasses, so he can't s-see me, and he can't hear, s-so M-meg... damn it!" Her head twitched. She took a deep breath and then spoke slowly. "She even tried shouting, and that didn't work."

"Siren powers are gifts of subtlety!" Hades shook his head and tsk-tsked. "You can't shout and get into people's faces. Oh no, my dears, your gifts will work, but you'll have to get close to him."

"We were right next to him." Exasperation laced my voice.

Hades twisted his large ruby ring, aligned the stone, then admired his reflection in its glossy surface. "Not close enough."

"Oh, skeeve!" Shar snapped, the image dawning. Hades meant *real* close. Bodily contact close, butterfly-kiss and whisper-in-the-ear close. The cake in my stom-ach threatened to throw itself onto his shoes. My face must have looked green because Hades stepped back warily;

maybe he remembered my reaction to Jeremy's unlucky fate in the subway.

"That's the only way it'll work. And once you have him under your spell, Demeter can't do anything. She can't reverse a Siren's power. Rules are rules." Hades winked and sat down. The chair spun once, and he was gone.

"R-remind me n-never to sit there," Shar stuttered.

"Steady there," I said. "When you talk fast, you start to caw."

"So now what?" Shar fumed, trying to speak slowly.

"You heard him—we have to get close."

"I don't want to."

"We have no choice. At least we can get to him in the office." I shivered, trying not to think about just how close I'd have to get to Arkady.

Shar cringed and pushed the half-eaten piece of cake aside. "We're not going to be alone."

"If we have to, we'll entrance Reynaldo just to get rid of him, and Jeremy still might be under the thrall," I said. "Once we have Arkady entranced, *he* can give the orders for everyone to get out of our way—they won't question him."

Shar shook her head. "We can't do this without some kind of a plan."

"Well, when Jeremy goes in, I'll stop him and entrance him again if I have to. He'll let us in, and then we both get close enough to do our thing." The thought made me feel like gagging, not just because of the condition and contents of the ear I'd be whispering into, but because I didn't want to use the power—again—on Jeremy. The effects of the first use were still unknown to me. "I'll tell Arkady to put on his glasses, so he'll see you. Then we can both work on him; he'll be assaulted from all possible sides."

Shar absently rubbed her beak. "I don't know. Then we have to get him out of there. There's going to be a lot of people in the way. Are you sure there's no other way?"

"Do you have any better ideas?"

She twitched her head, and I took that as a no. It was going to be a bad day.

For the first time since this affair started, I slept deeply, and when the alarm rang, I was reluctant to get up. Lazily, I stretched, and noticed that my blankets were gone. My bed was lined with molted feathers. *My feathers.* I leapt out of the bed and backed away. Feathers, talons, bird seed, and now nesting instincts! What was left? I didn't want to look at Shar; our transformation was dangerously close to completion. Arkady had to go, and something told me that if it wasn't soon, I'd be digging for worms and shiny objects.

At 7:30, we were out the door and headed toward the office.

"Third time's the charm, third time's the charm," Shar chanted as we walked along. I could hear her practicing slow speech, even through the scarf she wrapped around her beak. We stopped at a Duane Reade and picked up a package of surgical masks and more allergy pills.

"It's my turn to be sick," she said. "Not that it will earn

me any sympathy, but it might make Reynaldo keep his distance."

"And it's not like Arkady can catch something," I reminded her.

Deftly, she slipped the surgical mask on under the tangerine pashmina that she'd wound around her face. The weather was drizzly and raw, so she wouldn't look too out of place; neither would I when I kept my hat on all day. Ruefully, I had to admit that the feathers were very warm; if only they didn't keep poking out.

How good would it feel to let the wind ruffle them?
Stop thinking like that!

"Think they'd mind if we showed up to work in burkas?" I mused. Everything I wore was tight. My wings made it impossible for me to wear my coat, so I donned baggy sweats and plopped on a short cape.

"We will finish this today," Shar said in a determined voice. "I'm not walking around with a beak. And I think it's turning orange!"

We reached the House of Romanov, and went in and up with no problems from the security desk. Everyone was similarly bundled up. I was ready. I didn't care who was there—I was ready to march right down to Arkady's sanctum and deal with him. No one was going to stop me.

But when we got upstairs, it was deathly silent. There was no one *there* to stop us.

"Where is everyone?" I asked.

"Well, the runway show's done. Maybe this is their down time," Shar rationalized.

"But I know they had to go over the runway show, the reviews, and the orders," I pointed out.

"Then where are they?"

Slowly, we made our way through the elegantly papered hallways. Only the scuffing of our feet on the plush carpeting could be heard. Everything was open. Lights were on, computers were running, there was even a steaming coffee cup and a brownie with a hasty bite taken out of it on Reynaldo's desk.

"They're here. Or they were." Shar took off her coat, but kept her scarf tied firmly around her lower face. "But where are they now?"

"Let's check the king cobra's nest." I pointed in the direction of Arkady's office.

The doors at the end of the hallway were shut as usual, and a sliver of bright light cut across the purple carpet. As we got closer, we heard muted voices.

"The meeting today isn't supposed to start until nine thirty," said Shar, slipping out the folded schedule we'd printed out previously. I peeked at the paper; nothing was supposed to be going on during this early time slot. Shar looked at me as if she expected an explanation, but all I could do was shrug.

At that moment, Reynaldo burst through the door, slamming it behind him. He bustled down to his office, his hips swinging. He didn't seem to notice us skulking off to his right.

I cocked my head at Shar and we followed him at a discreet distance.

"Find out what's going on," I whispered.

Shar knocked on Reynaldo's door. He was in the midst of shoving the rest of the brownie into his mouth and nearly choked when he saw us standing there.

"Oh!" He plopped what was left of the brownie back on his plate. "What are you doing here?"

"We work here," Shar said through her scarf. "Did we miss the meeting?"

"Oh no no!" Reynaldo laughed—no, giggled. Whatever was going on in Arkady's office had put him in a good mood. I wondered what type of treatment could make him that jocular? I could use some.

Reynaldo shoved some papers into a briefcase then drained his coffee. He put on his coat and grabbed his Euro-bag.

"Where are you going?" Shar demanded. "What about this morning's meeting?"

"Oh, it's been canceled. I have to run, chicas!" Reynaldo waved at us and floated away.

Arkady's door opened and shut again, and then it sounded like Jeremy was on the phone.

"Stay here and see if you can find anything in Reynaldo's office about what's going on," I said excitedly. "I'm going to talk to Jeremy. With Reynaldo gone, that's one less person we have to deal with. This might be easier than we thought."

I scurried down the hall, but slowed down as I got near the door to Jeremy's office. I stopped in front of it and sidled my head around the door frame with trepidation.

Jeremy was sitting in front of his computer, his eyes moving back and forth quickly as if he was scanning the screen in front of him. *He looks normal.* I let out a breath and he looked up. My stomach did flip flops.

Was he still entranced?

A smile spread across his face when he saw me and his eyes softened, but they weren't glazed over.

"One sec," he said, tapping a few things into his computer that I couldn't see. "Oh this so great, Meggo, I think we're going to actually spend some more time together. Looks like things are going to slow down here—at least for a little bit."

He remembered me! And he seemed like himself. But I wondered what he meant by slowing down. I didn't like how that sounded.

I chanced one word. "Why?"

He jumped up and hugged me.

"You'll never guess what just happened!"

I pulled away slightly, cocked my head at him, and creased my brows.

"Oh, how could you know? Mr. Romanov called an early meeting to let us know that he'll be doing some traveling. But"—and here his whole face lit up—"I don't have to go with him. You have no idea how awesome that is!"

Oh, I think I do. You do NOT want to go where he's going. But what did he mean, Arkady traveling? And when?

I grabbed a paper and pen and wrote *where, when,* and *why?*

He leaned in close. "Apparently there's this really wacky

treatment for skin renewal or something like that. They only do it in Europe. Switzerland, I think." He made a disgusted face. "It's totally sick. Involves sheep placentas. Anyway, as soon as he heard about it, Mr. Romanov insisted on going."

Jeremy shut off the computer. "Wait, it gets better. I'm not sure how long he'll be gone, but from what Demi said, it'll probably be a while."

Demeter.

My smile faltered at the mention of her name. I could venture a guess as to where Arkady had heard about this miracle cure for his deep-tissue wrinkles.

"Demi's going with him, and she'll escort him home tonight. All I have to do is get them to the airport—they're flying out *tomorrow*!"

Shar

Seize the Day

*W*e saw no one for the rest of the day. Reynaldo never came back. Jeremy remained in his office, probably buying up pairs of eardrum-exploding concert tickets for him and Meg. And I bet Demeter was gloating. That witch. We left as soon as we were able.

"I'll text you tomorrow!" Jeremy waved excitedly **at** Meg as we left. She managed a weak smile.

"Do you think my phone will get a signal down in Tartarus?" Meg asked. "I'd like to call my mother for her birthday."

What could I say?

At the apartment, we plopped onto the sofa. Out of spite, I put my dirty boots on the spotless cushions. Dark smudges of something that was stuck on my shoe rubbed off on them. With a wicked grin, I let my claws slice holes in the fabric.

Suddenly Meg sprang up and danced in place.

"Is that some bizarre mating ritual? 'Cause I'm not interested." Birds did some pretty weird stuff to show off. "Are you okay?"

"Yes! Yes! Yes!"

I figured the situation had finally gotten to her and she was going the deep six.

"No, no, no! This is not the time to dance and be happy," I reminded her. "Arkady go bye-bye to Europe. We have reservations for a makeover in Tartarus!"

Meg stopped and stared at me like I was the one who was insane.

"Who's the *one* god who's helped us so far?" she asked, her eyes unnaturally bright. "Hades 'forgets' details; Demeter thwarts us every time we turn around."

"No one I can think of." I kicked off my boots. Even bird feet got tired.

"Persephone!"

My mouth, er, beak, dropped open. "You're delusional. She's threatened me numerous times, accused me of husband-stealing, and warned me away. That is *not* helping."

"She got us to the portal at the clinic, remember? I'm sure we would have finished it there if Demeter hadn't gotten wind of it somehow. If Persephone knew that you were about to get a one-way ticket to Tartarus, especially now when she's with Hades, she'd want to cancel Arkady's trip.

That's what convinced her to help the first time; she really doesn't want you in Tartarus."

I snorted. "Yeah, that's what I'm afraid of—her canceling me out. And what if Demeter shows up again?"

"She can't harm you, since you're under Hades' protection. We have to keep trying. Demeter seems focused on getting Arkady away from us, so we can hope that she's too busy to bother with you and me right now. Let's call Persephone."

"Sure. *You* call her."

Meg's jubilant mood deflated. "How?"

I stood in the middle of the room. "Persephone, come here! I demand you show yourself!"

"Not like that!" Meg hissed. "We can't afford to offend her. She's already leery of you because of Hades."

"Big deal. Let her get mad. Like you said, she can't hurt me."

But after several more shouts, I gave up. We needed to find a new way. I turned to Meg.

"There has to be something Persephone likes that we can bribe her with. What would she want? Too bad there's not a Greek god directory on the net," I mocked.

Suddenly Meg bolted and grabbed up her bag. She dug out the iPhone.

"The iPhone? Don't tell me it could be that easy!"

"It's worth a try." Her finger slid through the directory. "Hades said that we should take the time to use it, didn't he? And he said you could use it to call him. Maybe we can get in touch with other gods. Aha! Look at this!" She held it up for me to see. "Apparently they have 411." Her finger slipped over the touchscreen. "Here it is!"

"Give me that!" I snatched the iPhone. There was a contact file: *Acropolis Dog Grooming, Apollo, Athena ...* I scrolled down to Persephone's name and hit dial before I thought about it. After three rings, someone picked up.

"Hello," purred a sultry voice.

Persephone. Who did she think was calling? She wouldn't be expecting me. She was going to be ticked.

"Persephone, it's Sharisse."

Meg had to have heard the screech even without the iPhone being on speaker.

"What?! How did you get this number?!"

"Hades' iPhone. We need to talk. *Now.*"

"You *dare* speak to me that way?"

"I dare. If you want me out of Hades' life, you'll come over. *Now.*"

There were a few moments of silence. "I can't go to the apartment he's given you. I can only meet you on neutral ground. And not in a park, either."

"Fine. Times Square, half an hour."

The connection was severed.

"Put on your Batman cape, Meg, we're going out."

Meg had heard enough of the conversation to know the score. Wordlessly, we dressed and headed out into the darkening sky. Meg looked like a ninja with only her eyes peeking out; with my dark glasses on, I looked even more sinister.

We got to Times Square with only seconds to spare. We stopped under the huge electronic billboard to wait. Almost immediately, Persephone flashed in.

"What do you want with me?" she growled. "This better be worth my time, mortal!" She was sans dog. Lucky thing got a break.

"Let me," advised Meg, pushing me aside gently. She turned to Persephone. "We need your help."

"Why should I help you two again?" she sniffed.

Meg straightened her shoulders. "Your mother stopped us from succeeding yesterday, and now she's done something to guarantee that we'll fail to fulfill our contract. We would've been done and gone by now if it hadn't been for her."

"What? Mother!" she roared. Then she actually shook with rage. "We need a place where she can't eavesdrop."

Snap! The ground was covered with snow and ice; a ski lift glided up the side of a white mountain. We were seated on a deck. Persephone lounged in a cushioned chaise, while Meg and I had hard, plain wooden chairs. A fire crackled merrily in a stone pit. Persephone held a steaming drink, her hands in fur-lined gloves. We had nothing. Okay! Not the hostess type.

Meg quickly explained what had happened in the alley, and then Arkady's latest travel plans. I fought to keep my mouth shut as Persephone shot me dagger glances. She appeared more rational when dealing with Meg. When she was done, Meg took a sideways glance at me.

"And besides all that, you should know that Hades took Shar to—" Meg stopped.

Persephone's eyes narrowed dangerously. "Where? Where did she entice him to?"

"Huh! Like I want your secondhand scraps!" I snorted. We both jumped up, but Meg leapt between us. She pushed me back, and not so gently this time.

"Keep quiet! I'll handle this." She turned back to Persephone. "Please, hear me out. Shar has consistently refused him."

That seemed to suck the breath right out of her.

"I don't believe it," Persephone breathed. She kept giving me dirty looks, and I gave them right back. I was keeping my guard up. Persephone might be the only one able to help us, but I didn't trust her. True, she couldn't hurt me, but that didn't mean she couldn't send me to Cuba, or an African war zone, or a brothel in India. Or worse.

"I don't know what you think I can do for you," Persephone said finally. "I can't interfere in his agreements, and I can't speak to Mother right now because it's winter and I'm on Hades' time. And I told you before—I'm not allowed to interact with Hades while I'm on the mortal plane."

Meg's shoulders sagged. "There must be something you can do to help us," she pleaded. "You did before. We only want to send Arkady to Tartarus and go back to our lives. We—and I speak especially for Shar—*never* want to see Hades again. No offense!" Meg held up her hands as if Persephone would object.

Personally, I would have said something a lot nastier, but nobody was asking me.

Persephone stood silent for a moment. She was weighing her options. *Either she helps us, regardless of how much she hates me and blames me for seducing Hades, and we get free of our obligation or, she refuses, Demeter wins, and Hades gets us both. That would always make her wonder what was going on when she was with her mother.*

She blew the steam off her drink. "Maybe I can get you some information I might possibly overhear when I'm out and about. Beyond that, I'm not sure what else I can do. There are strict rules that all of us are bound by."

Not too all-powerful now is she? It really didn't seem like Persephone was interested in helping us, and she was fixated on blaming me for Hades' attentions. *Was she blind, stupid, or both?*

"Can we call you if we need to know something?" begged Meg.

Persephone pursed her lips, considering the question. "*You* can, *she* can't."

Bite me. Like I want to talk to you. I stuck out my tongue behind her back. Okay, second grade stuff, but I was limited. And tired.

"That would be great." Meg smiled prettily. Such a diplomat, and with few words too.

"Meg." Persephone glared meaningfully. "Don't bother me with little things." She jerked her head in my direction.

That's it!

"If you're done yapping, can you poof us into Arkady's penthouse? Or is that beyond your mighty all-powerful goddessness?" I jeered.

I landed with a hard thump.

But it didn't hurt near as much as it did when Meg landed on top of me.

Meg

Out of the Closet

"Get off!" Shar shoved me off her shoulder.

Slowly, I got up on my hands and knees, then stood. Wherever we were, it was quiet, save for the muffled hum of some electrical appliances that I couldn't see.

"Where are we?" I looked around; it all seemed very familiar. There was a wall of glass looking out over the city, and the shapes of modern furniture, all soft in the dim light of evening. Shar rose and wandered over to a sleek black table that sat under a huge mirror. She picked up a small statue of a woman in a draped, Grecian-style gown. The place reminded me of our apartment, but I knew that wasn't where we were.

By the door was an assemblage of large leather suitcases, all black, standing like soldiers. I went and flipped over a luggage tag and suddenly felt sick.

"Well, what do you know…" I said.

"What?" said Shar, coming over. "I don't know where she plopped us, but—"

"I'll give you three guesses." I pointed to the tag.

Printed in overlarge letters was the name *Arkady Romanov.*

"We're in his *house*?" Shar murmured.

I held my forehead in my claw-like hand, carefully so I wouldn't scratch my own eyes out. "Well, it's where you told her to send us. Everything was going so well until you opened that big beak of yours—"

"Shut up!" Shar cried, patting her beak. "A little empathy—you're usually the one who can't stop talking!"

I shook my head. "What are we going to do here? If we're found in his house, we'll get arrested, or shipped to the zoo! And we can't keep enchanting other people. Demeter might come before we get a chance to siren Arkady. If she whisks him off again before we get to him, I don't see us having any more chances to try. We have to get out of here. *Now.*"

"Are you kidding me? We can't leave!"

I threw up my wings in exasperation. "Why not?"

"We're *in his house*!" Shar eyeballed me with impatience.

"I know. And I want to go."

"Come on, Meg. Persephone just handed this to us. When are we ever going to get a chance like this? We'll cor-

ner him here—with no Reynaldo, no Jeremy, no Dem—"
She stopped herself. It was probably a good idea; better not
to accidentally invoke anything, or anyone.

"It looks like no one's here," I said grudgingly, walking
over to the window. "Hey, we're in the same building as
the office, look!" There were the familiar shops across the
street.

Shar rushed over and peered out. "You mapped out
the portals. Where's the nearest one?"

I dug the iPhone out of my purse and navigated to
the portal map app. It only took a second or two for the
grid to pop up. There was one portal close to the House of
Romanov, a mere four blocks away.

I looked at Shar, appalled. "We're going to the
morgue."

"Maybe it's in the lobby," she offered hopefully.

"I doubt it."

"Whatever happened to positive thinking?" Then, tapping a talon on her chin, she resumed her inspection of
the apartment. "No wonder he stays at the office so late;
he only has to come up here at the end of the night. Think
he'll be coming back soon?"

"I don't know. What time is it?"

Shar looked at her watch. "About 11:30. Let's have a
look around."

Nearby, on a small credenza, lay a long, thick, leather-
like envelope. Shar grabbed it, turned it over, and dumped
it out. The soft swishes and plops the contents made as
they landed sounded like thunder in the quiet apartment.

Shar sifted through the pile: tickets, passports, and other travel documents. She pulled one out and held it close to her face so she could read it. "Get a load of this. His passport says he's seventy-five." She laughed. "Guess they forgot the three in front."

"What time is his flight?"

"Noon." She stuffed everything back into the envelope and dropped it back on the table. "Be on your guard. If someone comes in, we'll have to hide, so we should stay together."

"Good idea. All I have left is some of my hair and my face. I can't afford a single feather more."

Silently, we moved into the kitchen. It was eerily identical to ours, from the marble floors to the giant cabinets and stainless steel refrigerator. Shar opened a cabinet, pulled out a box, and snorted violently.

"What's the matter with you?" I took it from her. It was a powdered mixture that claimed to be able to fix "creaky bowels." I dug a claw into my thigh to keep from laughing, but when I went to put the box back, I found every shelf crammed tightly with similar remedies—for hair loss, nail fungus, sagging skin, and other geriatric ailments. And they all smelled funky. The refrigerator was packed with drugs that I couldn't pronounce if I tried. I wondered how often Jeremy had to come up here, and if his duties included assisting Arkady dosing himself with any of this stuff. I stopped myself from picking up any of the boxes to read the instructions for application, ingestion, insertion, or whatever.

In a closet, in the hallway, we found a box labeled *Crème de la Mer*.

"Do you know how much this stuff costs?" Shar gasped. "Oh my God, the little bottles are like $150 and he has a crate!"

"What's so great about this?" I asked, unscrewing the lid from one of the jars and taking a sniff. "It smells fruity."

"It's made from lime and natural elements from the ocean," Shar said with authority. "And it's supposed to be a miracle cream."

"I don't think this would help him if he sat in a tub of it for a month straight." I said. "He should've been more careful about what he asked for."

"Like us, you mean?" She quirked an eyebrow at me.

"Hindsight," I rumbled, spinning her toward the hallway. "Moving on."

The hallway looked just like ours, tan carpet and neutral walls, except there was only one bedroom door.

"I heard humming before," I said.

Shar nodded. "Me too. It's, like, air conditioning or something."

"There's no air conditioning in January. It's coming from in here." I inclined my head toward the door.

Shar pressed her ear against it. "You're right. Do you think, you know … he's … in there?"

"I don't know."

"Open it," she ordered.

"And what if he *is* in there?"

"He won't see us unless he has his glasses on," she sang.

"In which case," I grinned, putting my hand on the door, "we get to work."

One turn of the knob and a gentle push, and the door opened without a sound.

The room was bathed in a soft blue light coming from the thing that rested in the middle of the floor. Shar inhaled sharply and I grabbed her hand. It looked like a giant coffin.

The sleek glowing monstrosity was the only thing in the room, and apart from its constant hum, there was no other sound.

"What *is* that?" Shar hissed.

We stepped nearer. The top had a glass lid that was closed, and inside, mist swirled. I squinted at the glass, trying to see through the moisture. After swiveling my head up and down and side-to-side several times, I heaved a sigh of relief. Whatever it was, it was empty.

"It's too dark in here to see." Slowly my eyes adjusted to the dim light, and I was able to make out some words printed on the side. "*Oxo-bed 8000*," I read aloud. "An oxygen bed?"

"Oooh! That's supposed to be incredible for your skin!" Shar squealed.

"It looks like an alien death pod," I said. "If it's a bed, do you think he sleeps in it?"

"Well," Shar said, now examining every inch of it, "the more time you spend in it, the more oxygen you infuse into your skin. It's supposed to be able to reverse sun damage. I've always wanted to try one of these!"

"You're not doing it now," I quipped. "Apart from someone coming in any minute, think about all the wrinkly skin that Arkady must have to infuse with oxygen. I guess he wouldn't be wearing much—"

"TMI!" Shar raised her hand. "Fine. I'll take a spa day in a clean, sterilized oxygen bed when we're done."

"That's better. Now, can we get out of this room, please?" I headed for the door without waiting for a response.

"Where is he?" Shar asked, closing the bedroom door with a barely audible click. "It's nearly midnight!"

"We need to get out of sight. Where do you think is a good place to hide?"

"How about the Crème de la Mer closet?" she suggested. "It wasn't totally filled. There should be enough room for both of us in there."

The closet wasn't small, but we still had to move a few boxes out of it so we could both fit—feathers, coats, capes, scarves, hats and all. We tucked the boxes under fluffy chairs and behind the heavy drapes that hung on either side of the glass wall in the living room; they wouldn't be noticed right away. I kept looking back at the door, expecting Demeter to walk in with Arkady on her arm. As we shuffled things back and forth, I strained to hear footsteps in the hallway, but no one came. Still, we huddled into the closet, dismayed that it was utterly and completely dark inside when we closed the door.

"Turn on the iPhone," Shar said.

I fumbled in my bag, pulled out the iPhone, and tapped its smooth sleekness. It flashed for a second, then glowed red in the gloom. Persephone's number, the last one we'd called, was still on the screen.

Shar yawned. "I didn't need to see that. God, am I tired!" Then she sneezed.

Even though I was sweating, I was wrapped up like a mummy to keep Shar's allergies in check. "I forgot we're in close quarters. Better put on one of those masks. The last thing we need is you sneezing and someone finding us in here."

"That would be awkward," she agreed. I held the iPhone over her bag so she could get the mask out. She slipped it over her beak.

"Can you breathe okay?" I asked.

"Uh huh." Shar closed her eyes. It was getting hotter in here, and I felt sleepy too.

"Stay awake!" I hissed. "We have to listen for Arkady. They should be here soon." I moved the iPhone around, illuminating the corners of the closet, but my arm began to feel heavy, so I laid the phone, screen-side up, on my lap. The closet glowed scarlet.

"I better turn this off," I whispered after what seemed like an eternity, but was probably only a few minutes. "So no one sees the light under the door."

Shar didn't answer. I slipped the iPhone into my bag and sat there in the warm dark.

A loud whirring sound jerked me awake. I fell against the wall with a thud.

"Huh?!" Shar grunted. "Where are we?"

It took me a couple of seconds, but it all came back.

Persephone, the apartment, the ghoulish coffin bed, and the closet.

"Oh my God…" I heard Shar say.

"Shhhh!" I held my hand up, not even sure if she could see it. I was beginning to make out shadows from the light filtering underneath the door. I didn't dare open it. Not yet.

"What time is it?" she whispered.

Clumsily, I dug in my bag for the iPhone, wincing as my stiff arms swished back and forth. I found it and ran a claw over the touch pad.

7:26 glared out of the red screen; it was early morning.

"He hasn't left yet." Shar struggled to her feet. "We can still do this."

She stumbled over a box and fell onto me.

"Not if we can't even make our way out of a closet! Stay still and be quiet for a minute." I put my hands in front of myself and felt for the door. Then I leaned forward and pressed my ear against it. The whirring sound continued, then suddenly stopped.

Click! Click! Click!

"I don't hear anyone, but something's happening out there—the humming stopped," I said softly.

"We can't stay in here forever." Shar was standing up now. "And it's stuffy in here. Open the door, I have to pee!"

I turned the knob slowly, trying not to make noise. As I pushed the door open, light flooded the closet and I had to squint. The suitcases were still by the door.

Shar stuck her head out. "I don't see anyone."

"That doesn't mean we're alone."

She took my hand and helped me out of the closet. We stood, blinking in the pale light streaming in from the glass wall. I could still hear the clicking, then a groaning sound. It was coming from the bedroom.

"I think he's home," Shar said through her mask. It was crumpled and smeared with makeup. I could only imagine what I looked like. Glancing down, I saw pin feathers sticking out of my pants.

Without saying a word, Shar started walking toward Arkady's room. When she got to the door, I gently poked her and she turned to me.

"Since his flight leaves at noon, we have an hour, max, before Jeremy gets here to take him to the airport. We need to entrance him and get him out of here before then."

Shar pointed to the bathroom and dodged in. I stood guard, hoping she'd be quick—she was. We made our way to the bedroom. Shar laid her hand on the doorknob and opened it, not even trying to be quiet.

The room was full of mist, more like a sauna than a bedroom. Arkady was sitting up in his oxygen pod, looking around. He had no shirt on; his skin was not only wrinkly, but translucent, hairless, and sagging in folds. Even from the doorway, I could see the blue veins underneath. He was skeletal skinny, his bones jutting against the thin skin.

"I'm going to be sick," muttered Shar.

"I'll join you later," I said. "Let's get started."

She nodded, and we both advanced toward Arkady's strange bed. He had no glasses on and probably couldn't see more than vague shapes, but he was startled by the motion.

"Ehh!" he cried in an abrasive voice. "Who the hell are you? What are you doing in my house?"

"I'm uh…" I started, trying not to shout, moving ever closer. "We're here to help you get ready for your trip, Mr. Romanov."

"Yes," Shar said, moving forward and looking around. Her face became suddenly bright and she quickly made for the small table by the bed. She snatched something up and held it aloft. Eyeglasses.

Arkady wagged his head and then waved his arms. "Where's Jeremy? Who let you in here?"

He struggled to get out of the pod, but lost his balance and started to fall over. I darted forward and caught him. His withered cheek fell against my shoulder.

Shar

When One Door Closes

rgh!" Arkady moaned, struggling. I grimaced, then motioned for Meg to get on with it.

"Calm down!" she snapped. Arkady, still in her arms, straightened up.

"Calm..." he repeated, his voice less harsh.

With horror, I watched as the last of Meg's hair fell away, leaving only feathers.

She bent her head so that her lips were only an inch or two away from his ear.

"Mr. Romanov," she breathed, "put your glasses on. That'll make this a whole lot easier."

I handed the glasses to Meg and she placed them on Arkady's face. His owl eyes blinked; he stared first at her.

I walked forward and forced his chin up with my hand to make him look at me, trying not to vomit at the feel of his cold, dry skin. "Arkady, time to give the devil his due," I said. His eyes widened and his lips parted to speak, but I shook my head very slowly and wagged a finger over his half-open mouth.

"No more yelling. No more fighting. You have an appointment with Hades." I crooked my finger, beckoning him. Mesmerized, he stood and began to make his way toward me, Meg at his side. I backed out of the room.

"Get dressed, Arkady," she whispered in his ear. "Something simple, don't fuss. Pajamas will work. You can leave your slippers on."

I laughed softly. "People will think he's crazy. No one will come near him or question us."

"Let's hope so."

We followed him from the bedroom into an oversized walk-in dressing area. Racks and racks of clothes, shoes, and hats hung at attention like good little cadets.

Closet envy!

Every flat surface was mirrored. I tried not to look at myself and kept my gaze fixed on him. With surprising agility, he pulled out black silk Armani pajamas, black slippers, and a robe with the initial *A* in a giant gold script. He started to slide the PJ pants over his baggy boxers.

"Come out when you're done!" Meg squeaked. We beat a hasty retreat, getting jammed in the door as we both tried to exit. I was taller, but she had the weight. She won.

I closed the door behind me. As soon as he was ready, we were morgue-bound.

Rrrrring!

Meg and I looked at each other. By the front door was a small television screen that gave alternating views of the street below, as well as of the elevator, the lobby, the hallway, and what looked like an area behind the building. This guy was completely paranoid.

What we saw now was Jeremy getting out of a long black limo. And Demeter. I swore in Spanish.

"How multicultural of you," snipped Meg. "What are we going to do?"

Arkady shuffled into the room and waited, a vacant look in his eyes. Meg grinned slyly and sidled up to him.

"Arkady, Jeremy and Demi are here. Ask Demi to wait in the car, and tell Jeremy to bring the driver and come up and get your bags." She nudged him forward.

He hobbled to the intercom. "Come up, Jeremy, and bring the driver to help you carry the bags. Demi, wait in the car." His voice was flat.

On the little screen, we could see Jeremy and the driver move toward the entrance. Thankfully, Demeter remained outside by the car, but she fidgeted impatiently.

"One last thing." Meg started searching around.

"What are you looking for?"

She hurried over to Arkady, and leaning really close, whispered, "Write Jeremy a check for $200,000, with a note on the bottom that says 'Romanov Grant.' When Jeremy gets here, tell him that he was a great assistant but he needs to finish school. Tell him to go back to the office right now and close it up, but first he should write a press release saying you're going to Switzerland to an exclusive health spa with Demi. You don't know when you'll return. Do it now, and fast!"

The goat shuffled quickly to his desk, pulled out his checkbook, and started scribbling.

"Meg, there's no time for this!"

"I just can't entrance Jeremy again," she hissed. "This will get him out of our way, plus give him a little extra for pain and suffering."

Arkady finished just as the doorbell rang.

"Meg, get behind the door!" We squeezed together. I pinched my nose to stop the sneezes that I knew would fight to get out.

"Answer the door and say what I told you to," Meg directed. "Don't let them ask any questions. And don't tell them that we're here."

I glared at him and nodded.

Arkady answered the door.

"Mr. Romanov! Are you ready to go?" Jeremy stood just outside, the driver waiting behind him. I knew he was staring at Arkady's outfit. I felt a sneeze and turned my head away from Meg. Should have kept the mask over my beak.

"Jeremy, you've been a great assistant, but you need to finish school. Here's a grant from the House of Romanov. Go back to the office and write a press release stating that

I'll be in Switzerland at an exclusive health spa with Demi. Then close up the office. I don't know when I'll return."

It was quiet for a few moments. No doubt the shock of the generous gift had left Jeremy speechless, not to mention Arkady's benign manner. Meg's body was tense. This all might be funny in a different situation.

"I don't know what to say," Jeremy replied slowly. "Mr. Romanov, why aren't you dressed?"

"No questions. Driver, get my bags. Jeremy, go!"

"But—" Jeremy sputtered.

"Go back to the office. Write the press release. Do it!" Arkady almost snarled. Sounded realistic to me.

"Well, uh, thank you, Mr. Romanov." Jeremy sounded uncertain, but he turned and walked slowly out, with the driver at his side carrying two bags. The driver would have to return for the last load.

We stood there—the fossil, Meg, and I—waiting. I heard the ding of the elevator, the doors opening and closing.

"He's gone," Meg sighed with relief and moved over to the window, only to motion frantically for me to come over. I got there just in time to see Jeremy walking away from the car, only to be stopped by Demeter. The driver loaded the bags and turned to come back in, but Demeter darted ahead of him.

"Oh my God, she's coming up here!" I hissed.

A few moments later, her voice was echoing down the hallway.

"Mr. Romanov!" She came into the apartment, not looking pleased. The driver was at her heels.

Before Meg could stop me, I stepped up and vamped the driver with my hazardous hazels. "The two of us will be riding with Mr. Romanov," I said, grabbing Meg's arm. "*Just us.* Meg, come on, last inning."

"No, Mr. Romanov is coming with me," Demeter challenged, holding out her hand to him. Arkady stared at her blankly. She waved a hand in front of his face, then did the same with the driver. Neither reacted to her. She stood, still as a statue. Then slowly, she turned to face us. Her stare was withering, but the tightness in her jaw said it all.

Well, well. For once Hades had been truthful—she couldn't do squat.

"Let's go," Meg said to the driver. He turned and left, and she waddled after him.

"Sorry Demeter." I smiled brightly as I led Arkady by the elbow. "And just so you know, when this is done, I'm going to buy alligator pumps and eat a big steak."

I was almost out the door when Demeter grabbed my arm.

"You're already doomed," she sneered.

"Bite me." I pulled away and turned my back on her. *Point, my favor!*

The driver assisted Arkady into the car and we followed. Once everyone was settled, the driver lowered the glass divider, twisted back, and asked, "Which airport, ma'am?"

I smiled prettily. "There's been a change of plans. City morgue, please." The window closed and the car took off.

It took about ten minutes with traffic. The whole way, we rode in silence. Victory was so close I could taste it. I was sure Meg was thinking about Jeremy, and who cared what Arkady was thinking. The driver pulled up to the grim, gray stone building.

Sure doesn't look like what I see on TV. Morgues were supposed to be shiny and silvery and high tech. This was depressing and creepy and dark. Like something out of a horror movie. The driver opened the door, helping first Meg, then me, then Arkady. If he'd understood what was about to happen, Arkady would have fought to stay in the limo.

"Thank you," Meg said to the driver. As she talked, I could see the pin feathers not only on her head, but starting to cover her face. She pulled her hat lower and her scarf higher. I did the same. This was going to be close.

She leaned closer to the driver. "Take the tags off the luggage in your trunk and drop them in a dumpster in New Jersey. Mr. Romanov and the redhead you picked up earlier were your only passengers."

He tipped his hat, ran around to the driver's side, and slid in. The car pulled away from the curb and disappeared into the morning traffic.

"Nice touch," I said. "Jeremy should have no problems when people start looking for Arkady." I squeezed her hand. "The finish line's inside." We each took one of Arkady's arms.

I would need a two-day soak in the Jacuzzi tub to feel skeeve-free.

The hallways of the morgue were crowded and bustling. Damn. We'd have to practically forge a path.

I looked at Meg. "Siren powers on!"

"I know," she replied morosely. I took off my sunglasses and tried to engage as many gawkers as I could in order to spare Meg, but there were too many people to deal with. Each time I glanced at her, she was more birdlike. I was guessing that even my face must be gone now. My backside felt different too, like it was elongating. I chanced a peek back. To my horror I saw some unfamiliar bulging. When I poked it, my butt felt like a feather pillow.

"Hurry!" I urged, beginning to drag Arkady faster. Meg followed suit. Now we were shoving people aside, not bothering to entrance anyone.

"Oh my God, what is that?" a woman screamed.

"I don't know, but it's got that poor man!" cried another.

"Someone call 911!"

"Meg," I huffed, "shout for them to forget what they see or something! I'll get Arkady to the portal!"

"Caw! Caw!"

Meg was a total bird now. With a mighty flap, she wriggled free of her cape and hat, her grey sweats shredded, and flew down the hall screeching, chasing the screaming people, a mascot gone wrong. The cacophony was deafening, but on I ran. I had to save us both.

I could *feel* the portal. My head darted back and forth, making it impossible to read any signs. I had to trust my instincts. I turned down one hall, then another, Meg's screeching caw in my ear. The pulse of the portal throbbed in my veins, beckoning me. Arkady flopped listlessly beside me, his feet not touching the floor. He seemed to weigh practically nothing. More Siren mojo?

A nasty right turn through double doors, and I stood, panting, in the refrigerated section where the cadavers were stored. A misty vapor seeped out of one body drawer. I hauled Arkady over to it. I yanked on the handle with my free claw, and the door opened and banged against the next one. I pulled out the stainless steel slab and pointed at it with a damning wing.

"Lay down!" I yelled at Arkady, my eyes blazing. "Do it!" I shoved my face within an inch of his. His breath was rank with decay.

He hesitated.

"Where am I?"

It was wearing off! I started to panic, remembering that the enchantment was stronger when Meg was with me.

"Caw!" I screamed. I meant to yell "Meg!" but my voice was gone. An answering cry came from the hallway. There wasn't much time. By the gift or not, he was going in. I grabbed his arm, almost wrenching it from its socket. He cried and protested as I lifted him up, resisting me with what little strength he had.

A harsh croak came from the hall, and Meg flew into the room. She wheeled around and slammed the door shut, throwing herself against it. Almost instantly there was pounding on the other side. Slowly, she turned and pecked at the bolt with her beak. *Click!* She'd locked it! She slumped against the door again, her feathered chest heaving and pumping, her bird body confined in what was left of the sweats and sneakers she couldn't discard on her mad flight through the morgue. Her beady eyes blinked helplessly at me.

I turned back to Arkady. And sucked in a breath. He sat there looking limp, pale, and disoriented. In spite of everything, I felt a small measure of pity for him.

Finally catching her breath, Meg pushed a metal table in front of the door as an added security measure and hopped over to my side. Together we stared at Arkady. Meg's head drooped a little. I wondered if she was thinking the same thing I was—that he looked so frail and so sad. His arm dangled at his side, probably injured from when I hauled him onto the table.

She warbled something softly in her bird voice that I couldn't make out. Whatever it was, Arkady sprang to life.

"What am I doing here!" he growled, trying to crane his neck and look around. "You fat, stupid vultures! You'll pay for this! I deal with powers that you'll never understand. I'll make sure you'll rot in the lowest corner of the Underworld!" Spit flew from his mouth and landed on my wing.

I'd felt pity for *this*? No one calls me fat! Or stupid! Or a vulture!

He wriggled like a maggot, trying to get off. I held his arms down while Meg knocked him flat.

"*Dosvedanya*, loser! Caw!" We shoved the drawer in and slammed the door shut together.

Meg

Some Sales Are Not Final

We stood panting in front of the body drawer. The mist that had been flowing out of it started to dissipate with a soft hiss. I was dimly aware of banging on the other side of the door to the room. It had been continuous since I'd shut it behind me.

"How are we going to get out of here?" I finally managed.

"Meg! You got your voice back! You're you!"

I glanced down. My sweats hung in tatters about me, but I saw my legs. I ran a trembling hand through my hair. It *was* hair! Still not believing it, I craned to see my reflection in the shiny surface of a metal door. I was me again!

I ran over to Shar and grabbed her by the elbows. Her

pert nose, sans the orange tint, was back, along with her elegant fingers. We were both plainly human.

"We did it! We did it!" I shouted.

Shar's exhausted expression immediately transformed into excited happiness, and every feature on her face lit up as she squealed.

"We're free! We're done!" We jumped around in a circle, holding each other and ignoring everything else. Then a muffled voice came through the door.

"Open up, this is the coroner! We've called the police!"

"Oh my God." Shar stopped jumping and looked around. We were in a cement room, with one wall of corpse cells—some likely occupied—and no windows. There was only one way in or out.

"We're trapped," I said.

Suddenly, the door of the body drawer closest to us rattled and shook. Then, with a screech, it fell off its hinges. The opening grew larger, and the banging on the door to the room stopped. It was absolutely silent.

Hades strolled out of the portal. "Ladies, I believe it's time to leave."

"Time to leave?" I choked out the words as I backed away, pulling Shar with me.

"Come with me. To Tartarus. Now." He pointed to the portal. I could see a set of rocky stairs leading down.

"Arkady went in!" protested Shar. "We delivered him! We made your deadline. In fact, we're early!"

"True, but not by much. And it seems that you had a

little help. You two were supposed to do this alone." He flicked a hand carelessly.

My skin went cold.

"As I recall," Shar said, her voice shaking, "we were the ones who slammed the door on Arkady. Poor Meg had to chase everyone away so I could get him in here. This was all Meg and me. No one else."

"Oh, I beg to differ." We turned and there was Demeter, sitting on top of the shiny metal table I'd shoved against the door of the room. She crossed her legs; her rubber rain boots, which matched her spring-green mac, dangled over the floor. "Much as I hate to admit it, I believe my son-in-law is right. There is no way that you two could have accomplished this alone. If Persephone hadn't placed you in Arkady's apartment, you never would have succeeded."

I could feel the color rising in my face. How did she know Persephone had helped us?

"Let's put this into simple terms even you two can understand." Hades spoke softly, casually leaning against the frame of the portal. "You had help. You cheated. What happens when you cheat in school? You fail. We live by the same rules. Demeter and I differ on some things..." he said with a twisted lip. Demeter gave an equally cringe-inducing glare. Then he continued, in an almost-brotherly *I-caught-you-doing-something-you-shouldn't-have* tone, with wide eyes and pouty lips, "But we all know that cheating is wrong."

"Cheaters never win," Demeter mocked, wagging a finger at us. Then she turned to Hades. "And weren't they supposed to keep mum about their assignment?"

"Why, yes, that's true!" Hades looked dramatically horrified. "They didn't speak with you about the arrangement…Did they?"

Demeter sighed. "I'm afraid they did, and I suspect they may have discussed it with Persephone as well. Why else would my dear, sweet, daughter involve herself with mortals?"

"You knew about it already!" Shar shouted angrily, pointing a finger at Demeter. "You mentioned it first! And Persephone chased *me* down to discuss Hades!"

Hades turned to us in mock pain. "I trusted you," he cried. "First cheating, and now this violation! You must leave with me now." His face hardened. "And even if the goddesses did know, you still had a nondisclosure clause, remember?"

"Next time," Demeter said, sliding off the table and strolling up to us, "don't try to get the last word with a goddess."

Hades sidled up to Shar, took her hand, and kissed it. "You should have taken the last deal I offered you, *ma chérie*. One night, that's all I wanted. You would have been well compensated, and you would have been free. But now, I have you anyway, and you've doomed poor Margaret too. Not a very good friend, are you?"

I moved quickly to Shar's other side, the angel to Hades' devil. "Don't listen to him, Shar! You'd have sacrificed yourself for nothing."

Hades turned his saturnine glance to me.

"Perhaps you'd like to make me an offer? I promise you it would be the most memorable pleasure of your pathetic life."

"No thanks." I showed him both palms, and turned my face away.

"Just thought I'd try. You might have been amusing. For a while." He sighed, sounding pleased with himself. "Very well. If that's all cleared up—"

"Wait!" Shar quipped. "If we failed at our mission, how come we're not birds anymore? We did it and you know it! You have to let us go!"

"I'm not saying that you didn't complete the mission. I'm saying that you cheated and violated the terms of the contract."

"And therefore," Demeter added, "you lose."

"Mother!" A muffled voice suddenly came from within another body drawer. "Mother!"

Demeter paled.

"Mother, you open this door!"

A great bang, and the door flew off its hinges and hit the wall. Persephone, wearing a glittering lamé halter and silver skin-tight pants, climbed out.

"Persephone, darling!" Demeter looked horrified. She glanced furtively at the ceiling, as if expecting something to come out of it, and laughed nervously. "What are you doing here? You have to leave *now*!" She rushed over and grabbed Persephone by the arm.

"Mother." Persephone glared at Demeter and pulled free. "You know exactly what I'm doing here. All of Tartarus is getting ready to welcome the newest Sirens home." She turned to Hades. "And, dearest, the room next to yours is being redecorated. In *pink*? You know I *abhor* pink!"

Hades raised both his hands as if he had nothing to do with it. "Come on, baby, why would I want to associate with ... that?" He glanced at Shar, who looked completely indignant. Persephone whirled around and faced Shar, who prudently stepped behind me.

"How did you screw this up?" Her tone was icy.

I pointed a finger at Demeter and Hades. "Ask them! He's saying we cheated because you helped us, and your mother agrees!"

"What?!" Persephone turned on Demeter. "Mu-ther!"

"Enough!" came a clear female voice from above.

"Wonderful, darling," Demeter grabbed Persephone's arm again and pulled her to her side. "See what you've done? You've broken the rules and gotten Hera's attention! Hopefully Zeus won't come with her."

Persephone shot her mother an evil look. "*I* broke the rules?" was all she was able to say before a statuesque woman, dressed in a gown made entirely of peacock feathers, passed through the concrete wall. She floated a few inches above the floor, her long, honey-colored hair flowing past her waist. She cast a furious glance at Hades.

"Hera, you can't interfere in my contracts," he said through clenched teeth.

"Hera! Queen of the Gods!" I whispered to Shar. "We're saved!"

"Maybe," she muttered doubtfully. I didn't blame her for being suspicious.

"Do you *think* I want to be *here*?" Hera looked at the rows of refrigerator doors and admired her reflection in one of them. Then she snapped her fingers, and all of us stood in a magnificent hall of white marble that gleamed in the sun.

"Is this heaven?" Shar murmured in a wistful tone, turning around and around.

"This is a vision of what your kind expects of Mt. Olympus," Hera said, bored. "Rare is the mortal who actually sees it."

"Why are we here? I have business to conduct." Hades' voice had risen a couple of decibels, and he looked meaningfully at us. We huddled closer and even though it was utterly pointless, shuffled away from him.

"Do not shout, brother-in-law!" Hera snapped. "You forget yourself. I suggest you speak with a lower volume and more respect if you don't want Zeus here. He won't be as willing to overlook your boorishness! Not to mention this last bit of knavery."

Demeter raised her hand and shook her head, trying to catch Hera's attention.

"Oh no, Demeter," said Hera. "It's not like you're innocent. This foolishness has gone on for long enough. Really, one would think the two of you had better things to do than torment mortals with your silly games."

"Games?" I dared to interject.

"Or should I say, wagers?" Hera shook her head, making her amber tendrils fly about her like she was floating in water.

Hades groaned while Demeter shifted her eyes from side to side.

Persephone looked confused. "Mother, what are they talking about?"

"Yeah," Shar broke in. "Someone explain this to us. What wager?"

Hades put on the same smile that he wore when we'd first met him in the subway. "You know the story. My lovely Persephone—" He walked over to her and kissed her hand. She gave him a pouty but suggestive look that I wished I hadn't seen. "Persephone stays with me for six months out of the year, and with her mother"—he wrinkled his nose—"for the other six. But when the season is about to change, sometimes the lines get blurred. It always happens at the beginning of February."

"You mean, like Groundhog Day?" Shar asked. "The six-more-weeks-of-winter thing?"

"Exactly," said Demeter. "And rather than argue about it, we made…" She hesitated.

"Go on," urged Hera.

"We made a bet." Demeter straightened herself and tried not to look guilty. "Hades had a contract he was going to call in, so he proposed—"

"I didn't propose anything!" Hades protested, and looked as innocently as he could at Persephone. A performance worthy of an Oscar.

"You did!" Demeter argued. "It was you—"

"I don't care who started it!" Hera thundered.

"All right, all right." Demeter cowered. "We made a bet where we agreed that the Sirens would go and collect on the contract—"

"Which I didn't want, because I knew they would screw it up," Hades interrupted. "And I was right. They delivered Arkady to me damaged." Hera shot him a look and he shut up.

Demeter continued. "We agreed that if the Sirens completed their mission, Persephone would stay with Hades for the additional six weeks, but if they failed, Persephone would come to me."

"And?" Hera prompted.

"And I got to choose the Sirens. I also stipulated that I be near Arkady to make sure Hades didn't cheat." She pointed angrily at him.

I looked at the goddess. "You chose us? Specifically?" I asked.

"Of course." Demeter waved a dismissive hand at us. "It seemed so obvious. I thought you two would never be able to work together to get this done. And you're not exactly smart. I still can't believe you fell for that train thing."

"What train thing?" Shar stepped forward, her eyes narrowed in fury and confusion.

Hera turned to her. "Didn't it ever occur to you that the train never stopped? Is that what happens in your world?"

We both shook our heads, and then it dawned.

"You mean," said Shar softly, "this was a setup?"

"One of my best yet." Hades' exuberant grin was almost boyish.

"Hades!" Persephone punched him in the arm.

"Oh, I wish we could get a shot at him," muttered Shar.

I kept going over what happened that night in the

train station—was it really all an illusion? "You mean to say that Jeremy was never harmed? In any way, ever?"

"Only the Fates determine such things," said Hera. "Your experience was completely engineered by Hades. I have to admit that he has a way of misleading gullible, slightly dim-witted—"

"No need to go on about it," I grumbled.

"So who's the cheater now?" Shar gave him a blistering look.

Hades shrugged carelessly. "I am what I am, ladies. It's what I do."

"And Demeter," Hera admonished, "the Fates decreed that Sharisse and Margaret would finish in the alley by the clinic, but they didn't."

"They got too close," growled Demeter.

"So you arranged to steal him, and then take him on a trip with you, putting him out of our reach," spat Shar.

"It is done!" boomed Hera. "Save for a few minor details."

Hades cringed.

"Persephone is not to be in your presence, Demeter, during her time with Hades. And she is not to meet Hades on the mortal plane ever. Yet here you all are."

"But—" Demeter started.

"No interruptions! There are rules, as you both lectured the girls. And there are more infractions on both your parts. Shall we review them?" Hades and Demeter shook their heads contritely.

"I didn't think so! Therefore, since both of you had a hand in this situation, Zeus, the Fates, and I decree that

Persephone will be spending the next six weeks with neither of you." With a wave of Hera's hand, Persephone was dressed in Daisy Duke shorts, western boots, a flannel halter top, and a cowgirl hat. "It's rodeo season in Texas." Hera smiled at her, then glared at Hades and Demeter. "Have a burger and a buckaroo on me."

Persephone giggled and blew a kiss to Hades. "See you in six weeks, cowboy!"

Hera flicked a bejeweled arm and all three deities vanished. Then she turned to us. "And you two. Honestly, you wreak havoc on all the planes like I haven't seen in millennia! I'm exhausted!" She rose. "I've had enough of you mortals for one day. It's time for you to return."

Before I could take a breath, I found myself standing in my room at home, alone.

Disoriented, I turned round and round, then started with surprise. My bed was piled high with clothes, bags, books, shoes, CDs—ill-gotten siren loot. Peeking out from a teetering stack of black was something...pink.

Shar.

"Shar!" I practically shouted her name, and scrambled for my bag. Finding my cell phone, I fiddled with the keypad and was about to speed-dial her when the thing buzzed in my hand. Somehow I managed not to drop it.

"Shar?"

"Meg?"

"We're home!" We said it together and started laughing.

"We really did it!" she squealed. "It's over!"

"Yeah," I agreed, though not so enthusiastically. It was

done, and in a few days we'd be back in school, and then … *do we go back to the way things used to be?*

"So," Shar's voice crackled in my ear, "what're you doing now?"

"Nothing."

"Me neither. Maybe we could … "

" … meet up somewhere? I could really use a double mocha latte!" I hoped I didn't sound too desperate, and it wasn't about the coffee.

"Chai for me."

"I know," I retorted, laughing.

Shar giggled. "I'll be in front of your building in about half an hour."

"I'll be downstairs."

After hiding my new stuff away, I quick-changed out of my shreddy sweats and slipped out unnoticed. Shar was punctual—and polished—as usual.

"Hera dumped us home at the same time," I said indignantly. "How the heck did you manage to do all this?" I waved a hand at her shiny-straight locks and deftly coordinated jeans, over-the-knee boots, sweater, and puffy vest.

"Professional pride," she said, stuffing her hands into her pockets. We started walking uptown. "It takes me all of five minutes to be 'meeting BFF for lattes' ready."

BFF.

I smiled to myself.

"And this isn't too bad," she said, assessing my ensemble, tugging at the sleeve of the sweater minidress I'd plucked from my Siren pile. "Is that … purple?"

"So it is," I beamed. "Let's get those lattes."

We walked in silence down the rainy street. It was cold and dreary, no doubt a reflection of Demeter's mood. I guessed she was probably pouting.

"Did you notice that everywhere we step, a puddle springs up?" Shar asked as she tried to avoid a lake-sized one unsuccessfully. "And deep, too! My poor boots are history!"

"We probably should invest in some wellies. I have these ones with—"

"Skulls on them?" Shar raised a brow.

"Yes," I answered defensively.

"Adorable. I should get a pair too—but no skulls."

"I've seen them with flamingos," I said.

"Do they make them in a ten narrow?"

I grinned. "I'm sure they do."

She flashed a smile as a taxi sped by.

We couldn't move out of the way and were drenched. But as the car passed us, I caught a glimpse of a dark and blurry face gazing out from the back seat.

"That—" I sputtered, muddy water dripping off my entire body, including my face.

Shar looked horrified. "It wasn't him in that taxi, was it?"

The cab pulled over a few feet from us. A man exited— tall, lean, and expensively dressed. Wavy dark hair. Chiseled cheekbones.

We held our breath.

"Can't be!" croaked Shar.

The man turned and stared at us with disdain, then moved on.

It wasn't Hades. Just a rude stranger with a resemblance.

"Hera said it was *done*." Shar's voice was shaky.

"Right," I muttered. We stood there dripping. "Now I really need a hot drink."

We ducked into the first coffee shop we came to, ordered our drinks, and snagged a cozy table in the window.

"Oh, this is nice." Shar cupped her hands around her mug. I was about to take a sip from mine when a husky voice came from the coffee bar; it seemed to rise over the chatter around us.

"It's hell out there! Give me something hot. And decadent."

Shar froze in her seat, and I closed my eyes for a long moment. When I dared open them, all I saw was a stocky guy in sloppy combats leaning over the counter. I nearly died when he spoke again.

"A triple caramel vanilla mocha. Full fat. Extra whipped cream. And a double shot of espresso. Supremio-deluxo size. Is that the naughtiest thing that you have?"

The voice did not match the package. I started laughing.

"What's so funny?" Shar demanded.

"We are! Look at us. Tensing up like scared cats at every overdressed or oily-voiced guy. And this is barely day one." I leaned in. "Are we going to keep looking over our shoulders for the rest of our lives?"

Shar grimaced. "I'm still in shock. It's gonna take me some time to get over this."

I nodded, understanding. "So what's the first step to sanity, then?"

She ran a finger along the rim of her mug, then looked

at me and smiled widely. "I say we start with the power of positive thinking. It's over. And he's gone," she said firmly. "We've come a long way, and the future looks bright!" She raised her mug in a toast.

Shar was right. There was a lot to look forward to, including Jeremy. And a new BFF.

"And it looks like you've learned something from me—" Shar began.

"What?"

"You've ditched the undertaker look. Somewhat." She didn't succeed in suppressing a cheerful smirk.

I started to raise my cup, but reflected in the glass behind her, I thought I saw … eyes.

Dark, smoldering, probing. As I stared, a face started to form.

"You okay?" Shar asked.

I looked at her; there was a twinge of concern in her expression.

I blinked and glanced back at the window. The eyes were still there, except this time I could see the face and the body they were connected to. Mr. Naughty, aka triple caramel vanilla mocha, was sitting at the table behind us. Our eyes locked and he winked at me.

I gave a him tight smile, then quickly turned to Shar and shook my head. Forcing myself to shrug off dark thoughts and wild fears, I lifted my cup in salute.

"I'm awesome," I said, and meant it. Tapping my cup against hers, I added, "Or should I say, *we* are?"

Acknowledgments

Charlotte Bennardo

No one writes a book alone; there are always people along the way who listened to me cry when I got rejected, offered brutal criticism that was (mostly) good even if I didn't like it, distracted me when I was on a rant, and promised to buy the book when it got published. And with a co-author you're never alone. It's time for me to pony up and say a humble "thank you, love you, don't leave me ever!" to all those wonderful, brilliant, and loyal people.

To Nat: more than co-author, you are shopping buddy, personal psychic, dessert partner, straight man, fashion consultant, sympathetic therapist, and most important, my "twisted little sister." It's been a rockin' roller coaster, Dahlink, and I hope it goes on many more books and years!

To Nick and my boys, Thomas, Alec, and Collin: You inspire my sick humor; be glad, it helped sell this book. Thanks for always asking how it's going and telling everyone "my mom's a writer." And no, no one's getting a Ferrari.

To my mother, grandmother, sister, and (miss you!) dad: most of you read my stuff, even when it was stinky! Everyone needs a cheerleading squad, and that's all of you! But please don't wear the little skirts. Thanks.

To my editor Brian Farrey and the team at Flux—Steven Pomije, Sandy Sullivan, and Courtney Colton: smart move! I promise to listen to most of your advice and work hard to make you glad you chose *Sirenz*.

To my agent Natalie Fischer: you recognized my late-budding genius. Now we just have to work on selling those other novels.

To all the friends: the other two of the Writing Wenches Fourum, Yvonne Ventresca and Elisa Roland; to Kathy Temean and Laurie Wallmark at NJ-SCBWI; to the Bunco Gals, and so many other family and friends along the way; not forgotten, but not enough space to thank you all, love ya. And if I'm ever really famous, please don't give up my dark secrets. Or I'll put you in my next book.

Natalie Zaman

There are so many people who played a part in bringing *Sirenz* into the world.

Super huge thanks to the NJ-SCBWI—without the existence of this fabby group of writers and friends, Char and I would never have met. A never-ending hug to RA Extraordinaire Kathy Temean, who works tirelessly to make sure every member of our chapter is given an opportunity to show, improve, and sell his or her work. Lyn Sirota—how can I thank you for suggesting that I join Char's critique group? Thanks bunches to Leeza Hernandez and Anita Nolan for helping us get the word out about *Sirenz* through Sprouts—the *best* SCBWI regional newsletter (IMHO). Ame Dyckman, who supported my projects big and small—*love* you! (And you still owe me an ice cream trip.) Susan Heyboer O'Keefe, good friend and—whether you were aware or not (you are now)—mentor and role model. Where would I be without my Writing Wenches? To the ladies of the WWF—Char, Elisa Roland, and Yvonne Ventresca—I only hope I can offer you the same support you've given me.

To Sr. Natalie, Mr. Curcio, and Ms. Latschar, thank you for instilling in me a love of reading and writing. Sr. Brigid Brady, Dr. Colette Lindroth, and much-missed Dr. Muriel Dollar—I carry your warmth, wit, and wisdom with me always. I am beyond fortunate to know Joelyn Melzl, Darlene Fraulo, Mari Cifone, Janeen Miller, Dawn Zerfass, and Suna—thank you for your boundless excitement, enthusiasm, and support for me and my projects. And of course, mega-thanks to the countless fellow writers, conference attendees, friends, and editor and agent mentors who read and reread the many incarnations of *Sirenz* and gave their suggestions, advice, and insights.

I will always be grateful for the fabulous staff at Flux for taking a chance on us, and to our agent, Natalie (!) Fischer, who made my decade when she said she enjoyed *Sirenz* as a reader. Thank you to my editor Brian Farrey for making *Sirenz* really sing and for helping me to hone my craft; I am a better writer for having worked with you. Without Sandy Sullivan, who caught, well, *everything*, this book wouldn't be the sparkly thing that it is—you're the best! Thanks to Steven Pomije and and Courtney Colton for telling the world about *Sirenz* and listening to our ideas. Our bright, eye-catching, and uber-fun cover is the work of Lisa Novak—thanks for making us stand out in a crowd!

Jane Reed Wilson, I never thought that I would enjoy

having my photo taken, but somehow you changed that—
TY! Marissa Miller—thank you for being our guinea pig.
And to the best nephew ever, Jesse Davidson, thank you
for sharing your time and talent for our little book.

Moo, Mert, Wink (Asim, Mari, and Vincent, respec-
tively; the world should know you by your real names
rather than the loony ones I call you), and Mom, there
aren't words enough to thank you for always believing in
me. And Raz—how do you properly thank someone for
putting his dreams aside so that you can chase after yours?
I love you.

And last but not least, thanks, Char, for letting me sit
around your house that summer—you know, the one where
you said, "Hey, we can do that!" and then we started writing that story…Thank you, dahlink, for sharing your amazing talent, your home, your time, your patience (perching!),
and most of all your friendship with me. My life is sweeter
because you are in it. xxxDimps

About the Authors

Charlotte Bennardo

A moderate shoe freak, Charlotte Bennardo divides her time between writing, her three sons, writing, her family and friends—and writing. When she's not wearing out her laptop keyboard, she likes to swim, garden, play with her cat, and hang out with her best friend and co-author, Natalie. Married, she lives in Bridgewater, New Jersey. Visit Charlotte online at http://charlotteebennardo.blogspot.com.

Natalie Zaman

Natalie Zaman learned that it's hard—but not impossible—to farm in high heels. When she's not chasing free-range chickens, she's writing, or plotting a road trip. She lives in New Jersey with her family—about five minutes from Charlotte. Visit her online at http://nataliezaman.blogspot.com.